Morningsong

A Novel

Morningsong

Shelly Beach

Kregel
Publications

Library of Congress Cataloging-in-Publication Data
Beach, Shelly.
    Morningsong : a novel / Shelly Beach.
        p. cm.
    I. Title.
PS3602.E23M67   2009   813'.6—dc22   2008054741

ISBN: 978-0-8254-2541-7

Printed in the United States of America

09 10 11 12 13 / 5 4 3 2 1

To Pastor Elvin and Elda Ann Harden.
Your gifts of faithfulness and love ripple out through eternity,
and we see Jesus in your faces.

Acknowledgments

I would like to thank my husband, Dan, for his unwavering love and support. Without his constant encouragement, confidence, and strength, my writing would not be possible. Dan, you are the love of my life and my true hero. Thank you for your faithful heart—for always being there and listening.

And my heartfelt thanks to the Guild, my warrior sisters who pour laughter, healing, perspective, and wisdom into my life. You have made me rich: Cynthia Beach, Angela Blycker, Ann Byle, Sharon Carrns, Lorilee Craker, Tracy Groot, Alison Hodgson, and Julie Johnson.

My special thanks to Dennis Hillman, Steve Barclift, and the wonderful family at Kregel Publications. It is a joy to work with each and every one of you. Many thanks to my editor, Dawn Anderson, for her keen eye, insight, patience, and encouragement.

Chapter One

Halfway through her morning walk on the streets of Stewartville, Mona VanderMolen made her final decision to kill Miss Emily.

She pondered her decision as she stood at the edge of the lawn facing Glenda Simpson's two-story, turn-of-the-century clapboard farmhouse.

What surprised her most was her numbness to the evil of it, even as her vision grew for how she'd carry out her plan. Sure, she'd done things she was ashamed of, things she and her girl-friends had laughed over at college reunions—things that kept her humble with memories of youth and stupidity. And then there were the years Ellen had blackmailed or manipulated her into being a silent accomplice to her rebellion—the times Mona had evaded her mother's questions or pulled her drunk sister through a basement window in the dead of night.

But something intentionally evil, premeditated, and cold? Never in Mona's forty-five years. Nothing like this. Since she'd moved to Stewartville, her public sins had been limited to an embarrassing unwillingness to observe the town's forty-five-mile-per-hour speed limit and running up the highest tab in town for overdue library fines.

Killing Miss Emily would change everything. But then, that was the point of it, wasn't it—to draw a line in the sand, to finally shut her up? Something in Miss Emily's skittery eyes told Mona she knew she'd changed and could hear the voices that rang in her head.

Doubt. Fear. Indecision. Guilt.

Killing Miss Emily was the only way out of it, even if it meant that everyone in Stewartville would know.

Mona VanderMolen was a good woman who had gone mad. Three months after she'd come out of her coma, she'd finally cracked.

The town would be stunned with the horror of it, and the sickening shame would separate her from the people she loved most: Elsie, Adam, Harold, Hallie, even Ellen. Mona pushed the thought from her mind.

The fact remained: it had to be done. She stared through the front window of Glenda's house as the chill November wind bit through her black, French terry sweat suit and the lime green parka she'd layered over the top for extra warmth. Her thoughts rolled back to her first glimmering thoughts of murder. They'd drifted into her mind easily, like the russet oak leaves that had wafted downward to Stewartville's lawns and sidewalks in gentle gasps and sputters of breeze as she'd headed west on Maple on her first lap that morning. By the time she'd turned north on Second, then east on Elm and south on Mercantile, the thought had grown to an idea, then to a resolve that hardened with the pain of each laborious step, until on her eighth lap, she found herself poised in front of Glenda Simpson's bay window, holding a driveway paver brick in her right hand.

With one small twinge of pain, Mona's vision had met flesh. The brick's rough edges bit into the hammock of flesh between her thumb and index finger as she adjusted its weight to get a better grip. She paused, then hefted it toward her shoulder, her arm trembling slightly as she drew it toward her chest. The weight was heavier than she'd expected, and she shifted her feet, then planted them wide apart for balance until the urge to lean to the right subsided.

Slowly, she closed her eyes and envisioned the throw. An overhand bullet that arched from her hand in a graceful swoop. The brick hurtling through the air and shooting through the pane of glass with perfect precision, raining glass shards into the juniper bushes below as the brick found its mark, leaving a starburst hole.

Then the sound of the thud, of stone meeting skull, and the sight of the body slumping to the living-room floor.

Mona opened her eyes and focused on the ripple of breeze through the juniper bush. If she thought about it another minute, she'd never follow through. It was pure evil, there was no getting around it, but some things in life weren't to be tolerated. Tyranny came with a price, as Miss Emily was about to find out. And insurance would kick in and help with expenses, she was sure.

She raised her eyes and looked through the window at the face that had tormented her day after day.

You're despicable, and I've taken all I'm going to take.

The face stared back silently. Mona could feel a trickle of blood running down the palm of her hand and the grit of the dirt on the tips of her fingers.

"I hate you." She spoke the words out loud.

The face in the window continued to stare. Not even a blink broke the gaze. It was the staring Mona hated most, the fact that, to Miss Emily, the hard, violating gaze meant nothing, just like it meant nothing to the other faces who took in her stubble of auburn hair and the scarred scalp that still showed through. A few months ago her hair had fallen thick to well-muscled shoulders on a tall, athletic frame that could heft hay bales with the best of Stewartville's men. But what did that matter now? Anger rose red-hot inside her like spewing lava, and she lifted the brick higher, staggering to regain her balance. But with the motion, her fingers lost their bite against the dirty chunk of concrete. She struggled to recover her grip, and the brick clattered to the sidewalk at her feet with a sonorous thud, landing inches from the raggedy hole where it had originally nested.

Mona blinked as she stood motionless and surveyed the streaks of blood on the palm of her right hand. Then she sighed, bent slowly to one knee, and nestled the brick back into place in the pattern of Glenda's walkway where she'd found it kicked loose, like a half-dozen others.

So here I am, Lord, a pathetic crazy woman wasting Your time, making You knock rocks out of my hand to save me from acts of insanity.

She eased the brick back and forth, working to make the edges lie even with the surrounding walkway.

This sure isn't where I thought I'd be standing three months ago, after Elsie brought me home from the hospital. Of course, You know that. I was supposed to be finished with rehab by now, but Your timetable and mine seem to be a little out of sync. And for some reason, praying and plowing through my agenda don't seem to be working this time, even though they've worked pretty well in the past. I'm tired of all this, okay? I just want to lie down and sleep for a few weeks and wake up again when I'll be able to walk without staggering or read faster than a third grader or push three-syllable words through my brain.

She gave the brick a final smack, then lowered her head to her hands and rested on one knee before she slowly stood and blinked against the spinning. She fought against the swells that rose in her stomach and the flash of frustration that coursed through her veins.

Dr. Bailey's warnings about post-craniotomy strokes and transient ischemic attacks, or TIAs, had been a doctor spouting necessary medical protocol when he'd released her from the hospital. The headaches, fatigue, dizziness, and flashes these past few weeks were nothing, and she'd prove it to him if she had to. She'd fought every other hard thing in her life—her father, Stacy's drowning, Hallie's rebellion, her own near death—and she could fight this. She only had to get past her three-month MRI and hope that Dr. Bailey didn't notice she'd already rescheduled it twice.

In the distance, the shriek of an ambulance approached as it headed in the direction of Stewartville Community Hospital's emergency room.

With each bad day, I'm more exhausted and one step closer to losing it, Lord. Part of me wants to give up and crawl off into the dark with the doubt and fear that keep shouting that this is as good as it will ever get. The other part of me is outraged that I can't control even the simplest things about my own body anymore. In five minutes, I swing from faith to depression to anger and then top it all off with a few ladles of guilt because I'm so weak.

And it's no secret to You that I can't walk by this house without fixating on killing Miss Emily because she's the living, breathing embodiment of all the things I hate about myself. She's as broken down and worthless as I'm becoming. Since we both know I'm losing it, what other excuse do I need to want her dead?

The calico with the flickering, crooked tail stared at her through the bay window that separated her from the outside world by a thin pane of glass. Mona had been told the story of Miss Emily soon after she'd moved to town. She was somewhat of a Stewartville celebrity, with her lightning-shaped tail, flinching fur, and skittery eyes that never rested anywhere for long unless she was shielded from the world in the protective recess of the bay window. Then, and only then, she would stare. She was one of Glenda Simpson's six well-fed and pampered cats.

Rumor had it that one Saturday Miss Emily had ambled into Glenda's dryer for an afternoon siesta, and Glenda had unknowingly tumbled both the cat and her husband's Carhartts on permanent press for a good fifteen minutes before she'd figured out that the high-pitched shrieking she was hearing wasn't coming from reruns of *Cops* in the next room. Miss Emily had emerged from the Kenmore with a walk that listed permanently to the left, a re-engineered tail, and an aversion to anything remotely resembling the fragrance of Downy.

For the first time, Mona traced the lines of the lopsided tail and noticed the angles of the two breaks. Miss Emily's eyes glared back, and Mona felt a surge of remorse.

"I'm sorry I'm staring. I understand why you must have a deep-seated mistrust of humans. And I'm sorry I was planning your demise in kind of an . . . imaginative way. I was letting my mind play with how good it would feel to just hurl something . . . you know, let it all fly, inflict pain because I'm hurting. We people commit murder in our minds dozens of times a day. I'm not saying it's right, I'm just saying we're more messed up than we like to admit. But I think I at least owe you a peace offering of canned albacore."

Mona tamped the brick with the toe of her tennis shoe as she glanced over her shoulder. The last thing she needed was for someone to see her apologizing to a cat. But no harm done. To the casual passerby, it would have appeared she'd taken a neighborly interest in replacing one of Glenda's loose bricks. Not for one moment would anyone ever guess that Mona VanderMolen had contemplated an actual act of violence like pitching a brick through Glenda Simpson's bay window in a random act of feline homicide.

She pulled a tissue from her jacket pocket, dabbed it on her tongue, and wiped the blood from her palm.

And what would Adam think if he realized he was dating a middle-aged wack job whose mind and body were disintegrating like cotton candy in a rainstorm? He was a good man who deserved a healthy, sane woman, not one who believed a cat could read minds and understand apologies.

Mona felt suddenly exhausted. After two months of laps around the same three blocks, she'd finally figured out why she hated Miss Emily so much. After all, she was just a beat-up calico with a busted tail and eyes that looked east and west at the same time. A cat with a mortal fear of household appliances. A cat that through a freak accident had been left to navigate the sea of life without a centerboard that went fully down, steering a little off-center and listing a bit to port.

Miss Emily was a reminder of who she'd become—one of the broken and dazed who listed a bit to port with a body that longed to be what it once had been. She wore her imperfections where everyone could see them, and people pitied her for it.

Mona shoved the blood-stained tissue back into her pocket. It was time to move on.

Chapter Two

It's 6:05 this foggy morning before Thanksgiving. If you're rushing out to do some last-minute shopping for that holiday bird and you're heading into Detroit, you'll already find southbound I-75 backed up clear past the Rochester Road exit. A three-car pileup is blocking all four lanes, and police are asking that you choose alternate routes.

Along the Ford Freeway, you'll find traffic sluggish for the morning commute . . .

Hallie's hand slammed the Reset button of the clock radio on the bleached white maple nightstand as she rolled to her stomach with a groan and pulled a wadded pillow over her head. She nosed into the sheets and snapped the red- and yellow-striped comforter over her shoulders with a decisive jerk.

"I am going to fail. I am so stinkin' going to fail that I'm going to need scuba gear to find my way up from the bottom of this class. And who gives a flying fig what a scarlet letter means anyway? Mother Teresa saved the starving orphans of the world, and I'll bet she did it without giving a rip about literary symbolism."

Hallie spit her muffled words into the mattress, then flipped onto her back. She sighed and opened her eyes.

"Stupid essay questions. I *hate* essay questions. Teachers just make up how they grade them anyway. Jill Emminga will get twenty out of twenty because the teacher thinks she's the best writer in the class, so it doesn't matter if what she says is a pile of horse pucky. Chelsea Delaney will get eighteen out of twenty for having a father on the school board, even though she doesn't know the difference between Charles Dickens and Charles Manson. And Hallie Bowen will get seven out of twenty for saying what she thinks."

Hallie slid from beneath the covers and headed across the plush yellow carpet toward her bedroom door, kicking a navy hoodie out of her path as she dodged the sneakers and jeans she'd left scattered the night before. An acrid odor rose from the clothes, and she wrinkled her nose as she shuffled past them and through an arc of light that spilled from a doorway that led down the dressing-room hallway to her bathroom. Ahead of her, a mirror on the six-panel mahogany door leading into the hallway reflected her image in the light from the dressing room as she reached for the oval brass knob. Her red hair was a jumbled mass, and she instinctively fluffed the curls that cascaded past her angular shoulders that were hunched in their usual, early morning slump. Her Tweety Bird T-shirt and gray flannel lounge pants were wrinkled and skewed from sleep, and she gave the pants a twist and a jerk before she opened the door and slipped into the hallway.

The upstairs bedrooms fanned out around the wide, vaulted hallway that was punctuated by a winding center staircase that cascaded to the floor below like the folds of a bridal gown. Hallie glanced toward the door to her mother's room directly across from her own. It was closed, and the crack beneath the door was dark. She rolled her eyes. What had she expected? She hadn't seen a sliver of light underneath that door before she'd left for school for the past two months. Some days when she got home at three, the waking up was just beginning.

Hallie hurried toward the stairs, her feet slapping quietly on the cold marble steps as she descended to the foyer. Imported Austrian etched glass windows on each side of the double mahogany doors glowed in the soft iridescence of the recessed lighting that had been installed to highlight them from dusk to dawn. During the school year, they were Hallie's silent timer, turning off automatically at 7:30. If she was still upstairs getting dressed when they turned off, chances were pretty good she'd be late. If she'd already come downstairs for breakfast, on most days she could grab a bagel and juice, walk the two blocks through the subdivision, and still make homeroom by 7:45.

Hallie turned and followed a long hallway past the library and dining room and into the kitchen, stopping in the doorway to flip on the lights. Several Coke cans and an empty Domino's Pizza box lay open on the cherry and granite island where she'd left them the night before, strewn among open textbooks, a spiral notebook, a camouflage book bag, and an open laptop computer with a screensaver that flashed photographs of beach scenes and lighthouses.

She headed toward a bank of country French cupboards on the far side of the island and pulled open a door, revealing a refrigerator bearing an assortment of condiments, salad dressings, wines, gourmet cheeses, and a Ziploc bag of pizza. She grabbed the bag and tossed it on the island behind her as she continued to rummage.

"We can't be out of Coke! How am I supposed to pass a test without a decent breakfast?"

She slammed the refrigerator shut and shoved a stray lock of hair behind her ear as she turned and scanned the countertops. Nothing. She grabbed the Ziploc bag, slid it open, and stuffed an enormous bite of pepperoni pizza into her mouth, then tossed the slice to the counter as she licked her fingers and headed toward the massive pantry off the hallway that led to the laundry room and back bathroom. She didn't know who she was angrier at—herself or her mother.

I can bet a month's allowance that Aunt Mona will ask how I did on this test when Mom and I show up tomorrow. Thank you, Mom, for giving her online access to my assignments and grades. I am so dead.

And I wonder what the rules of etiquette are for dinner conversation when your mom's sloshed so often that her brains must be pickled. "Well, Aunt Mona, I'm failing my classes because most nights I'm dragging my mother home from bars when she's too drunk to drive, or I'm cleaning up vomit when she does make it home. Now how about passing a little of that turkey and dressing!"

She stopped and leaned against a ladder-back chair that tucked into the built-in desk near the breakfast nook and stared at her knuckles as they gripped the spindles.

Today will be better.

The clock desk flipped from 6:10 to 6:11, then 6:12 before she forced her feet and her mind to move once again.

Today. She promised.

Hallie released her grip on the chair and reached to flip on the hall light. The important thing was to just keep moving, to do the next thing, to take the hurdles in front of you, one at a time, even if they felt like they were set a bit higher than the day before. Look down the road, and you'd never make it.

Hallie moved into the hallway toward the pantry. If she hurried, she'd have time to meet Abby and read through her notes a few more times before the test. Maybe even pray. Thank heaven for one friend who hadn't suddenly disappeared when she'd come home from Aunt Mona's this summer with a new interest in prayer and God. Abby was one of the few people who'd asked her honest questions, listened to the answers, and then begun to ask questions herself. Some of the questions had been about Aunt Mona and the accident. Others about Hallie's anger at God and why it seemed to be fading. Then one day her voice had joined Hallie's at the end of a prayer, and Abby began to look for answers on her own. She'd even bought a Bible.

Hallie hadn't been sure how Abby was going to react—if God might be the one subject that might scare her off. Nothing else had seemed to. In the two years since Stacy had died, her friend had pretty much seen it all and stuck by her through depression, counseling, drinking, and running away. And when it came to hauling her mother around, Hallie would have never guessed a scrawny ballet dancer would be tough enough to help carry her mother up the stairs to the master suite. The girl had pretty much freaked out the first time she'd discovered Hallie had gone out in a cab in the middle of the night, loaded up her mom, and driven her home in her Corvette Z06 when she'd found out her mom was too plowed to drive herself. But after the shock of the first time, Abby had seemed to understand there weren't a lot of options. It wasn't like Hallie's dad would have shown up, even if she'd bothered to call him. And even though she wasn't a licensed driver, Hallie was a good driver. Her dad had taken her out a few times in her mother's car. Abby had even told her parents selective parts of Hallie's situation, carefully leaving out her identity. They'd responded with sympathy when she'd told them she was "helping a friend with a substance-abuse problem whose parent was having trouble facing the issue."

Hallie laughed out loud as she walked down the hallway toward the pantry. "Pretty funny, Abby. How about 'I'm helping a screwed-up parent who won't face her substance-abuse issues'? Of course, if we actually said the truth out loud, my mother might have to face who she's become. Now wouldn't that be the day?" The words spilled from her as she rounded the corner to the pantry and reached for the light on the wall beside the door.

Hallie stood, frozen, as her eyes swept over the scene.

Boxes of Special K, Triscuits, Quaker Apple Cinnamon Rice Cakes, and assorted groceries were piled in a heap to the right of the door. A five-gallon plastic container had burst open, and a carpet of yellow Nutra Sweet packets and single-serving gourmet creamers blanketed the travertine tiles. Canned fruits and vegetables lay strewn in every direction.

Hallie surveyed the mess. The pantry shelves had been nearly emptied and dumped to the floor as though someone had swept them clean. The jumble of food and paper products made no sense until a familiar shape caught her eye. From beneath a mounded pile of Bounty paper towels and Charmin toilet tissue, her mother's size 6 Christian Dior sneakers jutted at an odd angle from the debris.

For a split second, Hallie stared at the skewed legs and sneakers beneath the mountain of nonperishables and wondered if perhaps her mother had simply chosen to rest on the floor in the wee hours of the morning. But that, of course, made no sense at all. Then she noticed the odor and the slick of liquid and the bottle that had skittered across the room and rolled beneath the lip of the oak cabinets.

Like a Magic Eye puzzle, the pieces floated into perspective. The scene before her was just another morning, another evening, another afternoon—different, but still the same.

"I'm so sick of this, Mom." She crouched and pulled aside the bundles of tissue and paper towels. "Are you sick of it yet—of sleeping in your puke?"

Hallie hurled a half-dozen packages of toilet paper into the hallway as she unearthed her mother's slumped form. Ellen Bowen lay faceup, her skin pale and clammy to the touch. Her shoulder-length blonde hair lay in a tangled web across her face, and Hallie brushed it back.

She slapped her mother gently on one cheek, then the other.

"Mom, wake up! Answer me. How much did you drink?"

Hallie's eyes scanned the room for other empty bottles, but she only saw the one that had slipped beneath the cabinet. She knew it meant nothing, that her mother could have been drinking all night, that other bottles could be in the trash, in the car, in her bedroom.

"Mom!"

Hallie rubbed her mother's cheeks as though warming her from the cold, then took her hands in her own, slapping the palms sharply. Her eyes searched her mother's face for signs of life. The eyelids were still.

Slowly, Hallie pushed herself to her feet and stepped back until she felt the resistance of the closet door where the vacuum, mops, and brooms were stored. Her eyes never left her mother's face as her right hand slid across the wood panel until her fingers found the knob.

She was suddenly aware that her feet were cold, and she glanced down. She was standing in a slick that had poured from the spilled bottle of vodka. Her hand dropped to her stomach as the familiar knot in her gut began to contract. Like a mist settling over a lake, she felt the slow descent of coldness over her heart. She stood motionless and staring as it enveloped her, her feet growing more chilled as the puddled liquid saturated her soles. When she spoke, her words were clear and steady.

"I have a test scheduled this morning, Mom, but maybe this is the real one. I don't think I'm supposed to be doing this anymore. I can't do it. This time you're going to have to clean up your own mess."

She turned off the light and walked back toward the kitchen, her feet leaving moist prints on the travertine tiles in the hall behind her.

Chapter Three

Mona turned toward the Yoders' gazebo and made her way through the dusting of fall leaves that lay strewn across the heaved-up sidewalk between Glenda's house and Chuck and Cissy Yoder's extra lot.

Life inside her own head would have been a lot less complicated if Glenda had turned on her dryer one warm day last spring and simply gone for a walk. The stupid cat would be dead, and she wouldn't be battling warring voices that percolated to the surface of her brain like a spiritual game of Whac-a-Mole every time she laid eyes on the decrepit creature.

Miss Emily seemed to bring out the worst in her. At the very sight of her, thoughts would bubble up that Mona wouldn't have believed possible—mangled, misshapen thoughts she'd tried over and over to beat down. Anger at God for allowing her to be flung upon the rocks in the Lake Michigan surf that had bashed her skull to oatmeal on the seawall. Or allowing her brain to be slivered and sliced, then leaving her in a coma for weeks as Hallie and Ellen had kept vigil at her side.

And what about the agony of Stacy's drowning—of the niece she'd lost to the grip of Lake Michigan's riptide in the instant when she'd turned her back and stepped away? Mona had prayed through that grief and anger in steady increments, letting it fall from her cupped hands like water as she'd parted her fingers of guilt. She'd fought against Ellen's attempts to refill her hands again and again—blaming her for not staying with the girls for those few seconds on the beach that day, for not coming faster, for allowing Hallie and Stacy to swim at all. It had taken almost two years for Ellen to begin to speak to Mona again, much less trust her to spend time with Hallie. None of them had been the same after Stacy's drowning, but the guilt and anger had gradually slipped from Mona's soul over the years until new pain and familiar voices of inadequacy had slipped into their place.

Mona's left toe caught on an edge of uneven pavement, and she stumbled, catching her breath as she staggered and caught her balance against the trunk of one of the many oaks that stood between the sidewalks and the streets of Stewartville. She assessed the distance as she caught her breath. Another forty feet, and she'd be home free.

She pushed off and set out over the grass, limping across the frost-laced lawn and heaving herself up the wooden steps of the Yoders' gazebo and toward the benches that had been built by the four boys and their dad. If Chuck Yoder had chosen a storage shed for the family project last summer, Mona was certain she would have perished mid-lap the morning of her first walk after she'd finally been released from Muskegon Mercy General and sent home to Stewartville. Some days, she still thought it might have been better if she'd just curled up in a heap and let the angels pluck her up. But most mornings, she focused on how good it felt to gulp deep draughts of loamy air on a crisp morning as her dragging feet sent heaps of auburn and yellow leaves billowing in her wake.

She slumped on a redwood bench encrusted in an icy glaze as her head fell back like a rag doll. Spikes of red hair jutted out from her head in crimson exclamation points as she massaged her left thigh slowly and focused on slowing her jagged gasps. Her breath rose in smoky wafts that hovered over her damp and splotched face before dissipating into the morning air like cream swirling through a coffee cup.

I'm not bolted down too tightly these days, Lord. One minute, I'm thinking about beaning a cat with a brick, and the next, I want to lie down and die myself. Part of me is grateful I'm alive, and the other is angry I'm not who I was before my accident. It seems like when I'm praying these days I'm spending most of my time apologizing for not being who I think I should be and being ashamed at who I am.

Half a block back, she'd thought long and hard about giving in to the pain and tucking herself neatly beneath Verna Leffingwell's butterfly bushes. She glanced down at the green jacket layered over the Saks sweat suit that had been Ellen's parting gift when they'd said good-bye at the beach house in August. Her sister had always had impeccable taste, right down to her Louis Vuitton bags and Hermès scarves. Mona smiled, envisioning Ellen's horror at discovering that her sister sweated publicly and prolifically without even a hint of mascara to soften the horror of it all. But makeup or not, if she collapsed today, at least she'd be in a designer sweat suit.

A trickle of blood traced its way down her palm, and she slipped her hand into the pocket of her jacket, searching for a tissue. Her fingers met a slip of paper as a car horn tooted, and she raised her hand to wave, not bothering to glance up.

An image flashed before her eyes of her body laid out in death. She was sure she'd make a striking corpse, her five-foot-ten frame nestled neatly in the autumn leaves beneath Verna's late-blooming pink blossoms, peacefully snoozing her way to Glory. It would give the folks of Stewartville something to talk about for the next few years—the day Mona VanderMolen just laid down and died under Verna Leffingwell's butterfly bushes on the eighth lap of her morning walk.

Mona's thoughts were interrupted as Bobby McGuirk sailed by on his Spree motor scooter and offered a vigorous wave, a half tail of his blue twill shirt flapping in the breeze like a wounded duck. Mona zipped her jacket higher under her chin. Even in the dead of winter, the boy never wore a coat.

She offered a half-hearted wave in return and squeezed her eyes tightly shut against the pain in her leg. She imagined Bobby would most likely find her body while he was cruising to work for his shift at the Crystal Flash gas station. Everyone in Stewartville knew you could set your watch by Bobby, who through promptness and meticulous attention to windshield washing, had proudly risen to the rank of assistant manager at the age of eighteen and had earned the privilege of wearing a navy twill shirt with an oval patch bearing his name. He'd most likely make the front page of the *Stewartville Sentinel* and revel in celebrity status at Trina's Café for weeks to come.

The hammering rhythm had eased to a familiar throb. Mona raised her head slowly and pressed her palms to her temples as pinpricks of light danced behind her closed eyelids. Her thoughts beat a familiar rhythm of their own cadence.

I didn't think I asked for a lot. Just ten blocks by Thanksgiving— walking, not running or jogging or doing the Hokey-Pokey. Just a simple, ten-block walk without a cane.

Just ten blocks, Lord.

It didn't seem like a lot to ask from You—the God who designed mosquito wings and the northern lights.

The wind brushed her shoulders, and a chill passed through

her. She glanced up. At the edge of the lot, Verna's bushes shook in the wind, and a shower of blossoms fell to the ground. She shoved her hands into her pockets for warmth. The paper brushed her fingers, and she pulled her hands back out and tucked them hastily beneath her legs.

Everyone in Stewartville knew Verna's butterfly bushes were always the last to succumb to the fall frost. By the time Ellen and Hallie arrived tomorrow, the bushes would be naked. And by the time Adam came on Thanksgiving, the blossoms would have dried and drifted into obscurity. Mona smiled. She knew he'd bring his own flowers. The man seemed to be positively obsessed with them, and if he had to have an obsession, he'd chosen a good one, even if he was directing his attentions toward a deranged woman.

Beneath her thighs, Mona's fingertips burned. The electronic sign on First Federal Bank had read twenty-eight degrees at ten o'clock as she'd made the swing from the back alley behind the antique shop west onto Maple and north onto Second Street. She knew she couldn't sit long, or the Stewartville paramedics would have to thaw her from the bench. A fleeting vision of blowtorches and water cannons aimed at her backside flickered through her brain, and she squirmed as the icy planks of the bench bit into her thighs.

Does even sitting have to be hard, Lord? And when did I turn into a whiner—a middle-aged, brain-damaged, broken-down whiner with really bad hair, for that matter? I can hardly stand myself like this, and I don't see how You can stand me. I'm frustrated and angry, and I'm tired of being who I've become. I want to take care of myself again. I want to walk without collapsing in a heap like a snowman in a spring thaw. I want to think without groping for words. I want to be who I was before I got flung on the rocks like a rag doll.

It didn't seem she was asking for much—not for the parting of the waters in Fish Creek or for the sun to stand still over Miller's IGA. Just to do the simple things she'd been able to do in the *before* time rather than to be defined by the things that had disappeared in the sweep of a wave. The small things, like jogging on a summer morning, or reading a newspaper without the words dancing off the page, or sitting in a crowd without her head exploding like a supernova.

The small things had worn her down and become her enemies, things she'd tried to keep people from seeing. Things she'd tried to tell herself didn't matter, except they did. They'd crawled into the nooks and crannies of her mind where fear and fatigue lived, and she'd tried to keep them hidden there, but hiding had only deepened the pain.

She shrugged her shoulders against the icy breeze that pinched her ears and raised a hand to her hair. Her once-tangled mane of curls was gone, sacrificed to the craniotomy that had saved her life. At least a dozen times a day, she lifted her hands to run her fingers through the familiar curls, only to be met by the spiky shafts. She bounced her palm against the points as though patting herself on the head like a child.

At least one thing that's gone is coming back, she assured herself. She crammed her hand back into her pocket and touched the familiar slip of paper. She clenched it in her fist.

So do you plan to go through with it or not? What are you afraid of? It's not like finding out the truth changes anything.

The burning in her fingertips had moved into her hands, and her toes were beginning to tingle. She flexed them inside her tennis shoes, hoping the movement would stimulate circulation. She let the paper fall from her fingers, pulled her hands from her pockets, and slapped her fingers against her thighs. Down the street just beyond Junie Clarence's overgrown juniper hedge, Mona caught sight of Officer Spencer's cruiser passing slowly through the intersection of Mercantile and Elm, heading east. She raised a hand limply and waved. From inside the cab, Officer Spencer nodded as the cruiser eased down the street.

Mona checked her Timex—10:48. If she didn't make it back to the shop soon, Elsie would be calling. The woman was positively maniacal about Mona's morning routine.

I am not moving yet. Just two more minutes before I have to face the questions again, even though I'm turning to ice.

She tried to silence her thoughts and soak in the final moments of solitude, but her inner dialogue buzzed like an irksome fly.

The doctors had said to rest, so she'd rested. Life had become a predictable cycle of therapy, naps, Adam's calls and weekend visits, and Elsie's constant hovering to make sure she was towing the line. But recovery? What did that even mean anymore?

What if this is all there is? Am I ready to live with that? And how can I be sure I won't lose what I've fought so hard to get back?

There was no way of ignoring it. She couldn't stand the cold much longer. It didn't matter, anyway. The only thing that mattered at this moment was that at the end of her walk, she'd have to face Elsie. Once again, Mona considered lying down beneath Verna's bushes and calling it quits.

What seemed like a hundred and one times a day, Elsie had found reasons to slip upstairs from the shop and into Mona's apartment on rehab days and scrutinize the therapist's every move, scowling, scolding, and offering constant correction. It didn't matter that Elsie McFeeney didn't know one iota about occupational therapy or that she knew even less about rehabilitation from brain injuries. When it came to advising anyone on anything, Elsie had been Stewartville's resident expert for almost three-quarters of a century, and God bless anyone who tried to tell her differently.

For weeks, Mona's early morning walks had been her secret escape from Elsie, from everyone. No medical personnel. No rehab therapists. No well-intentioned neighbors and church friends. No furrowed brows or pursed lips or awkward silences. No need to be perky if she wanted to kick rocks or cry or plot the murder of a cat.

Just the silence of morning, the anticipation of another day, and the hope that perhaps the legs that wobbled and shook might carry her just half a block farther than the day before.

Until the morning that Elsie discovered that Mona was walking the streets of Stewartville in the early morning hours when "only God knew what wacko was up and about lookin' for trouble." And so the walks were pushed back to a "decent" hour of the morning. Some battles Mona no longer had the strength to fight.

The strains of "You Are My Sunshine" broke into her thoughts, and she reached into her pants pocket for her cell phone.

"Do I need to come get you?"

Mona sighed softly. "No, Elsie. I'm fine."

"I've been watchin' out the window, and you haven't passed for ten minutes. You sittin' at the Yoders' again?"

"Just for a minute. I'm fine, really."

"You and I know, girl, that you don't sit unless you're fixin' to pass out cold in your tracks, so's you just wait there until I call Harold and have him come to pick you up. He's home bakin' cherry pies for tomorrow, and he needs to take a break for a spell. Just sit tight until he gets there."

"I'm just heading back now, Elsie."

"I said sit, child. Now how far did you get this morning?"

Mona fought back the urge to remind Elsie that a forty-five-year-old woman did not need to be called a child or reminded to sit like one. "Almost eight."

"Well that's almost ten. Don't go all mule-eyed on the world and lookin' at your life like a half-empty glass, Mona VanderMolen. That's five more times around the block than you could walk when you came home from the hospital in August, praise the Lord, with your brains all smashed in. By Christmas, it'll be ten, and by next summer at the beach house, you'll be walkin' all the way to Grand Haven and back. Now hold on just a splickety-second and Harold will be there for you. I'm givin' him strict instructions to take you directly to Trina's for a farmer's omelet before he brings you home. Gotta get some meat on your bones before the snow flies, or you'll die your death of cold this winter."

Mona set her lips. She had no intention of allowing Harold to pick her up or to take her to Trina's for any kind of omelet. She was walking home herself and would tell Elsie so in no uncertain terms. But she also knew that the biggest hitch in her plan was that Elsie never recognized uncertain terms unless they were her own.

"I'm fine, Elsie. Harold's got enough to do today with his baking."

A police car rounded the corner of Mercantile and Maple and pulled up in front of the gazebo. Mona threw Officer Spencer a smile and waved as he opened the door of the cruiser and stepped out, then walked slowly toward her. One hand rested on his hip, and he paused as he noted the phone at Mona's ear.

"Joe Spencer just pulled up, Elsie, and I'm sure he can give me a ride home if I need one."

She refused to lie. She had no intention of asking Joe for a ride, but he would certainly be willing to provide one if Mona asked. The look in his eyes as he approached, however, told her he hadn't stopped for a morning chat. For a moment, she wondered if he'd seen her clutching a brick in front of Glenda's house. She felt her cheeks flush.

"Gotta go, Elsie. See you soon."

Mona rose slowly as Joe Spencer approached. His brow was drawn into a furrow over brown eyes, and he pulled his officer's cap from his head as he stepped into the gazebo and stood before Mona.

"Miss V, you feeling all right?"

"I'm fine, just a tad winded. Anything I can do for you?"

The officer shifted his weight. He was one of Stewartville's two and a half finest, and Mona had known him from the first day she'd driven into town and discovered the speed trap that had helped boost Stewartville's revenues over the years.

"As a matter of fact, yes. If you could step into the car with me, I'll be glad to offer you an arm. I need to ask you to come down to the station so we can discuss a police matter."

Mona felt the blood drain from her face. Even if he'd seen her in front of Glenda's, he couldn't possibly have known what she was thinking.

"What police matter?"

The muscles worked in his jawline as Mona's mind raced. He cleared his throat. "With all due respect, I know your health hasn't been strong, Miss V, and it won't be easy to talk about this. I think it might be helpful if you called a close friend or family member— maybe Elsie McFeeney or Harold Rawlings? I'm sure one of them would be willing to meet you at the station. If I could just get you to the car first, I can offer an explanation once you're settled inside."

Mona felt the pressure of his fingers as he took her gently by the arm and navigated her toward the ice-covered steps. The pain in her leg and the throb in her head dissipated into a faint, hovering awareness—pressing and pulsing in a silent rhythm as she felt herself being led away.

The last thing she remembered as the door to the cruiser closed behind her was Miss Emily staring at her behind the glass of Glenda Simpson's bay window.

Chapter Four

Mona was certain the Effinghams' cows had plotted to melt down her brains by causing her migraine.

She sat slumped in a straight-back oak chair, facing Joe Spencer across his desk in the first of four rooms that defined Stewartville's police department in city hall. Her head was cupped in her hands, her eyes closed as she sat and waited for Joe to get off the dispatch radio. Between thoughts of panic about why she was there, she tried to screen out the thought that her pounding head was about to blow her pupils clear to the Meijer store in Greenville.

It was impossible to sit in the room and not hear every word broadcast on the dispatch radio. Stewartville was in crisis. The Effinghams' Jerseys had instigated a rebellion against their electric fence, and half a dozen or so had taken possession of M-57 on the east side of town. Traffic was backed up nearly to the Middleton Mennonite Bakery, an event that seemed to be warranting the dispatch of Stewartville's only other full-time police officer, not to mention a flurry of conversation between Nellie Krell, the front-desk receptionist, and Alvira Miller, the city clerk. As soon as the call had come in, the women had moved as one to the hallway drinking fountain across from Joe's open office door. Minutes later, Mona had heard Nellie dialing the *Stewartville Sentinel.* Mona made a mental note to check this week's paper to see if errant cows made the front page.

Between throbs, she prayed for the cows to go home and for Joe Spencer to end her speculation about why on earth she'd been dragged into the station. In the two minutes it had taken them to drive to city hall, she'd envisioned a garish kaleidoscope of possibilities. She was certain her blood pressure was rising with the speed of each flashing image.

"Miss V?"

Mona's eyes flew open, and she pulled herself upright.

"I took the liberty of calling Harold and asking him to come down and join us. I hope you don't mind. He should be here any minute."

"Mind? Why should I mind? And what on earth is going on that you'd be calling a seventy-six-year-old man to sit with me? You're scaring me here, Joe. And let's cut the 'Miss V' stuff. I get the fact that you respect me and this is police business, but you're Joe and I'm Mona. Now could we please move on to why I'm here?"

Joe Spencer cleared his throat as he picked up a pen and began to drum on the coffee-stained calendar covering his desk.

"Mona, earlier this morning I pulled over a vehicle coming west into town down M-57. The driver was doing seventy in a fifty-five, but that was only one of my concerns. She was underage and unlicensed."

Mona swallowed and felt her head growing light.

Pulled over. That meant she was alive, thank God.

"The other, bigger problem was that she had an intoxicated passenger passed out in the backseat. The passenger was so drunk that I immediately called an ambulance and had her transported to the hospital because I was fearful of alcohol poisoning. I know this may be difficult for you to hear, but I have Hallie in the lounge down the hallway. Your sister, Ellen, has been admitted to Stewartville Community Hospital and has been placed in intensive care. The doctors are giving her the very best care they possibly can, but she's very sick."

For a moment Joe Spencer's face faded beneath Mona's stare. She blinked and willed her eyes to refocus, to pull the whirling details in both her mind and her vision into perspective. Only two things mattered, and she knew what they were. She stood.

"I've got to see Hallie. Where is she?"

Joe rose and stepped to Mona's side. He laid a hand on her arm, his brown eyes catching hers and holding. Mona wondered how old he could be. Twenty-eight? Thirty? His job had to be tough—knowing everyone in Stewartville and their families. She could see how hard he was trying to make this easy on her. His smile was warm and tinged with a gentle awkwardness.

"She's in the break room. I got her a Coke and some chips. She was pretty shook up when the ambulance arrived with the EMTs. She kind of freaked out when they mentioned the word *coma*, and she kept repeating that she thought her mother had just passed out like all the other times, that she didn't know it was alcohol poisoning, she didn't know she should have called 911 right away."

"Alcohol poisoning?" Media images flashed through Mona's mind, of frat parties and tightly zipped body bags being rolled into ambulances. So it had gotten this bad. As far as she knew, Ellen had never let it go this far before.

Panic gripped her, and she turned and hurried from the room and down the long hallway, dragging her hand lightly along the paneled wall as she made her way to the end of the corridor. She paused for a moment before she pushed open a door marked Break Room.

Hallie sat on a gray vinyl loveseat facing a Coke machine, her back to the door. Her feet were planted on the seat, her chin resting on her knees and her arms clasped around her legs as though she were holding herself together. A mass of shoulder-length red hair poured from her head in a wild jumble of curls that spilled onto her gray hoodie.

Mona walked across the room and slipped her hands around Hallie's shoulders as she bent to hug her, the red curls enveloping her face as their cheeks brushed.

"I'm here, Hal." She whispered the words.

Mona felt the muscles draw taut.

"I'm so very, very sorry, honey. I should have seen this coming, should have figured this out sooner. If I'd only known . . ."

Hallie pulled away and looked up. Her face was puffy and swollen, but her green eyes were dry. "If you'd only known, then what? You'd have called and talked some sense into her? The only thing she listens to is a bottle. Or maybe you could have come down for a weekend? On a good day she might have noticed you were there. What about locking her in her room and throwing away the key? I played around with that idea a few times."

Mona ignored the sarcasm.

"How bad has it been?"

Hallie choked out a humorless laugh. "You don't want me to answer that question."

"I wouldn't have asked if I didn't want an answer."

Mona clutched the back of the loveseat as she straightened to stand, then stepped to the other side, sat beside Hallie, and took her hands. The faint odor of liquor drifted to her nose.

Dear God, no, please no. She shoved away the image that leaped into her mind as possibilities formed. How could she have been so blind and not asked more questions, not paid more attention?

"I didn't know what to do." The voice was wooden.

"You brought her to me. That was the right thing to do."

"I might have killed her—I should have called an ambulance right away. Did the cop tell you she's in critical condition—that this time she drank so much her heart and lungs were shutting down?"

A wave of nausea swept over Mona. She turned toward the door and looked into Joe's eyes. He drew in his breath and nodded.

Dear God, it's Stacy all over again. It can't be happening. Hallie can't take this again. This child has already lost her sister and her father. When is enough going to be enough?

She closed her eyes for a moment and forced herself to focus. No matter how she felt right now, where was the truth? She opened her eyes. Hallie was staring at the Coke machine, her fingers picking at the hem of her jeans.

"Hallie, you brought your mom to me because you knew you needed help, and I should have been there to see you got it long before this. You brought her here because you're smart. For the past three months, you've been doing the best job anyone could ever do in the middle of a horrible mess. Not even an adult could handle this alone. I should have figured this out months ago and never let you go home alone with your mom at the end of the summer. After your dad left, she just couldn't cope. She'd already lost Stacy. It was too much for her to handle, and I should have seen it.

"But you—you did the right thing. You brought her here because you were trying to take care of her."

Hallie lifted her head, and her green eyes reflected a hardness Mona hadn't expected to see. She had expected tears or anger, maybe even fear. But not the calm coldness that radiated from somewhere deep, where scars and wounds had hardened the soul.

"No, you're wrong. I brought my mother here because I'm sick and tired of playing nurse to someone who doesn't care a thing about me. I've given up on her. I've been cleaning up her puke for three months. I'm failing every class in school because I'm nothing but a babysitter for someone sucking on a bottle of vodka every night. I can barely take care of myself, much less her. My dad's shacking up with some chick who could be my sister, and I want to go live with him as much as I'd like to poke a stick through my eyeball. So I was bringing my mother to you, Aunt Mona. Your half-dead, drunk sister and your delinquent niece who may have killed her own mother by being too stupid to call 911 have landed on your doorstep. Happy Thanksgiving."

The words hung suspended between them as Mona searched for a response. The only one that came seemed hollow, but she spoke it, trusting the truth that lay beneath the words, knowing she had to speak them as much for herself as for Hallie.

"We're not giving up, Hal."

In the hallway behind her, slow steps echoed on the vinyl floor, and Mona tightened her grip on Hallie's hand as she turned. Beside Joe Spencer, Harold Rawlings stood in the doorway in his bib overalls, his plaid flannel shirt buttoned clear to his Adam's apple. He held a Perrinton Grain Elevator cap in his hands. Hair that at one time was blond had faded to a gray-streaked wheat and was parted neatly to one side with bangs cut straight across his forehead like an Amish schoolboy. At seventy-six, Harold's face still held the look of a child who had grown taller, more round-shouldered, and whose eyes had gathered up the span of his years and held them there. He was leaning lightly on a cane, and Mona shook her head. The winter months were a bad time for his gout to be acting up again.

"Is it okay if I step in? Joey Spencer here, who I'm proud to say I taught to use his first router, gave me a call and asked me if I could come down."

Hallie's feet dropped to the floor, and she whirled where she sat.

"Harold?"

The old man's face broke into a smile.

"Yes, Miss Hallie Bowen."

The girl jumped up and ran to the door, wrapping the older man's lanky frame in a long embrace. He smiled, the long lines of his face softening as he leaned forward, awkwardly holding his cane and raising his free hand to her shoulders.

Joe stepped into the room. "Mona, I've asked Harold if he'd sit with Hallie a few minutes while you and I talk briefly in my office. Is that all right?"

Mona gripped the arm of the loveseat as she stood, then walked toward the hallway as she watched Harold draw back, point to Hallie's bare feet, and shake his head as she smiled back.

"It's okay, Aunt Mona. The cop probably needs to talk to you about what to do with the delinquent kid and the drunk sister. Adult stuff you can talk about privately so you don't upset the kid. Harold and I will sit here and discuss why teenagers today wear flip-flops in November. And what's with the cane?"

Harold held Hallie at arm's length and looked her up and down. "The kid looks too big for her own britches, if you ask me. The cane is for whacking teenagers who get out of line. Sounds like she could use some lessons in manners from a man who doesn't have to provide explanations to curious teenagers for the aches and pains of getting old." He took her by the arm and steered her toward the loveseat. "Now teach me a thing or two about flip-flops and how teenagers manage to keep from getting pneumonia in those things." He turned to Mona. "We'll be just fine here for as long as you need us to be."

Mona watched, astounded, as Hallie dropped willingly into the loveseat.

"We should only be a minute," Joe said, reaching to close the door behind Mona as she turned to face him. She glanced right and left down the corridor. No chair. It appeared they'd be talking where they stood. She leaned heavily against the wall and shoved her hands into her pockets, wishing she could slide the full weight of her body down the wall and collapse onto the floor. How long had it been since she'd left the apartment that morning? It felt as if she'd been gone for a week.

"Mona, I'm afraid the news about Ellen isn't good. Her blood alcohol is almost six hundred, and they've placed her on a ventilator. It's important to get you to the hospital as soon as possible, but we need to make sure your niece is going to be all right. Just let me know how I can help. The hospital called and asked how soon you might be coming so you can help provide a history."

"Aspirin."

"Aspirin?"

"She's deathly allergic to aspirin. But I don't suppose they treat you for alcohol poisoning with aspirin, do they? Write this down!"

Instantly, the officer's notebook was in his hand as details poured from Mona's mouth.

"She's O positive, and she had an appendectomy when she was eleven. She's had cosmetic surgery, a face lift or something like that. Anything else, she hasn't told me about. And she's on meds—tons of meds. I'm just not sure what. Something for her nerves, and something for migraines. You need to call this in and tell them I'm coming just as soon as I've made arrangements for Hallie."

Joe Spencer glanced up from his notebook. "Will she be going to the hospital with you?"

Mona had decided the answer the moment she'd seen Harold.

"No. She can't right now. Later, maybe, when her mom's better."

Mona watched as Joe Spencer's hand hovered above the paper, then drew a final flourish.

"Let me know when you're ready, and I'll drive you."

Mona felt a knot rising in her throat. "Thanks, Joe. I'll just be a minute or two, I think, but I'd like you to understand one thing. I love my sister very much, and I'm praying with every fiber in my soul that she makes a full recovery. But right now, I'm confident she's getting the very best treatment she could possibly receive. So I'm not leaving here until I'm sure Hallie's okay, do you understand? This kid's been through more than I could possibly explain, and right now, she's the conscious one. I'm not abandoning her."

The officer closed his notebook and slipped it into his pocket. "Just let me know when you're ready." Then he turned and walked down the hallway and disappeared into his office.

Mona closed her eyes, and her lips moved in silent prayer as the murmur of voices drifted through the door. She shifted her weight, and her hand slipped deeper inside her pocket, her fingers brushing paper.

She pulled the slip from her pocket and carefully unfolded the familiar creases of the yellow form that had been given to her at her last neurology appointment.

MRI with and without contrast, cerebellum. Three month follow-up, craniotomy. Scheduled for November 3 at 3 PM at Muskegon

Mercy General Hospital. The first date had been crossed out, and a second date handwritten beneath it: November 17, 1 PM. The second date had also been crossed out with a red ink pen.

I've got no time for this, Lord. You see what I've got on my hands. If there's something going on in my brain, You're going to have to patch me together.

She gripped the slip tightly in her hand as she reached for the door, but before she had the chance to turn the knob, Hallie flung it open.

"I'm going home with Harold to help him bake pies. Since you and my mom can't even handle frozen bread dough, this may be my only chance to learn anything remotely domestic. I figure you have to say yes. Harold gets a little help, I get a little education, and everyone breathes easier knowing Hallie isn't doing something stupid."

Mona opened her mouth, then closed it. At the precise moment she was certain she needed to be in charge, a fifteen-year-old had taken over. Or maybe not. Perhaps it had been Harold or God. She couldn't be sure whose idea it had been, just that it was a good plan.

"I could use a little company, Mona. I felt a little peaky this morning, so I'm glad for the help." Harold had joined Hallie, and they stood side by side, as mismatched a pair of friends as Mona had ever seen, a senior citizen in a grain-elevator cap and a renegade teenager in a hoodie and flip-flops. Mona couldn't imagine anyone she'd rather have beside her niece.

"I agree. Officer Spencer has agreed to drive me to the hospital. I need to get there soon to give them your mother's medical history, and I'll need to stay as long as she needs me—possibly overnight or a few days. Harold, if you'd call Elsie and tell her what's happening, I'd appreciate it. Hallie, I'll call with details about your mom as soon as I know anything."

Mona's fist clenched the paper in her pocket as she wadded it into a ball. Then she angled her body away from Harold and Hallie and turned toward a blue plastic trashcan in the hallway, where she dropped it. It ricocheted from the rim and skittered toward the wall.

Dr. Bailey had told her what symptoms to watch for. But her face wasn't drooping, and her vision wasn't blurred, and her head hadn't exploded yet, although some days it felt like it might. She had everything under control. The lights and the dizziness were simply some wacky new form of migraine to add to her list of post-craniotomy symptoms.

They had to be.

"Drop something, Mona?" Harold asked, glancing back as he directed Hallie toward the door.

"Just tossing something I didn't need." Mona stepped in front of him and headed down the hallway to Joe Spencer's office.

As she spoke, a starburst of light cascaded through her right eye. She fought to blink away the pinpricks as she shoved away a growing fear that pulled at her heart: that when Ellen woke up—if she woke up—she would see glimmers of the hard-hearted stubbornness that had brought her through the doors of Stewartville's emergency room reflecting from Mona's own eyes.

Chapter Five

Adam slammed the door of the blue Suburban behind him and crunched through the piles of dead leaves that had drifted in soft mounds on the gravel parking lot of the Pentwater Artisans' Center.

Just one hour to get in and get on, then on to the tough job—sweet talking Aunt Florence out of her recipe for butter crescent rolls. Mona VanderMolen, what have you done to me—giving me the nerve to take on Aunt Flo just to coax an extra smile from you?

He'd worked extra hard for Mona's smiles in the past few weeks. They'd grown fewer and farther between, and the thought worried him. Something was wrong, and she wasn't talking about it.

Like Julie.

He refused to let the idea take root. Mona wasn't Julie. Mona could be trusted, and when she figured the time was right, she'd talk about whatever it was. She certainly didn't owe him explanations of her every thought and action. In the meantime, he had a project to finish and baking to get started. Tomorrow was Thanksgiving, and if he didn't stay focused, he'd never get everything done.

The single car in the lot told him Gene Davidson, the center's founder, had come in to do paperwork before the early morning crowd arrived to work on their painting, pottery, woodworking, and assorted craft projects. When Adam had moved to Apling-ton and his uncle Elmer had told him about the Pentwater Arti-sans' Center, Adam had been struck by its founder's vision. The center had become a community where area artists and trades-men could access tools and equipment to hone their skills and develop their crafts. People from the community paid a small membership fee and used the center to work on projects not in-tended for profit.

In Adam's profession as a skilled tradesman who sold his pieces, he'd never had a reason to use the center until the day he called Gene to ask his advice about brands of shapers, and Gene had told him about a friend named Linas Hallett.

"Heard you know a woman in Stewartville name of Vander-Molen who owns the antique store that used to be Hallett's Hard-ware," Gene said. "I have a friend who grew up in Stewartville who'd like to meet you and talk to you about something he thinks might make you sit up and smile."

Gene had been right. Every time Adam thought of his first meeting with Linas, he smiled. And every time he envisioned Mo-na's surprise at what Linas had sold him, he broke into a full-faced grin.

Adam stepped through the gray metal rear entrance door and inside the expansive workroom. He made his way quickly through a line of lathes, band saws, table saws, and other woodworking tools and toward the beauty that had preoccupied his thoughts and stolen so much of his time the past four weeks—a turn-of-the-century, general-store counter embellished with hand-carved acanthus leaf moldings. His grin broadened as he drew closer, not-ing the deep luster of the red oak and the triple panel insets. He stopped just short of its massive length and placed his hands on his hips, then moved nearer and laid his palms on the surface of the countertop.

Squinting, he ran his fingers across the grain of the wood in a slow, circular motion. It had taken him a week to decide whether to refinish or restore the piece. In the end, he hadn't been able to bring himself to disturb the aged luster of the wood. Instead, he'd simply buffed it to a deep sheen and let the beauty of the grain speak for itself. It had only seemed right.

Now, as he inspected his work, he knew he'd made the right decision. His fingers searched for the slightest snag of imperfection but were met with only the silky surface. His smile widened. The wood beneath his fingers became Mona's skin as he held her arm on Saturday walks and felt the press of her weight as she leaned into his side for support. He saw her head tossed back in delight at the sight of a friend or a call from Hallie, and he heard the deep timbre of her full-throated laugh.

Adam pulled his thoughts back into the present. He needed to focus on the moment and the truth that had wrestled him to the floor weeks before—there was no going back. Every phone call, every commute to Stewartville over the past three months had been one more decision to move forward. One day at a time, he'd pulled Mona into the center of his life, and he couldn't see any way of moving toward his future without keeping her there forever.

Forever?

The word carried weight. He'd tested his strength beneath it once before, and it had almost crushed him.

And what's behind her silences, the hesitation that seems to be growing? How do we move into a future if she won't even trust me for the present?

He shrugged off his jacket and tossed it over a radial arm saw mounted on a stand. The truth was, he didn't know. He wasn't sure what Mona was trusting right now. The only thing he knew he could bank on was that tomorrow they'd be together, and for the first time since Mona had come home from the hospital, they'd be with Ellen and Hallie. When the day was over, he'd be sure they made time to talk—a long, relaxed conversation at her apartment. And she'd never suspect that his well-crafted plan had been unfolding right beneath her nose the entire day.

If he could get Ellen to cooperate.

Ellen, of course, was the one potential glitch in the plan. Too much hinged on Mona's sister, and it worried him. The woman was a loose cannon. He had no reason to believe she'd give him the time of day, much less trust him. In the end, he could be risking it all on the gamble that Ellen would be willing to help him surprise Mona with the most monumental gift of her life.

He crossed his arms as he examined the piece he'd so painfully negotiated to purchase. It was a beauty. An eight-foot expanse of red oak that stood like a queen commanding her subjects among the lathes, drills, and other woodworking tools. From the moment he'd laid eyes on the piece a month ago, he'd known it would be perfect.

And how could it be more perfect: the original counter from Hallett's Hardware in Stewartville—the building that had become a pizza and an ice-cream parlor, then Stewartville Antiques. This would be Mona's Christmas gift.

"Please don't mess this up for me, Ellen. You're the one person who can torpedo all the details I've set into motion for this woman."

He stepped around the counter and bent down, pulling two slabs of fresh red oak from the open back. Then he turned and walked across the workroom toward a table saw.

Negotiating for Linas Hallett's family treasure hadn't come cheap. Through the Pentwater grapevine, Linas had heard the story of a love-struck furniture craftsman and his antique-dealer lady friend, and he'd played his cards like a pro. Hallett's Hardware had been built in 1891, and even though the Hallett building had been sold by the family in the 1930s, the counter had graced the same store in Stewartville for more than three quarters of a century before the pizza store owners had pulled it out to remodel in the sixties. When Linas Hallett got word that the counter was being sold off, he'd purchased it and put it into storage in his barn at his home near Pentwater where it had collected dust for more than forty years. It had cost Adam three lunches at the Brown Bear and a check for twice what he'd hoped to negotiate. But in the end, both Linas and Adam had gotten what they'd wanted. And the men agreed on one thing: the piece deserved a second life in its original home, where it would be admired and put to use for another generation.

Adam stopped in front of the table saw and stacked the boards on two sawhorses as he pulled his safety glasses from his denim shirt pocket and held them up to the light. A thick film of sawdust coated the lenses, so he reached for his front shirttail to wipe them before settling them over his eyes.

A lot had changed in the past three years since Julie had died, and a lot more since he'd met Mona. He hadn't seen any of it coming, the good or the bad. And as much as he'd planned in his life, God always seemed to come up with an alternate route, sending him down roads he'd never have chosen. But the Lord had dropped a good woman into his life and had given him courage to set a new course. And tomorrow, he'd set the first step in motion.

Adam pulled a note card from his pocket and checked the

measurements for the shelves he'd taken three days earlier, then selected a board and laid it on the deck of the table saw as a scene flashed before his eyes.

Julie pulling a chambray shirt off a rack and their tug-of-war as he protested. The determination in her shoulders as she carried it to the check-out, then her grin as she'd tugged him into a pretzel shop as an act of penance.

He blinked, as though for an instant the image had truly been there. Then he slid the card back into his pocket.

Are you ready to risk it again, this time for a woman who may end up being an invalid for the rest of her life? What about five years from now or ten, when things could get worse?

And every time you try to talk to her about how she really feels, she pushes you away. Ellen can't stand you, and Hallie's had enough trauma for ten teenagers. Is that the family you want?

You live in a guest house and work for your aunt and uncle. They're getting ready to retire and sell the business out from under you. Only an idiot would be looking to commit to a woman in this mess. Admit it. You're crazy.

Adam readjusted the safety glasses and snugged the nosepiece firmly against his face. A crazy man? Was it crazy to be falling for a smart, beautiful, compassionate woman who loved God?

A door slammed behind him, and he turned. Bill Mulligan was headed his way, lifting his oil-stained John Deere hat and running his fingers through a few wisps of graying hair as he ambled with the rolling gait that announced he was overdue for at least one knee replacement. He stopped near a mammoth Shop-Vac next to a lathe and plopped his hefty frame onto a gray metal office chair. His red flannel shirt was untucked on one side, and his worn jeans rode a tad high over a well-used pair of steel-toed boots.

"Got that cabinet of yours rubbed down to a toothpick yet, Adam? Heaven knows you've been polishing it like a man possessed. You've sure been zip-lipped about who you're giving it to—we've all decided it's gotta be a lady, the way you're working yourself like a crazy man."

Adam laughed. "That's pretty funny, actually, Bill. So what makes you think I'm a crazy man?"

"Well, it's not just me, really. All the woodworking guys and the pottery folks, we took a vote. You put in more hours on that cabinet than the rest of us combined. You're sure not doing it for money because we'd have to throw you out of the place if you was going to sell the thing, so you must be doing it for love. You must be nuts over somebody. I don't suppose you'd like to fill us all in on the name of the mystery woman?"

Adam reached for the card and a pencil in his pocket and inspected the measurements for his cuts. Then he pulled a measuring tape from a hip pocket and began marking cuts as Bill spun his oil-stained hat in his hands.

"Sounds like you've wasted your time doing a whole lot of assuming, Bill. Now if you'll excuse me, I've got more work than time here."

With a flick of Adam's thumb, the table saw sprang to life, and he drew the blade down into the fresh wood as a spray of dust rose into the air. Within seconds, the safety glasses he'd so carefully cleaned were coated again with a film of dust.

Seconds later, the whine of the saw hung in the air, then faded. Adam glanced at Bill, then pulled the glasses from his face. He rammed them into the pocket of his chambray shirt at the sight of Bill's broad grin as the question echoed back.

Mona VanderMolen, what have you done to me?

He'd known the answer for weeks. The time had come to face it or let it go.

"If you'll excuse me, Bill, there's a call I've got to make." Adam reached for his cell phone and headed for the back door.

Whether she would cooperate or not, the time had come to call Ellen.

Chapter Six

Mona was only vaguely aware of the three-block ride to the hospital or of Joe Spencer's hand on her back as he guided her through the hallways into the intensive care unit. Something inside her relaxed under his control for those moments, and she relinquished her thoughts to a kaleidoscope of fears for Ellen, guilt over Hallie, and prayers for them both.

But the somber gray eyes of a thirty-something doctor brought her back as though she'd suddenly wakened from sleepwalking, and he delivered the report of Ellen's condition. She wished, as he spoke, that his expression would not seem so certain, that he would glance at the papers he held in his hand or announce an overlooked fact or new lab result. But his eyes stared straight into hers as she leaned heavily against the wall outside Ellen's door in the critical care unit. Something inside her told her that if he would just stop talking or if she could think of the right question to ask, the world might rewind to the way it had been before, except that the "before" time held the horrors that had brought them all here.

But the doctor's eyes never looked away, and his quiet stream of words continued.

"Elevated blood alcohol content . . . repressed respiration . . . ventilator . . . unknown resolution . . . possible long-term implications . . ."

With each phrase, new realizations pressed her soul until the weight of his words felt as if they would crush her to the floor. The rhythm of her heart pulsated in her stomach. Whispers of fear had been lying in wait from the moment she'd heard Joe Spencer's words, and the doctor's pronouncement gave them full voice.

Ellen could be brain damaged. She could die.

Mona's fingers drifted to her throat and hovered at the scar. She saw the doctor's eyes follow her motion, and she forced her hand to her side. The only thing she could do was push ahead, to pray, wait, and give whatever strength she had to her sister and to Hallie.

"I need to see her."

Mona felt the gentle pressure of the doctor's hand as he took her arm and guided her into her sister's room and to the end of her bed. A jumble of memories coursed through her mind—dim shadows of Hallie and Ellen hovering over her. The smell of disinfectant and Betadine. The beep of monitors, the sound of gurney wheels, and the *whoosh* of the power doors that had opened to her unit just outside her room. A giant fist pressed into her abdomen, grinding its way toward her spine with each breath as she took in the IVs, ventilator, and heart monitor attached to her sister. She closed her eyes.

"Are you going to be all right, Miss VanderMolen?"

She forced her eyes open and turned to face him. "I'm fine. Just a bit short on durability. And memory. I'm sorry, I seem to have forgotten your name."

"Dr. Jeffreys."

"Dr. Jeffreys, thank you for everything you've been doing for my sister." For the first time in their conversation, Mona actually saw him, a tall, slender young man with solemn gray eyes that reminded her of her father—eyes that seemed to say that something inside him had been broken long ago. She wondered if he was a kind man, if he had children.

She turned toward Ellen's still form on the bed. Her blonde hair was splayed over the pillow as though she were drifting underwater like a sleeping mermaid. Her makeup had been scrubbed clean, and her pale cheeks were flushed. Mona couldn't remember the last time she'd seen her sister's face naked. The lines of her fine cheekbones had disintegrated to hollow caverns, and a bruise had formed on her left temple.

A mirror image of Ellen's face flashed before Mona's eyes—gaunt and pale against the hospital bed linens, fine featured, with deep-set eyes and a chiseled jawline. Her mother's face. The last time she'd been struck with that resemblance had been eight years ago when she and Ellen had stood together beside their mother's casket. Until now.

Mona's hands crept back to her throat.

"When can you get that thing out of her? I can't tell you how much I hate them."

The doctor pulled a turquoise vinyl recliner from a corner near the sink and directed Mona toward it. "Right now, the ventilator is keeping her alive. Taking it out depends on a lot of factors like when she begins to wake up and her ability to breathe on her own. I hope you'll excuse my directness, but you're looking a bit worse for wear here. Are you feeling all right yourself?"

Mona moved toward the recliner and eased herself into it. "I plead the Fifth. But I don't suppose you have any Diet Coke around here?"

She scooted the chair toward the bed, then leaned forward and slid her arms between the safety bars as she reached for Ellen's manicured hand, which was resting on the neatly tucked sheets. "Are we going to be here long?" She looked toward the doctor as he made a notation on Ellen's chart.

"I'll have someone bring you a sandwich and some fruit from the family pantry. We like to avoid admitting people on the family plan if we can avoid it. And yes, your sister's going to be here a while. Could be a day or two or much longer. Based on her numbers, I'd assume she's been drinking for a number of years."

The doctor looked up from the chart, and Mona glanced toward the window. The discussion wasn't new. She simply hadn't had it for years. The faces of police officers, high school teachers, and concerned friends flashed through her memory. How many times had she told herself that with Ellen's marriage she'd transferred responsibility for these kinds of conversations to Phil?

The ventilator rasped as it rose and fell beside her. Had she been wrong? And did it even matter right now? Should it have mattered two weeks ago? Six weeks ago? Six months ago? She turned and faced the doctor.

"More in the past few years and especially the past three months, I think, but yes, pretty heavily since she was in college."

Dr. Jeffreys made a notation. "I'll be back in a few minutes to take a more complete medical history. I also need to ask if your sister has an advanced directive for medical decisions. With her history, I'm assuming you're familiar with what that entails and the types of decisions we might be looking at on her behalf right now."

Something inside Mona froze. She swallowed. "I don't have any idea . . . she's never discussed anything like that with me. I should probably call her husband. I'm just not sure where he is right now. They're separated, and with the holiday weekend . . ." Her grip tightened on Ellen's hand.

"I'd advise you to call him immediately, no matter how strained their relationship might be. It's important that we know her wishes, especially in light of the fact that she's on artificial life support at the moment. I'm sure you understand the implications."

The word hung in the room, then settled in Mona's soul like a glowing ember. *Implications.*

Within seconds, the ember flamed into an inferno. What could a thirty-something doctor possibly know about implications? How many loved ones had he lost? How many ventilators had been crammed down his throat? Mona forced herself to pause and draw a deep breath as she felt the words pressing against her chest.

"My craniotomy was three months ago. Maybe that will help you understand that this punk look isn't my hairstyle of choice and I know more than I want to know about implications."

Mona swallowed and felt the anger ebbing from her as she leaned forward and stroked back a lock of Ellen's hair that had fallen to her cheek.

"I have a very personal understanding of ventilators and waking up in places I never thought I'd be. I know what it's like to wonder if I was going to get a second chance and being afraid of what it might look like if I did. And I know my family had no idea what my wishes were when my feet were dangling in the grave. So when I sit here with my sister, I understand a lot more than I think you understand yourself."

Mona's words, spoken barely above a whisper, had come out with the force of a torrent. A flood of embarrassment washed over her.

"Dr. Jeffreys, I'm sorry . . ."

The gray eyes remained unblinking. "No, I'm sorry, Miss VanderMolen. This is a difficult time, and I know you're under a huge strain. You don't owe me an explanation or apology. I'll send a nurse in later with advance directive papers so you can have some time to call Ellen's husband or consult other family members."

Mona opened her mouth to break in, but the doctor continued.

"Your sister's purse is in the closet. It's the only personal item that came in with her, and I'd advise you to take it if you leave the room. Cell phones aren't permitted in this area of the hospital, so if you have one, please turn it off. If there's one in your sister's purse, please check it. There's a lounge just across the hallway in case visitors come or you need a change of scenery. You can use your phone there. Now if you'll excuse me, I'll be sure someone brings you that sandwich." He laid his hand briefly on Mona's shoulder, then turned and was gone.

She drew her legs beneath her and rested her head in her hands. Mona stared at the pattern of the teal jacquard window curtains that had been drawn to dim the midday light. The sound of the ventilator wheezed against the silence.

Dear God, I'm lashing out at people who are trying to help, and this has barely started. Where's the strength I'm supposed to feel? Hallie needs me, Ellen needs me, and I barely have strength to stand on my own.

She felt the heat of tears rising in her eyes.

And an advanced directive. Dear God, no.

The words slowly saturated the corners of her mind. A dozen *what ifs* flew through her thoughts as the sound of the ventilator punctuated the minutes.

What do I say to Phil—that this time his wife drank herself into a coma? That she's on a ventilator in Stewartville? And what are the chances he'll even care?

Mona weighed the likelihood of Phil's indifference and knew it was the greatest likelihood of all. Running away from Ellen's drinking had always been his way of coping, and more than once Mona had found herself furious at the other end of a conversation that had gone silent. So why should she expect him to act like anyone other than who he'd always been? Phil had always found a way to put himself first while parading in false benevolence, and Ellen had known it when she'd married him. With Phil distracted by a new girlfriend and the fact that he'd know Ellen was already in Stewartville, Mona knew the chances were slim to none that he'd offer anything more than condolences and a fat check.

The man's inability to truly care for his family had fired a rage so deep in Mona that she'd struggled to rein it in. For years, she'd told herself it was a righteous anger, that she was entitled to it. Then after Stacy's death, guilt had crushed her, and she'd struggled with her own desire to run, to shut down, to hide from pain. In those dark days, she'd found something of herself in Phil.

Then she'd found a freeing glimmer of truth.

Pastor Cunningham's words had pierced to her heart on her first Sunday at Stewartville Community Church. She was certain that before she'd moved to Stewartville, someone must have ratted her out, or he must have tapped her phone or bugged her house.

Years later, she could still clearly remember his words: *"Because of the Holy Spirit in us, we are never stripped of our power to care for others and the freedom to choose what to do with our anger. We're always called to forgive out of the forgiveness we've received."*

Even in the first flash of indignation that had fired through her, Mona was certain the sermon that day had been God's neon billboard flashing to her soul. The former English teacher in her told her not to waste a word, and she'd grabbed her notebook and scribbled copious notes. Later, she'd prayed over them and wept as she'd confessed her anger and pride. She'd even apologized to Phil face-to-face, forcing herself to forgive him again when he'd laughed and turned away. Afterward, over a hot fudge ice-cream brownie, she'd thought in a new way about how hard it must be to live life in Ellen's shoes.

There were days she still struggled, when exhaustion robbed her of the desire to care and she ignored the truth and acted out of her emotions. In the months since her accident and surgery, exhaustion and pain had frayed away the edges of her resolve. She couldn't remember the moment when they had overpowered her strength; she only knew they had overtaken her in the tiniest of steps and in the silent spaces of doubt suspended between moments of pain.

"I've got to make some calls, darling," she whispered. "I'll be right back."

Mona stood slowly and felt for the cell phone clipped to her waistband. She couldn't remember the last time she'd called Phil. It must have been when they were arranging scholarship money for Dan Evans as thanks for the part he'd played in her rescue at the pier. She was sure her cell phone held only Ellen and Phil's land line and Ellen's cell numbers. Mona walked to the oak-veneered closet on the other side of the room and opened it. Ellen's brown leather Gucci bag hung on a hook at the top of the space. She slipped the cell phone and wallet from a side compartment and slid them into her pocket. Then she turned and walked out the door, forming a prayer as she made her way into the hallway.

God, You know sarcasm and a whole lot of other ugliness are on the tip of my tongue right now because You know every word I've already thought and will think. You know I'd like to take a few potshots at Phil because I'm frustrated with a father who walked out on my niece and a husband who walked out on my sister.

But I know what I'm supposed to do is lay all that ugliness down, whether I want to or not, because You have a better plan, one I don't understand. So I'm going to dial this phone and speak for You, but You've got to help me because if this man trash-talks my sister, I'm going to want to lambaste him. So I'm asking for Your power because I've sure got nothing to offer but a prideful attitude and a whole lot of exhaustion. So I'm handing those over to You because I can't be trusted with them.

Mona made her way past the nurses' station and through a set of power doors that swung open before her, her lips moving as she walked. She would pray herself through this if it killed her. She rounded the corner to the right, toward the lounge, gripping the wall as she turned, then stopped short.

Elsie stood facing her, her hands on her hips, her feet set wide apart like a drill sergeant waiting for fresh recruits. Her wispy lavender hair was swept into an updo and held in place with a row of silver bobby pins with tiny rosettes. A purple- and yellow-striped blouse topped her lilac polyester slacks, and the toe of one tiny lavender running shoe tapped a rhythm. Before Mona had a chance to speak a word, the barrage began.

"And what makes you think you're s'posed to be takin' care of everybody in the universe yourself, young lady? I came just as fast as I could. Heaven knows, the last thing we need is you collapsin' and endin' up in a bed next to your half-wit sister. You'd think a mother who has a teenage child of her own to look after would know better than—"

A fresh rage shot up from Mona's belly and grabbed her by the throat. She'd been prepared for insults from Phil, but not her friend, not Elsie. She lowered her voice to a whisper and leaned forward, grabbing the wall for support as words flooded out of her.

"A half-wit, is that what you're calling my sister? If you've shown up to spout lectures, Elsie, you can head straight back home because that's not the kind of support we need here right now from family."

Elsie's head drew back and her eyes went wide, but Mona pressed on.

"My sister's in the other room with a tube crammed down her throat. I really don't care what your personal opinions are about her alcohol, her manners, or her mothering, but you're not going to insult her in front of me! I certainly didn't get up this morning and earn my righteousness. Heaven knows, in the past fifteen minutes alone I've given God a hundred reasons to give up on me, but for reasons that boggle my mind, He claims me even when I mess up. The last time I checked my Bible, God's grace was the same for all of us, so slip off the self-righteousness, Elsie. I want Ellen to see you for who you really are when she wakes up."

Mona's legs were trembling. With her final words, a brilliant shard of light flashed through her peripheral vision, cascading into rivulets that shimmered as they drifted toward the floor like fireworks on a hot summer night. Her face was burning, and she was suddenly aware of a hot stream of moisture slipping down her cheek. She blinked, but Elsie's face had become a blurred squiggle.

"I will not cry!" She swatted at her face.

She felt a hand grip hers, and a lavender blob placed a tissue in her fingers. She dabbed at her eyes, and Elsie's face took shape as the tears cleared. Pale blue eyes stared straight into Mona's. There were tears there.

"This drinkin' thing hits close to home for me and a lot of people who love you. I don't expect you to know why. People don't always talk about their griefs. But knowin' your sister's in there because she made bad choices, it hurts a lot of us because we know where it leads, we know the price Ellen may pay and what it could cost you and Hallie. Some of us have lived long enough to see it too many times. Drinkin' like this ends up leavin' a big wake. A lotta people get pulled under in that wake, but you know that."

Elsie's hands fell from her hips, and she crossed her arms over her chest.

"Now about that self-righteousness. Nobody talks to me like that, young lady"—she paused, and her eyes narrowed—"unless they're right. Got a bit uppity there for a minute, I did. Seemed to forget my place at the foot of the cross with the rest of the sinners of the world. But I'm sure you can pass on some of God's forgiveness to an old lady who's sincerely askin' you, for yourself and on behalf of your sister. Because once we can get on with the forgiveness, you and me got things to do.

"You got a mess on your hands, and you can't do this on your own. You've got decisions to make. You probably can't remember the last time you ate or what you ate. You probably need to call Phil. You can do that while I check on Hallie. I brought you a toothbrush and clean clothes and a copy of *Sense and Sensibility* from your bookshelf. I thought you could read out loud to that sister of yours. I heard somewhere it helps to wake people up, and it seemed to be a good title for a woman that spends more in a year buyin' panties than I spend on my car.

"And you need a nap, girl. I'm not takin' no back talk or eye-rollin'. So if you're ready to get on with forgivin' me, we've got things to do. Let's not drag it out. We got people lookin' on."

Mona had no intention of eye-rolling or back talking, and she didn't care if people were looking on. Her only desire was to lean into Elsie's hug and to hold on, and that's what she did.

Moments later, Mona's body was jammed next to Elsie's on a small couch in a crowded waiting room as she scrolled through

Ellen's cell phone directory and searched for Phil's number. She rehearsed her words as she dialed, then counted four rings before the phone rolled over to an answering machine. Phil's voice greeted her in his most professional tone. She was halfway through the recording before she snapped the phone shut.

"I can't leave a message like this on his machine."

Elsie patted her hand as she pulled a bag of peanut M&M's from her purse and handed them to Mona. "Relax, child. You can hardly hunt him down and tell him in person."

Mona stared at the clock above a painting of a wooded winter scene hung on the wall at the end of the room and forced herself to wait. Four minutes later, she redialed. With a second click of the answering machine, a swell of fear crept into her thoughts.

"Where *is* he? Why doesn't he just pick up?"

"It's only been five minutes, and you need to breathe. And nothin' you do on this end short of prayer's gonna move that man to do any dad-blamed thing."

Mona stared at the phone in her hand. Elsie was right. Was Phil recognizing Ellen's number and ignoring the call?

The phone in her hand rang, and Mona jerked.

"Gracious, child, you just took five years off my life, and I don't have 'em to spare. Now calm down. It's probably Phil, all stirred up thinkin' Ellen's pesterin' him. Prepare to get your head bit off when you answer that thing."

Mona knew Elsie was right. She glanced at the number, and her heart stopped. She read the number twice to be sure.

It must be a mistake. It didn't make any sense.

The phone rang a second and third time, and eyes in the waiting room flickered toward her. There was no time to escape to the hallway before she answered.

Mona pressed the green button and put the phone to her ear.

Hallie slipped into the bathroom and pulled the door closed be-hind her. She'd expected something masculine and rustic, cer-tainly not a sea of pastel and floral bouquets. The long, narrow room was wallpapered in powder-blue-striped paper with pink roses above white-painted wainscoting. Even the muslin tieback window curtains at the end of the room had been edged with pink rosette embroidery.

Harold—a fan of embroidery and flowers. Who would have thought?

She pulled a lime green cell phone from the pocket of her jeans and pressed the number five as she lowered the lid on the toilet and perched across from a claw-foot tub. A plastic shower curtain hung in an oval from a pipe suspended from the ceiling by a series of meticulously engineered hooks.

The number dialed automatically as Hallie listened. She knew if her dad didn't pick up by the third ring there would be no an-swer. Midway between two and three she heard a click, then the muted sound of voices finishing a conversation.

"Dad?"

"Hallie?"

"Where are you? Am I interrupting something?"

"You're never going to believe this, but Heather and I are with my boss and his wife at their apartment just outside Paris. I can't remember if you ever met the Sorensons. We're cultivating a new client for an international account—probably the biggest opportu-nity of my career."

Hallie plucked a piece of invisible lint from the leg of her jeans.

"When will you be home?"

"We're hoping by Christmas, but the women are cooking up a few side trips—Rome and maybe Greece. I'm sure my salary increase and bonuses are being devoured by the shopping mania I'm witnessing over here. We've only been here four days, and Heather already knows every shop owner on the Champs-Elysées. What about you? What's up?"

Hallie stood and drew back the muslin curtain at the window that looked out onto the back yard. A cracked path of concrete led from a small wooden deck to a white, painted, single-stall garage that leaned slightly toward a neat hedge that bordered the lawn.

"We're in Stewartville."

"How nice. I'm glad your mom's deciding to get out a bit."

Hallie let the curtain fall back into place.

"Out. Yes, I'd say she's definitely there. More than a bit."

"You know, I called her last night to let her know I was out of the country and to give her my new cell phone number. You don't happen to know if she got the message, do you?"

The key was not to pause too long in her answers. Not to think but to just let the words flow. It had always been the easiest way to deceive him, and it helped that he couldn't see her face.

"Probably not. She's been pretty busy. But thanks for having Heather call me with the new number last week. I put it in my phone, so I figure we're covered."

From the other side of the bathroom door, Hallie heard a timer go off in the kitchen, then the squeak of Harold's oven door as it opened.

She turned and faced herself in the small, oak-framed mirror. Her eyes were puffy and red, and her cheeks were splotchy. She looked like her face had been shoved into one of Harold's hot pies.

"I've gotta go, Dad. I'm helping with some pie baking. I just called to ask you . . . when you'd be coming home. I wondered when I might be seeing you with the holidays and . . . everything."

"Can't come home now, Hal. Everything I've worked for these past eight years at the company has brought me to Paris for these meetings. And you're in Stewartville with your aunt Mona and your mom and pie baking and who-knows-what-else. I shouldn't tell you this, but Heather's shopping for a Movado watch for you. How could it get any better than all that?"

"I don't imagine it could, Dad. After all, I imagine we could probably fix everything that's wrong with the world with home-made pies and expensive jewelry."

Hallie willed lightness into her voice. She couldn't let him know. It would spoil everything for him. And having him in Stewartville wouldn't make any difference to any of them. It never did. At least that's what she was supposed to believe.

She heard his laugh. "I never thought I'd hear you sounding like Heather. That's something she'd say."

"I never thought I'd hear it myself."

"Tell your mom Happy Thanksgiving for me."

"Of course."

With a click, the line went dead.

In the kitchen, the sound of pans rattled as Hallie slid her phone back into her pocket. She wrapped her hands around her elbows and drew her arms close to her body.

Beyond the door, the kitchen timer went silent.

Chapter Seven

Mona drew in a breath as she put the phone to her ear. It didn't make sense. Why would Adam be calling Ellen? But there was no time to imagine a possible answer before his voice broke into her thoughts.

"Ellen, this is Adam Dean. You're probably a bit surprised to be getting my call."

Words fell from Mona's mouth before she had a chance to think. "You can't imagine."

There was a pause. Had he recognized her voice? Should she ask? But he pressed on.

"You might find it odd that I'm calling you, since we barely know each other, but frankly, I need your help for something extremely important. You can probably guess it's about Mona. I've planned something really incredible for her for Christmas—it's all too complicated to tell you now, but I need you to know that I absolutely need your help to carry this off. It's important that she doesn't suspect a thing, or everything I've been working for over the past few months will be blown to smithereens. This means everything to me, Ellen, and I want it to mean everything to your sister, too."

The air had been slowly draining from Mona's lungs as she listened, her head growing lighter with each sentence. "Adam . . . I . . . don't know what to . . ."

"I don't have time to explain right now. I'm actually in a bit of a hurry. I'm running errands, and I've been trying to call her all morning, and she's not answering her phone. Frankly, I'm starting to get a little worried.

"I know this might sound a little crazy, Ellen, so what I'm really asking right now is for five minutes tomorrow to explain the rest of it and why I need your help. You're Mona's family, and having you be part of this would mean a lot to me. I hope you'll give me time tomorrow to explain it all."

The phone went dead for a moment, then clicked back to life while Mona searched for words.

"Adam, I—"

"That's my call waiting. I've got to go, Ellen, it could be Mona. Just five minutes tomorrow, that's all I'm asking. Think about it."

A dial tone sounded in Mona's ear for a full thirty seconds before the thought occurred to pull the phone away. When she finally did, she was surprised to find herself staring at a sullen-faced teenage boy in a Detroit Tigers baseball cap sitting on the far side of the waiting room beneath the winterscape painting. She slid the phone into her pocket and smiled in embarrassment.

"That the husband?"

Mona turned toward Elsie, confused.

"Excuse me, what did you say?"

"The husband, Phil. Was that him?"

"No, it most certainly was not."

"Then who was it?" Elsie had busied herself digging through a pink floral tote bag and was arranging an array of fruit, Tupperware storage containers, and plastic silverware on a Formica-topped coffee table in front of them. "They got a microwave in this place?"

"It was Adam."

Elsie slapped a Bartlett pear into Mona's hand. "Eat it. Now why in blazes would Adam be calling your sister? To swap recipes? Sounds fishy to me. And why didn't I hear you tellin' him he was talkin' to you?"

Mona busied herself arranging silverware. She could practically feel the heat of Elsie's glare boring into her head.

"Woman, don't go playin' fast and loose with the truth. Call him back and set it straight. Keepin' secrets is the best way to tell someone they can't be trusted." Elsie stood and marched toward the door, waving a Tupperware container. "I'll be lookin' for a microwave, just in case you needed some privacy to make a call." Then she disappeared into the hallway with a wag of her lavender hair.

Mona felt a flush at the base of her skull as the boy in the Tigers cap crossed his arms and cocked his head to one side, his eyes locked on her. She evaluated her options—walking out of the room and not returning, which would have required too much energy, or willing herself to disappear into the pattern of the carpet, which would have required a fairy godmother. She chose a third option—tossing Elsie's pear back into the pink floral tote bag and ripping into the peanut M&M's she'd placed on the table in front of her.

Life had turned into a surreal kaleidoscope of emotions, all tumbling so fast into changing shapes that she would have had to have been an Olympic sprinter to keep up.

Her sister was in an alcohol-induced coma and clinging to a life Mona wasn't certain she wanted to live.

Hallie was smoldering with so much rage that at any moment she might spontaneously combust before their eyes.

Mona's own body and mind were plummeting out of control in a death spiral, with the possibility of impact rushing toward her with head-spinning intensity.

In the middle of the free fall, Adam Dean had chosen to swap secrets with Ellen. Secrets about her.

Her head fell into her hands. It was all coming too fast. She couldn't keep up.

And why didn't I tell him who I was? What have I done?

In a split second, a voice answered.

You deceived him.

Mona raised her head as the boy in the Tigers cap turned away. The realization crashed in on her. In less time than it had taken to draw a half-dozen breaths, she'd subverted three months of trust and deceived the man she'd come to lean on and laugh with, the man who listened when she rambled and when she was silent.

She stared at the floor and locked her gaze on a blue and gray carpet square near her feet. She had to call him back and explain—she just didn't know how or when. Certainly not at this moment, when Elsie might come through the door at any second and when Ellen's condition was so volatile. She needed time to be alone and sort out the words in her head. It was too important. It would have to wait—at least for now.

Mona closed her eyes and thought back. Her relationship with Adam hadn't come easily, but then, she hadn't expected to be so sick for so long, to be so tired, to have to fight for every movement and every thought. Somehow, she'd thought that, when Adam had walked into her life, her recovery and their friendship would unfold together smoothly and naturally. But she'd been wrong.

In the first weeks after her release from the hospital and return to Stewartville, her progress had been encouraging. Her legs had gained strength. Her headaches had waned. Her vision and memory had improved. She'd pressed for a full recovery until the week she'd hit a wall. It had taken her weeks to face it, but her improvement had plateaued. Then came the days when she felt herself slipping backward.

Rehab had been grueling, but she'd pushed herself, prodded by Elsie's incessant hovering, Harold's quiet presence, and Adam's constant encouragement and weekend visits. Over the months, he'd grown from supportive cheerleader to closest friend until the day came when she realized the joy in her life had come to be measured in cell phone calls and Saturday visits. She reveled in the thought for nearly a week until the day she stood in front of her kitchen sink as a shower of light cascaded through her vision and she'd collapsed to the floor. Thirty minutes later, she lay at the foot of her bed and wept as she dialed Dr. Bailey's number.

For weeks, she'd told herself nothing had changed as she'd carried a slip of paper for an MRI in her pocket and distracted herself with details of the shop that had gone unattended during her hospitalization. When Adam came for Saturday visits, she'd worked through the fatigue and refused to give in to the migraines. She'd forced the strain from her voice and called Hallie and Ellen twice a week, extending invitations for visits she was sure would never be accepted. She'd kept Excedrin in her purse, the truck, and in the pockets of her pants, and she'd never left the shop without sunglasses.

As the weeks had passed, Mona began to see the obvious. There wasn't time in her life for a man. And as difficult as it had been, she'd forced herself to carefully spell it out to Adam. He'd listened quietly as she'd explained. She was over forty, for heaven's sake.

She had a business to run and complicated family commitments. This certainly wasn't the time in her life to begin dating.

His response had been perfectly clear. He was over forty, for heaven's sake. He had a business to run and complicated family commitments. He was a widower and didn't plan to ever begin dating. But he'd met a wonderful friend. He liked her. He enjoyed spending time with her. And he fully intended to continue showing up until she told him to stop.

Of course, that thought had seemed impossible. It would be too emotionally exhausting to cut things off completely, even though it had seemed on the surface to be the right thing to do. It had suddenly become too complicated. Mona couldn't envision a life with Adam erased from it any more than she could envision moving ahead with him at the center. And so she'd slipped into quiet denial as Adam's calls and visits had continued. But each day, his life had woven itself more deeply into hers, and each day, her fear had grown—fear that perhaps he would leave first and not give her the choice.

But if she'd seen anything in Adam Dean in the last three months, she'd seen faithfulness. She'd worked hard to see into the heart of the man on their afternoon walks or drives in the country, and their time together had shown her what she had discerned even before her accident at Lake Michigan—there wasn't a duplicitous cell in the man's body. If a question called for a straight answer, he gave it. If a situation called for a direct question, he asked it. With a glance, he knew if she needed rest or escape from the shop, silence or conversation.

But his perception also frightened her. Over the years, none of her friends had ever penetrated the defenses she'd built. And the closer she and Adam became, the more he gently tried the locks to the places she'd kept bolted. There were days when she could feel him standing quietly outside these doors, and she threw the weight of her battered body full-force against them.

When Adam asked about her rehab appointments, she became evasive. First in increments so small she refused to admit it, and then in a hundred isolating decisions that forced her heart away from his. Time and time again, she'd pushed him away, yet he always came back.

Someone in the waiting room coughed, and Mona looked up. A young woman in the corner held the hand of an elderly woman beside her. Mona crumpled the empty bag of M&M's and tossed it back into Elsie's bag.

You have to call him. He deserves honesty.

Her head was throbbing, and her back ached. The thought of telling Adam he'd been pouring out his heart to her instead of Ellen seemed too ludicrous to imagine.

She dropped her head into her hands.

Dear Lord, how can I mess things up by just sitting still and minding my own business? This is an amazing man, and I've managed to ruin something wonderful for him by just breathing too long.

Her eyes were burning, and she rubbed her palms across her lids.

I've got to call him and face it. And call Phil. And figure out what I'm going to do when Ellen wakes up . . . and with Hallie . . .

She refused to let herself finish the list. Just thinking about walking back into Ellen's room seemed more than she could manage. She could feel her mind and body slipping into low gear. The work of finishing the next thought seemed suddenly more than she could bear.

She needed Ellen's lab results from Dr. Jeffreys for Phil. She needed to call Harold and check on Hallie. She needed to call

Pastor Cunningham and get the prayer line going. She needed . . . Mona's mind trailed off as she stared at the blue and gray geometric pattern of the carpet tiles.

She needed to do the right thing.

Deep inside, Elsie's words prodded her. "Keepin' secrets is the best way to tell someone they can't be trusted."

She reached for her own phone, clipped to the waist of her pants.

Adam deserves more than drama and complications. And it's only going to get worse. I have to tell him not to come to Stewartville tomorrow.

She flipped open her phone as she stood and walked into the hallway.

In the end, Mona's good intentions to call Adam were swept away in a whirlwind of mayhem that blew through the waiting room doors, swirled around her, and drew her into a surreal vortex until almost midnight.

Swept away by the nurse who brought news that Ellen had begun to wake from her coma and who had rushed Mona to Ellen's bedside with Elsie's pink quilted Bible tucked into her arms. Swept away by the sight of Ellen coming to life, her hands responding to touch, her fingers restless against the white sheets, her eyes moving behind the still-closed lids.

Then by a call from Harold telling Mona that Hallie had slipped out for a walk after lunch. She'd seemed upset. Had they seen her? Then waiting for reports from church friends and Joe Spencer while Elsie held Mona down and insisted she not run off looking for her.

Swept away by a flood of emotions as Pastor Jake and his wife, Debbi, from Stewartville Community Church held Ellen's and Mona's hands and prayed, then headed out to drive the streets in search of Hallie.

Then the surge of hope at the sight of Hallie outlined in the doorway of her mother's room, her silhouette backlit by the brightness of the nurses' station beyond the threshold as Mona sat in near darkness in the recliner beside the hospital bed. Exhaustion had overtaken her, and she hadn't moved from her chair as she watched Hallie silently looking at her mother's still form.

Just two more steps, Lord. Just get her inside the room.

She stood in the darkness, and minutes passed before Mona spoke.

"It's nearly nine o'clock, Hallie. Do you realize how long you've been gone?"

Hallie's hands were shoved into her jeans, her shoulders high and cupped as though she was bracing herself against an icy wind.

"I'm sorry. And I know I need to apologize to Harold. It will be the first thing I do when I leave."

"Leave? You just got here." Mona rose slowly. A pain shot through her leg, and she winced.

"I'd really rather you sat down, Aunt Mona. This shouldn't take very long. There's something I needed to say to my mom. This is my chance to say it in the presence of someone who's not half drunk, and this time I can talk without getting sworn at or having excuses thrown back in my face."

"Hallie—"

"Sit down, Aunt Mona, before you fall down." Hallie's tone softened. "Please."

Mona eased back into the chair. Her head was pulsating.

"It's taken me a few hours of wandering around and sitting in the Stewartville cemetery to get up the courage to come here, but I had to. I've been giving this speech for months in one way or another, but I'm here to say it one last time.

"I'm sick of not counting for anything, Mom. I'm sick of coming in second to a bottle of booze. I'm furious that my life doesn't count for anything to you, that my education doesn't count, that I don't get to have a normal life with friends because my life is all about cleaning up your messes.

"I'm tired of being ashamed of you and fighting to keep from puking up my own guilt and anger and shame. And I'm tired of forgiving you one day and fighting not to hate you the next."

Waves of nausea rolled over Mona, and she covered her mouth as she glanced at Ellen's face. The lids were still closed. Her eyes moved down her sister's body. The fingers of Ellen's right hand, farthest from the doorway, gripped the sheet tightly.

"God knows what I've been forgiven in my life, Mom. Every day I live with the pain of that reality." Hallie's hand flew to a chain and heart-shaped pendant around her neck. "I love you, and I've forgiven you. I'm still choosing to forgive you every day. I need to say those words out loud and have someone hear them for both of us. But I'm also angry. Angry that I've got to fight for myself because I don't have a mother who'll fight for me."

The hand gripped the sheet more tightly, and Mona drew in her breath slowly and held it.

"I can't do it anymore the way we've been doing it, Mom. I can't take care of you—it's too much for me. So I'm here to tell you that, even though I love you, you've got to find a different way to deal with the drinking. I'm not going home with you when this is over. I'm looking at other options." She shoved her hand back into her pocket, and her shoulders relaxed. "That's really all I have to say for now. Except that I wouldn't even be standing here if it wasn't for God. I had to figure out who He was—a liar or a sadist or someone who forgives people who really screw up. You probably don't want to hear it, but that's what this is really all about, Mom.

"I'm heading back to Harold's now. I'll call him as soon as I get outside and let him know I'm okay." Then as quickly as Hallie had appeared, she was gone.

The room was silent except for the sound of the ventilator. Hallie's words tore through Mona's chest as if they had come from her own child. She was certain Ellen had heard every heart-piercing word. She leaned forward, resting her head on the cold bedrail as she reached for her sister's hand. Ellen's carefully manicured fingers slowly closed around her own in a grip as tight as death.

Mona's head snapped back, and she looked into her sister's face.

Ellen was staring at her with the grieving eyes of a mother who has just lost her only child.

Chapter Eight

The aroma of hazelnut coffee drifted warm and hazy around the edges of Mona's dreams. The smell teased her awake, and she fought the desire to follow, savoring the veiled darkness between her and the world. Reality—and the press of decisions—lay on the other side.

Her eyes were sticky from sleep, and she opened them slowly and ran her fingers over her face, then through the clumped and matted spikes of her short hair. Her left leg ached, and a familiar tingling radiated through her thigh. There would be little walking today to stretch the cramped muscles. Just waiting and praying.

Ellen lay sleeping on her side, her legs drawn up in a fetal position beneath the blue cotton blanket. Memories of the previous night played through Mona's mind as she waited for the early morning fog to clear her thoughts, and she kicked off the blankets in the window seat where she'd made a makeshift bed.

The night had been a blur. Elsie's hovering, interspersed with three attempts to call Phil on Ellen's phone before the power died. Then the early morning extubation of the ventilator tube. Finally, Ellen's transfer from critical care to a private room and Mona's collapse into her window-seat bed in the early hours of the morning.

She folded the blanket quickly and glanced at the hospital tray. A tall, lidded cup of tea from Trina's Café sat next to a take-out box. She opened it carefully as she scanned Ellen's face for signs of waking, but the gaunt face lay still on the pillow. She looked into the box. An enormous Belgian waffle lay mounded in the center, smothered in strawberries and whipped cream.

Mona glanced at the clock: 7:22. She dipped her finger in the whipped cream and stuck it in her mouth, then walked to the door and looked down the hallway. Except for two doctors charting notes at the nurses' station and an aide pushing an IV stand, it was empty.

She walked back into the room and sat cross-legged on the window seat as she settled the take-out box carefully on her lap.

"Elsie, my love," she murmured to herself, "you must have read my mind."

Ellen woke at 8:15, moments after Mona had returned from washing up and changing into fresh jeans and a Stewartville Antiques sweatshirt.

She asked Mona to leave at 8:17. The words came like a bullet shot.

"Get out."

Mona sat in the window seat, folding her dirty clothes. Her hands continued to smooth creases as she glanced at her sister. Ellen lay angled upright in bed, glaring, her gray eyes hard and her mouth pressed into a thin line. A familiar mask had settled over her face.

"I guess that means I can pretty much skip right past the polite 'How are you feeling this morning, Ellen?'" Mona slipped the clothes into a bag, aware that even the rustle of the plastic would annoy her sister by diminishing her importance.

"You heard me. Get out!"

Mona picked up a toothbrush and tube of Crest and added them to the bag.

"It's good to see that you're well enough to talk again. Do you know where you are, how you got here?"

Ellen struggled to support herself on one elbow, and Mona winced as an IV line strained at the back of her sister's right hand. Ellen didn't seem to notice. Her eyes bored into Mona's.

"Don't turn this fiasco into something it's not. I know what you're up to. I heard Hallie's 'poor me' speech last night. I know the two of you put your heads together and came up with that 'exploring other options' crap so it would look like it was her idea to come and live with you. This is what life has always been about for you—taking my daughters. You took one, now you're going for the other one."

Her voice was hoarse from the ventilator, and her muscles strained against the sides of her neck as she rasped out the words.

"After all I did for you—sitting up night after night after your accident—and this is how you repay me—by taking the last thing in the world I have? This was your perfect chance—waiting until Phil left me and I was nearly dead so you could get what you've wanted for so long. Did you show up today to see if there was something of mine you might have missed? Maybe the six hundred bucks I had in my purse, or maybe my checkbook?" Ellen flung back the blankets on her bed as she searched wildly to find the release for the guard rails.

The rage in her tone tore through the room with deadly force, landing like a weight on Mona's heart, pummeling her spirit with each new sentence. Then in one flashing instant, she saw Hallie standing beneath the rage, deflecting lies that rained down upon her in the torrent of anger. A burning rose in Mona's gut and hovered in her chest. She felt the rhythm of her pulse in her temples as she reached for her purse on the floor.

"Has it ever occurred to you, Ellen, that Hallie isn't another one of your possessions—that she isn't something you *have*—that people couldn't possibly take her from you like cash from your wallet? Love doesn't work like that. Yesterday she asked you to start acting like a mother, to stop doing things that hurt her, but she can only ask. What you decide will be your choice. But I'd think long and hard about that choice because whatever you decide in the next twenty-four hours is going to define the relationship you have with your daughter for the rest of your life. You've been given a second chance at life, Ellen. Consider what you're going to do with it. I'd recommend you figure out what it means to live like a mother instead of a victim."

Ellen flailed in the bed as she still searched for the release to the guard rails. "Shut up, Mona! You've got a lot of nerve—"

"No, I've got a lot less nerve than you might think, really, but I'm sure it's a matter of perspective." Mona shoved her feet into her sneakers and stood. "You've asked me to leave, so I have no desire to overextend my stay. But before I go, I think you should be aware of some of the important details of your life.

"You're in the Stewartville Community Hospital. Hallie drove you here because she's resigned from parenting her alcoholic mother—it's a tough job description for a fifteen-year-old whose job should be growing up and going to school.

"In case you're curious about how you got here, you were in a coma, so she drove you here—illegally. When the police pulled her over for speeding, they were naturally concerned about why an unlicensed teenager was at the wheel and transporting a parent with a blood alcohol level of almost six hundred. These facts didn't impress the local police or the social workers in charge of child welfare."

"You've got to be kidding!" Ellen lunged forward in the bed. "What kind of moron would call social services over something like this? I'm a good mother."

"Who said I disagreed? I'm just catching you up in case folks from law enforcement or social services begin stopping by asking questions. You might want to begin thinking about the kinds of answers they might be looking for.

"One final piece of information—it's Thanksgiving, and we're celebrating at Elsie's. Everyone has been hugely worried about you. I'll let them know you're out of the woods—they've been praying like mad and lining up in the waiting room, even though they couldn't get in to visit. They couldn't be more grateful to hear you're alive and won't be living the rest of your life on a respirator. They really care about you, Ellen, and they want you to know that."

Mona flung her purse over her shoulder, gathered the plastic bag and jacket from the window seat, and made her way toward the door. "I'm sure the social worker will be in later to discuss rehab options with you. If you want to go home alone, that's your choice. There's one catch, however. The police have temporarily impounded your Corvette—something to do with marijuana they found in the glove compartment. I think the social worker and cops may have an opinion on where both you and Hallie spend the next few weeks."

Ellen had grown suddenly quiet, and she fell back against the pillow and pulled her blanket around her chest. The bruise over her eye had blossomed to a deep blue and inched toward the bridge of her nose. Mona wondered if her sister had a clue how horrible she looked or if it would even matter to her. She'd never seen Ellen like this. She wondered how many times Hallie had.

"My suggestion is we talk as a family—you, me, and Hallie—but I'm not going to beg you, and I'm not going to beg her. Heaven knows, I can't force either one of you to do anything. But living life on your terms sure seems to have brought you to the edge of nowhere." She slipped her arms into her lime green parka.

"I'll be back later today, like it or not, with a chocolate shake for your torn-up throat. Right now, I'm going to go and help your daughter try to figure out what her options are. She seems to think she has a plan, and I don't have a clue what it is. You might want to give some thought to your own options and where you'd be right now if Hallie had turned her back on you yesterday and not brought you here for help. She did it because she loves you, Ellen. Even if she's trying to force you to stand on your own two feet."

With those words, Mona walked out the door.

Mona's thoughts came together in bits and pieces as she walked the four blocks from the hospital to the antique shop. She'd put off talking to Adam for too long, and she unlocked the guilt and let it wash over her as the cold November wind burned her lungs. The only thing she knew for certain was that it would be impossible to explain the chaos of the past twenty-four hours during a four-minute drive from her apartment to Elsie's or while the two of them were surrounded by family and friends in the middle of holiday mayhem. He was due to pick her up at her apartment in a couple of hours, and she'd have to find a way to face him and ask him to wait for an explanation until they could have time alone together. Maybe it would be best to arrange to meet him at Elsie's. And what if he'd called Elsie or Harold and found out the truth about why she hadn't been answering her phone? Could he possibly have figured out that she'd answered her sister's phone instead of Ellen?

She mulled over her choices from different angles as she walked, trying to diffuse the nagging sense of guilt that hung over her. It would only take one call to tell him she'd headed to Elsie's early and to meet her there—one more call that would be another thinly veiled deception. It didn't seem right, but none of her options seemed right. The only thing she knew for certain was that she wanted to lie down on her bed and sleep until spring planting.

By the time Mona reached the antique shop, exhaustion had kicked in. She let herself in through the alley door, made her way through the empty shop, and slowly climbed the stairs to her apartment. A note in Elsie's thin, spidery scrawl was taped to her door.

Brought Oscar home this morning. Fed and walked him. Take a nap before you come.

From inside her apartment, the sound of toenails skittered across the floor.

"I'm coming, Oscar," she called as she pushed the door open. A wiggling black form slammed into her shins like a live battering ram, and Mona knelt to stroke the squirming black dachshund.

"I missed you, too, sweetheart. If Adam runs for his life, I'll always have you."

She glanced at her Timex. He'd said he would be there at eleven thirty, and it was nine o'clock. If she hurried, she might have time to lie down for half an hour before heading to Elsie's.

She eyed her bed. First things first.

She showered and changed into a pair of khakis and a buttery cashmere turtleneck Ellen had bought her for Christmas four years ago.

"The last gift I'll ever see from her," Mona spoke aloud as she settled herself on the antique, four-poster bed in the spacious single room that served as her living room, dining room, kitchen, and bedroom. A knot throbbed at the base of her neck from hours of bending over the side of the hospital bed. She rubbed it gently to work out the kinks as she dialed Harold's number on her cell. Hallie's voice startled her.

"Harold Rawlings' residence."

"And what are you doing answering Harold's phone, Hallie Bowen?"

"Doing what I was told to do—treating Harold's house as if it were my own. He's given me permission to use his woodworking tools and play his piano."

"His piano? I've never seen a piano at Harold's. And I wasn't aware that you played a note. Did your mother teach you?"

"It's in a bedroom. Mom made me take a year of lessons when I was eight. I still know "Off I Go to Music Land" and "O, Really, O'Riley.""

"Your talents never cease to amaze me."

"There's even a coal bin in his basement, and his bathroom has this really weird bathtub—"

"Hallie, I really didn't call to talk about Harold's house. I wanted to tell you about your mom." Mona waited, but there was only silence.

"She's doing much better this morning. I thought that after dinner, the two of us might go up to see her. You can't avoid talking to her forever."

Mona heard the sound of a door opening, then closing in the distance. "As far as my mother's concerned, I've said all I need to say. Now you and I, we need to talk about what comes next. But right now, Harold's standing beside me, so I'll put him on and leave the room so you two can talk about me and say whatever you think you need to say. I'll be in the basement listening through the floor register."

"Hallie!"

There was a clatter of footsteps, and Harold's voice came on the line.

"She's been downstairs since yesterday, working on a birdhouse I got her started on. She's right, though—you and her got to sit down and talk. And there are a few things I'd like you and me to chew on together. You've got a lot on your plate, Mona, and I thought you could use a little extra perspective. You can take or leave what an old man has to offer, but I thought I'd be able to give you some options you didn't know were there."

Mona's eyes fell on the bookshelf that held her father's diaries. She couldn't remember the last time she'd had the perspective of an older man who cared about her.

"Hearing what you have to say would mean more than you know, Harold, especially since I'm feeling rather slim on options at the moment."

"Well, don't go trusting what you feel in the hurting times, Mona. Looking at God's big picture is the only way to know how to move forward. Keep that in mind. And I'm holding you to your word that you'll listen to all of what I have to say, even though it might not be what you expect."

"Should I be expecting something, Harold?"

"Yes, you rightly should. Expect that people around you see that you're in a pinch and want to help. I'll be seeing you this afternoon at Elsie's, then."

Mona hung up and dropped the phone onto the red, yellow, and blue Dresden Plate quilt on her bed.

It had all become too much for her brain to bear. A homeless niece and an alcoholic sister. Adam's secret plans and her accidental deception. A body and brain that were crying out for rest. Her life had become too complex to comprehend.

She slid from her bed and walked to her couch and scooped a dazed and dozing Oscar from beneath a yellow crocheted afghan.

"Someone needs you, darling."

Then she plopped back down on her bed and slipped between the quilt and the top sheet, tucking Oscar beside her.

"Just half an hour, Lord. That's all I'm asking for."

She was asleep before Oscar's body had warmed the sheets.

Mona awoke with a start. She flung the quilt aside and glanced at the clock on the bedside stand: 11:17.

"Oscar, how could you! Why didn't you wake me up a half hour ago?"

Oscar stared at her indignantly as she hit the auto-dial for Adam's number and slid off the bed to look for her shoes and car keys. The sound of faint ringing drifted up from the antique shop below, and she quickly hung up.

"Stupid shop phone. I'll never make it." She listened for a second ring and a third as she hurried toward the door that led to the landing and down the stairs to the store below, but the ringing had stopped. She turned and headed back to look for her keys and pressed the redial button. The sound of ringing once again drifted up from the shop, this time louder. She paused and stared at the phone in her hand as she heard the sound of footfalls on the stairs outside the apartment.

Good night, he's here.

Mona froze as she listened for the tell-tale creak of step eleven.

Dear, Lord, what should I do? Tell him the truth about the mess of my life or wait? What on earth do I say? That I've been in the hospital with my half-dead sister for the past twenty-four hours, and I never found time to call him? That I let him spill his guts to me and think he was talking to Ellen?

A knock sounded on the door as Mona turned. Tingling radiated down her left arm as she slid her phone into her pocket, hitched up a weak smile, and opened the door.

Adam stood facing her, wearing navy slacks and matching suede jacket open over a cranberry crewneck sweater. He carried a lidded cup of coffee from Trina's Café in one hand. His sunglasses had been shoved to the top of his short sandy hair, and his smile was as natural and disarming as the first day Mona had met him.

She breathed an inward sigh of relief as she searched for the right words.

"It's you . . . I . . . you surprised me. You're a bit early, and I was just getting ready to leave, actually."

He stepped into the apartment and scooped her into one arm, carefully holding the coffee away from the two of them. The faint scent of Dial soap drifted over her as her face brushed his sweater.

"Somehow, I was hoping for a greeting that would be a bit more affirming. 'I knew you were coming, so I'd planned to leave' doesn't do much for the male ego. Do you charm all your guests with that opener?"

Mona pulled away and blushed. She was suddenly aware of his

steady gaze sweeping over her face. She turned to look for her purse.

"That didn't come out quite right. I was just thinking that Elsie might have a lot to do this morning with all the company . . ."

"I see. How thoughtful of you. So you were thinking of Elsie." From the corner of her eye, Mona saw Adam take a slow sip of his coffee, but his eyes never left her face. She spotted her purse hanging from the spindle of her mother's rocking chair, and she walked across the room to get it, grabbing her jacket from the end of the bed as she turned and faced him. She rested a hand on the bed to steady herself as she felt the surge of words rising within her. No matter how difficult it would be, she had to tell the truth.

"Adam, in the last twenty-four hours, my life has turned into an episode from a soap opera, and I've suddenly become responsible for two lives besides my own. I don't think I slept two hours last night, and my family would qualify for their own cable TV series. I'm pretty sure that, when you and I get a chance to finally sit down and talk about what's happened and how messy my life has become, you're probably going to think long and hard about how wise it is to be spending time with me. So I'd thought that today it might have been better, easier . . . if we'd just met at Elsie's, talked afterward, and gotten it all over with."

Even as she spoke the words, she realized they were coming out all wrong. She'd wanted to explain it all in well-crafted sentences that hedged the starkness of the facts. She hadn't called him, hadn't found time for him in the middle of the drama of her life. And if she'd just had time to find the words, she might have understood why herself.

A horn honked in the street below as her hand drifted to the spiky stubble of her hair. She watched as Adam took another long,

91

slow sip, his eyes narrowing as he drank, as though the liquid was burning his throat. The silence hung in the room as he pulled the cup away from his lips and moved toward her, setting his coffee on the small kitchen table that sat in the center of the room. His eyes had narrowed, and Mona tried to read the look as he drew closer.

"Gotten it over with? And what would we be getting over with?" He stopped just inches from her and stared directly into her eyes. For the first time since she'd known him, she was overcome with a sudden urge to turn from that look and run.

She shifted her weight. "There are things you don't know—things I need to tell you." A pain radiated up her left leg, but she steeled the muscles in her face not to wince.

"A great starting point, telling me things you think I need to know. And what would those be?"

She drew in a deep breath. "That my sister's here in the hospital. She drank herself into a coma, and Hallie drove her here yesterday. That Hallie won't speak to her mom, and Ellen thinks I'm trying to take her daughter from her. That I don't know what I'm supposed to do about either one of them. Those, for starters."

Adam's eyes searched her face. "Anything else?"

Mona shifted her eyes to the top button of Adam's jacket. "I think that's where we should start for now."

Adam settled his feet wider apart and tipped his head to the side.

"And during that twenty-four-hour period when life was spinning out of control for you, did the thought ever occur to you to call me, to ask me to pray with you or for you, to ask me to come and be with you? Did the thought pass through your mind that I might be able to help, might want to help, even if that meant just showing up to sit in the waiting room? Or in the middle of your crisis, would I just have been in the way, another visitor, another 'friend'?"

The navy button at the top of Adam's jacket had four holes. Mona counted them six times before she could find the words to answer. She knew they were stupid words before she even spoke them, but they were the only words she could find. Exhaustion had stripped her to a painful rawness.

"I wanted to call, but it seemed like too much. I couldn't make myself do one more thing. I was overwhelmed. I barely knew what to do next."

In her peripheral vision, Mona saw Adam's head draw back. She counted the button's holes seven more times in the silence before he spoke.

"So in a crisis, calling me was something you would have had to force yourself to do, not something that would have helped you, relieved you in some way, given you a sense of comfort."

It was a statement more than a question. His tone had changed, and Mona heard the calm finality that had settled into his voice by the end of the sentence. A rush of heat washed through her gut.

"Adam, no, it wasn't . . ."

With a gentle pressure on her arm, he turned her and guided her toward the door. "I see that you were right, Mona. Meeting at Elsie's would have been best so we could have saved this awkward discussion for later."

They drove the few blocks to Elsie's house in silence, the truth isolating them in its starkness. She hadn't called him, hadn't found time for him in the middle of her crisis. Adam had found a way to say the words correctly, and in his words she discovered the thing she'd so lamely tried to disguise as procrastination.

Fear.

She just didn't know which she feared the most—the fear that Adam would see the mess of her life and walk away.

Or the fear that he would see the mess and commit to stay.

Chapter Nine

Mona slammed the door of the Suburban, her only thought escape.

Don't talk to me, then.

She hoisted her purse to her shoulder and hurried up the winding sidewalk toward the wide verandah that led to Elsie's crimson-painted front door, hung with a pine-needle wreath. The painful silence of the ride had been excruciating. Mona's only thought was to melt into the crowd and chaos that waited behind the door.

Women in the kitchen cooking, men in the library watching football. This should make it easy enough for you to shut me out. A pang of conscience tugged at her thoughts as the warring voices in her head formed ranks.

And didn't you shut him out first when you made the decision not to call? And what about your choice not to tell him the whole truth?

She grabbed the wrought-iron stair railing and pulled herself up the steps.

And why didn't you call? What are you so afraid of?

The sound of a car door thudded as she crossed the porch and reached for the doorknob. Her hand hesitated for a moment as she waited for his footfalls behind her, then she turned the knob and stepped across the threshold.

The smell of burnt marshmallows assaulted Mona's nose as she paused in the tiny, wainscoted entry. The dining-room table stretching the length of the room before her was set with Royal Albert china, crystal stemware, and colorful Depression glass serving dishes. Through an archway to the right, a matted golden retriever with glittery butterfly wings strapped to its back careened into the room, chased by two tiny fairy princesses brandishing magic wands with cascading purple tinsel. The dog skittered across the hardwood floor and thumped into a potted dieffenbachia near the archway to the kitchen, sending up a spray of dirt as the plant tumbled to its side. The fairies squealed, turned, and headed back into the living room as the retriever disappeared through another archway leading into a library.

"Somebody get this mangy mongrel outta my kitchen before I set its wings on fire!" Elsie's voice rang from the kitchen, and Mona let the pandemonium of sound and sight flow over her like a summer shower. She'd walked into the midst of McFeeney family mania, and she savored it. A gust of cold wind brushed across her back as the door opened and closed behind her.

"That woman does have a powerful set of lungs. I'd guess folks clear to Hubbardston just heard her threaten that dog." Adam had stepped into the entry, and Mona could feel the closeness of his presence in the tiny space. His tone seemed warm, inviting. She willed him to speak again—to say anything that would erase the silence of the car before the noise and chaos of the house enveloped them.

She slid her purse from her shoulder and unzipped her brown leather jacket. In an instant, Adam's hands moved to her shoulders, easing the coat free of her arms. She felt the weight of it fall away behind her as she watched the squealing fairies dash through the room, this time chasing a German shepherd with a pink cowboy hat strapped to its head.

Why didn't you call him?

96

An ache in her neck tightened. She stepped toward the dining-room threshold and leaned against the doorframe. Behind her, she felt the brush of movement as Adam hung her coat from a peg near the door, then turned and stood next to her.

"This is the way I see things, Mona. This house looks like a pretty intimidating place to me, what with screaming fairy children and crazy cowboy dogs. We could stand in this tiny room for a long time, or we could take life by the throat and step out into the chaos. We might get knocked down or have to clean up a little spilled dirt, and we might eventually be asked to scrape a few burnt pots and pans. But I figure that's the price you pay to enjoy a feast with the family.

"Whatever you want to say to me later, I want you to know that I see messes as part of life. We're all broken, and some of us are a little more cracked than others. You don't scare me, and your family doesn't scare me, but maybe knowing that frightens you more than you'd like to admit."

Mona felt the force of his eyes on her cheek as she slowed her breath and turned to look at him.

"Adam, you know it's more complicated than . . ."

Elsie's voice echoed from the kitchen. "If that's you Mona, you and Adam will have to do your courtin' later. Bessie Bender called a half hour ago and kept me on the phone with a recital of every ailment she's had since her mama powdered her fanny. Made me burn the marshmallow toppin' on my candied yams. So park that good man of yours in the library with the other men and get out here and make yourself useful."

Mona felt the flush start at her neck and head toward her hair. Adam stepped in front of her and leaned in as his hands grabbed hers in a quick squeeze. His smile was quick and easy.

"It's okay. It doesn't matter what anyone else says. Know your own heart and don't speak it until you're ready."

He turned and headed into the library, his words suspended like a thread between them.

Elsie had put Hallie in charge of the seating arrangements, and by the time Mona had scooped her first bite of pickled beets to her mouth, the girl was making her think seriously about the dieffenbachia near the archway. Mona was sure she'd heard somewhere that it was a poisonous plant, and she wondered if anyone would notice if she secretly shredded it into Hallie's salad.

Hallie had seated herself across from Mona and Adam, between Harold and Elsie's fairy great-granddaughter Daphne, who spent most of the meal quietly scraping dabs of butter from her crescent roll and licking them from her fingers. Elsie's daughter, Jessica, her husband, Dennis, and their three married sons with their wives and children filled in the remaining fifteen places at the table of twenty. But Hallie barely glanced at them. Her eyes were glued on Adam as she shot out a steady stream of questions.

What exactly was it that he found appealing about Aunt Mona?

Did he like her with short, spiky hair, or did he think she was prettier before the accident?

Wasn't it getting to be a drag, driving all the way over from Aplington every Saturday just to see her?

Had she ever told him about the time Aunt Mona and Stacy and Hallie had gone out in the middle of the night and wrapped the neighborhood cars in toilet paper?

Mona wondered if Joe Spencer would arrest her if she stuffed the child's mouth with candied yams and taped it shut.

Ellen's call came as the cranberry sauce, homemade applesauce, and corn relish were making their third pass around Elsie's expansive dining-room table. Mona breathed a sigh of relief, carefully folded her ivory linen napkin, and pushed her chair away as she watched Hallie's eyes shift to the window and stare to the street beyond.

"I'm not going home with her. Just so we're all clear on that. And trying to force me would be a bad idea, if you catch my drift."

Adam rose, drew Mona's chair from the table, and helped her stand.

"Hallie, your 'drift' is usually a gale-force wind," Mona said. "I think everybody who knows you has figured that out. If everyone will excuse me, I'll just take this in the kitchen."

Mona walked through the archway and into the familiar red gingham warmth of Elsie's kitchen. The butcher-block counters were piled high with crusted pots and pans, and the sink was brimming with soaking bakeware and cooking utensils. By the fourth ring, Mona had reached the red Formica dinette that sat in the alcove near the back door. She snapped open the phone as she dropped into a chair.

"They're discharging me tomorrow, and I need to talk to you. When can you get over here?"

Mona ran her fingers through her hair as she forced the exasperation from her voice. "We're in the middle of dinner, Ellen. I'm not really sure."

"I'm not asking you to come right now, Mona. I just need to talk about some things, and I don't have much time."

Mona glanced at her watch: 3:10. "How about at supper time?

They bring your meals around five or six. I'll make a plate and bring it up. They're letting you eat, right?"

The line was silent.

"Ellen?"

"They're forcing me into rehab, Mona. Hallie talked to the cops and some social worker. She's blaming everything on me. She told them her father's in Europe indefinitely."

Conversation drifted in from the dining room, and Mona heard the low murmur of Harold's voice, followed by Elsie's quick laugh.

"Rehab? That could be good—it would be helpful. But where?" Mona leaned forward and rested her head in her hands.

"Back home, or they have programs here." Ellen's voice was quivering. "Two weeks inpatient, then a long-term, outpatient program. They're trying to make it sound like they're giving me choices, but they're pushing me into a corner."

Mona forced herself to speak the question that always triggered the excuses and the running. "And what do you want?"

Again the silence, then the sound of ragged breathing. "I want to know my daughter doesn't hate the sight of me when she looks in my face. I want fifteen minutes without the thought of a drink. I want to rewind my life to when I was nineteen, to the time before I began throwing good things away in tiny pieces."

The words came faster. "In spite of all the horrible things I've said and all the reasons I've given you to want to push me as far away from you as possible, I'm asking if I can stay in Stewartville, Mona. I have nowhere else to go, and I can't do this alone. I'm asking you to help me. I don't even think I know what that means. I know I don't want to keep drinking, even though I know I don't act like it. I know I almost killed myself. I need help, and I'm scared. Is that what you've been waiting to hear?"

From the dining room, the sound of Adam's and Hallie's voices rose above the murmur and mingled, then dissolved into the hum of conversation. Mona blinked as the words sank in.

"Do you think this is about what I'm waiting to hear? Because if it is, we can end the conversation now and save a lot of time."

Again, the silence.

"Ellen, are you telling me you want to move to Stewartville? Permanently?" Tightness gripped Mona's throat as a wave of questions flooded her thoughts.

"I'm not sure. Probably not . . . but maybe. I've just been thinking about my options, and I don't have many at the moment. I thought you and Stewartville might be one if you were willing to consider it."

Mona sat, stunned, and stared at the dirty pans stacked in a lopsided heap high above the sink. With one wrong touch, one heavy step, the entire pile would crash to the floor.

In Ellen's silences and tone, Mona had felt the first inner pulse of hope. Her sister was going into rehab and was asking to move to Stewartville. Equally stunning was the fact that they had just carried on a civil conversation for more than thirty seconds. None of it seemed possible. But then, Harold had called earlier in the day suggesting that there might be other options, and that didn't seem possible, either.

"Mona?" Ellen's voice broke the silence. "It would mean a lot to me if you'd come by so we could talk."

"I'll be there in an hour. With dessert."

"It would mean a lot to me."

Mona scooped up the words and carried them back to the dining room.

Mona sat at the kitchen table, drying silverware and sorting it back into a velvet-lined maple box, as she watched Hallie swirl water through the bottom of the turkey roaster.

"This is the most disgusting thing I've seen in my life. There are hunks of fat and skin globbed all over the bottom of this pan. I say we throw it out and buy a new one."

Elsie stretched a red gingham dish towel taut and snapped Hallie's leg. "Why don't you just work up enough gumption to finish somethin' that takes a little elbow grease, Miss Bowen? Don't go talkin' lazy in my kitchen unless you want your fanny whacked. Don't you agree, Harold?"

Harold stood in the archway, leaning into his cane, with Adam behind him. "The entire community of Stewartville took a vote years ago, Elsie, and decided that we must always agree with you. I believe it's in the city council minutes." He smiled and gave his plaid shirt collar a quick tug. "Now if you'll excuse us for a few minutes, Adam and I are going to abduct Mona and that gumptionless child for a few minutes and head upstairs for that meeting you and I talked about earlier."

Elsie looked up from the expanse of counter where she was arranging stacks of freshly washed Royal Albert china and directing various granddaughters to the proper china cabinets scattered throughout the house. She placed her hands on her hips.

"Harold's already heard my mind on this, and what he speaks he speaks for the two of us. Go on upstairs to my sittin' room and close the door. Anybody else heads toward those stairs to do any listenin' in, and they'll be dealin' with me. Now get these ladies outta my kitchen, especially this complainin' one." She snapped Hallie a second time with the dish towel.

"And just so's you don't feel you missed out, Miss Hallie, the messy bits will still be in the bottom of that roastin' pan when you come back down."

With a flourish, Elsie shooed Hallie and Mona from the kitchen and up the stairs behind Harold and Adam.

Mona chose a mission rocker near the window that overlooked the roof of the back porch. It was the seat that offered the nearest thing to an emergency exit in the claustrophobic room, and her eyes could escape to the trees and the streets beyond the small space. Her eyes caught a movement below as she waited for everyone to settle in. A calico with a crooked tail was meandering down the sidewalk at an odd angle.

Miss Emily.

Mona quickly turned away from the window as Adam closed the door to the tiny room behind the four of them. He folded his arms and leaned back, his head barely clearing the slope of the ceiling, which angled sharply toward the exterior walls.

Harold had already eased his long, angular frame onto an overstuffed, powder blue loveseat tucked beneath the slope of the roof and stored his cane out of sight in the space behind him near the wall. His navy plaid shirt was buttoned all the way to the top and neatly tucked into a pair of light blue, belted dungarees. His poker-straight, pale hair was parted on the right and combed neatly down his forehead. Hallie sat beside him, perched on the edge of the cushion, her chin cupped in her hands and her elbows resting on her knees. For the first time since Mona could remember, Harold opened the conversation.

"Your sister doing okay, Mona?"

She nodded. "As well as can be expected. She's being released in the morning. Social workers and police are encouraging her to go straight into a residential rehab facility. I'm heading over to the hospital soon to try to work out some details."

Hallie pointed at Adam. "Why is he here? This is weird."

Adam shrugged his shoulders and smiled. "I was invited. Ask Harold. He's the man in charge of the guest list."

"I wouldn't say I'm in charge of anything, but Adam's here because I asked him." Harold reached into his front shirt pocket and pulled out a rumpled piece of paper. The instant he unfolded it, Mona's heart sank, and she felt a sudden urge to check on Miss Emily, but she forced her eyes to remain in the room. She eyed a copy of *Gone with the Wind* lying on a coffee table at the side of the loveseat.

"This is something Joe Spencer found at the police station yesterday. When I picked Hallie up, he gave it to me because he thought it might be important. I wanted to ask you about it, Mona."

Harold leaned across the room, and Mona's hand shot out as she snatched the paper from him. She folded it and slid it into the pocket of her khakis as a flash of anger burned through her.

"Thank you, Harold. I'll take care of it."

"Pardon an old man for intruding on your life here, Mona, but if that was something you planned to take care of, you wouldn't have thrown it away in the first place. I'm afraid you tossed it because you didn't plan on doing anything about it, and I think Hallie and Adam should be concerned about that. That's the reason I asked them to be here. They'd do anything for you. Adam here should be your hero. Any man who can fast-talk Trina into opening up at the crack of dawn on a holiday for one order of Belgian waffles is braver than a grizzly hunter sportin' bacon grease."

Mona felt the color drain from her face.

Good heavens, Adam brought me breakfast this morning! That means he knew about Ellen and never told me.

So has he figured it out—that the voice on the phone was me and not my sister?

Her eyes flickered to the window as she considered escape, mentally calculating if her ankles would break in the drop from the roof to Elsie's concrete driveway below. In her peripheral vision, she could see that Adam was focused on her.

"What's on the paper Joe Spencer found, Mona?"

She fought to make her tone sound nonchalant. "It's nothing, Adam . . . a note from my doctor."

She continued staring. This wasn't their business. Couldn't a person even throw paper in the trash in this town without someone else rifling through it?

Harold crossed his arms. "An appointment slip for an MRI of her brain. Ask her if she plans to have it done. Ask her how many times she's cancelled it. And while you're at it, ask her how she's been feeling lately. We can't be having you freewheeling with your health, young lady."

Anger exploded inside her. How dare he expose her like this in front of Adam, in front of Hallie? Her choices were hers, nobody else's. She didn't owe anyone in this room or this town an explanation.

Mona stood, and her voice was shaking. "Harold, thank you for your concern, but in an hour I've got to be at the hospital helping Ellen make decisions that are going to impact her and her daughter for the rest of their lives. I haven't got the strength or energy for an interrogation right now."

She made a move toward the door, but Adam stepped in front of her, his eyes locked on her face.

"So how many times have you cancelled it, Mona, and why would you do that? And when do you plan to go ahead and have it done?" His eyes drilled into hers, and she looked away. The sight of Miss Emily staggering down the sidewalk flashed in front of her. She hated that idiotic cat. Maybe she'd find it and run over it on her way to the hospital.

"This is stupid. It's just a stupid three-month follow-up for my surgery. I'm fine, everyone." She placed her hands on Adam's chest and tried to push him aside, but he wouldn't move.

"Then think of how much it will mean to us to have the MRI confirm it." His voice was steady. Mona's hands shoved against him one more time, and he reached for them and eased them back to her sides.

Behind her, the window beckoned, and something inside her snapped.

"Just stop it! It's hard enough to do what I have to do these days without everyone in my face telling me how to live my life! And what makes you all think you know what's best for me? The last time I checked, I was an adult and in charge of my own medical decisions." She turned, slumped wearily back into the chair, and crossed her arms across her chest.

From across the room, she heard a giggle. "I wish I had a voice recorder so I could play that back to you sometime. You've been in my face for the past two years, preaching to me about facing the tough things, and I imagine an hour from now you're going to be preaching the same thing to my mother.

"So since when did you get to be exempt from your own sermons? If we've got to take care of us, you've got to take care of you. We're family, so now it's your turn to listen. You've found a man willing to spend Saturdays here in Booney Town for you, who brings you waffles gobbed in whipped cream, who doesn't seem to mind that your skull is cracked and that your family could give Dr. Phil a run for his money. If I were you, I'd stop whining and start listening to people who seem to be trying real hard to take care of you."

For a moment, Mona wasn't certain if she should throw Hallie out the window or jump out herself. She was only certain that she felt as though she'd been punched in the gut. None of them knew what it meant to face that stupid MRI alone. She hated every second of clattering, pounding claustrophobia. She hated the feel of the tube sliding past her arms as it sucked her in. She hated the cage that encased her head. She hated lying half-naked, draped in a hospital gown that had shrouded the bodies of hundreds of other patients. She hated the reassuring voices of people she didn't know telling her she was doing fine when she knew she was not. She hated walking in alone, walking out alone, and waiting alone.

She forced herself to speak, to keep her tone even, to smile pleasantly and face them all, especially Adam.

"I'm grateful for your concern, really, and I'll give Dr. Bailey a call and reschedule. I promise. Just give me some time to figure things out with my sister and Hallie.

"Adam, I don't even know where to start, but thank you for surprising me with a wonderful breakfast and for showing up when I give you reasons to drive in the opposite direction."

Adam nodded, but there was no hint of a smile.

"Thank you, Hallie, for reminding me I can dish it out but

not take it. And thank you, Harold, for . . . for quietly loving me, no matter what shape I show up in, day after day." Mona smiled tiredly around the room as she ran her fingers through her hair. She needed to leave, to get out of that small space and into the air, to think about what had just happened. She needed to just get it over with and talk to Adam about the call, about Ellen, about everything and clear the air.

"If that's it, I'd like to head out to the hospital. Ellen and I have some things to discuss before tomorrow."

Harold pointed at a footstool next to the mission rocker. "Adam, this other thing may take a moment. If you wouldn't mind sitting down."

Adam settled his long frame onto a cream vinyl footstool to the side of her chair as Mona prayed the emotion and drama would be over. She needed some emotional reserve left over for her time with Ellen.

"Is this gonna be as good as watching Aunt Mona eat her own words?"

"Well, we don't want to be keeping you from your greasy pans, so I'll try to keep it short." Harold smiled, proud of his quick comeback. "First of all, since I've known Dr. Bailey for twenty years and I'll be seeing him on Tuesday, I'll just casually mention the little two-step you've been doing, rescheduling and avoiding your MRI. I'm sure he'll join us in getting after you. And don't make me bring Elsie into this. I don't think you want to know how persistent she could be if we added her to the team on this one."

Mona swallowed as she watched Harold's wide grin. In all the time she'd known him, she'd never seen him exert control over someone else's circumstances. This was bizarre. Disagreeing and bantering with Elsie had come as easily as breathing. But arguing with Harold? The idea seemed absurd. What had come over the man?

"I'm thinking you might be a touch peeved at me right now, but you're too polite to show it, what with Hallie and Adam here. Probably thinking Harold's gone a little off his gourd. Me and Elsie been seeing a struggle in you, Mona, and I learned too late that love does hard things when someone is struggling. So when I saw that MRI note you'd throwed away, I couldn't stand by. I'm too old to make the mistake of standing by again."

The room was quiet except for the sound of children's voices drifting up the stairs and through the sitting-room door.

"These last few months have been hard for everybody, and right now I think God wants family together. Ellen needs her sister, Hallie needs her aunt and mother, and Mona needs all of us. I believe the Lord's got it all spelled out for these next few months. The Lord's asked me to open my home to Ellen and Hallie for a time."

When Harold had finished talking, Mona turned toward the window. Thoughts of escape were gone.

When she left moments later to head for the hospital, she was not alone. Adam walked beside her down the front steps of Elsie's house. This time he was holding her hand.

Chapter Ten

Mona sat in the recliner and watched her sister spoon whipped cream from a slice of pumpkin pie she'd opened from among the plastic containers piled on her hospital tray.

"You want me to live where?"

"With Harold Rawlings."

"Elsie's boyfriend? What is he, a hundred years old? You want Hallie and me to move in with an old man? You must be out of your mind."

"Harold is most certainly not Elsie's boyfriend. He's simply an old friend who was her business partner. And what's your suggestion, Ellen? That the two of you move into my loft apartment and sleep in my bathtub? Rent a room at Rusty's Roost and share a twelve-by-fourteen space? Maybe you could ask for a room-and-board arrangement with one of the wonderful Mennonite families in the area. How do you feel about simplifying your wardrobe, wearing a head covering, and learning to can vegetables? We don't have a lot of options here."

Ellen stabbed at the pie. "What about Elsie?"

Mona smiled. "Elsie, by the way, adores your daughter and is keeping her for the night so I can get a good night's sleep. But no offer has been made to take you under her roof. If you're brave enough to ask a woman who doles out opinions like a human PEZ dispenser, it's up to you. However, I believe that you and Mrs. McFeeney might find yourselves butting heads from time to time on everything from childrearing to politics, if you're willing to take the heat. And let me tell you, Elsie can make a solar flare look like a polar ice cap."

Ellen shoved the pie across her tray. "So what am I supposed to do, Mona?"

Evening had fallen. The fluorescent lighting cast stark shadows across Ellen's face, and the circles beneath her eyes had deepened.

"You're supposed to do the hard work of rehab—not just for you but for Hallie. She's going to be out of the house soon, maybe out of your life. I know she doesn't want to talk to you right now, but she's angry, and you have to give her permission to be angry. You can't change her, Ellen. You can only change you.

"Harold's giving you and Hal a chance to be together in his house. That's just two weeks away, and Hallie and I can cram into my apartment until then. It won't be your house in Bloomfield Hills, but you have to see the big picture—that he's offering you all he has for nothing in return, knowing you and Hallie are going to be a major inconvenience to his life. Would you do that for a friend, much less someone you barely knew?"

"How much does he want?"

"You're kidding, right?"

"Of course I'm not kidding. The man knows where I live and what I drive. How much does he want a month? A thousand? Two thousand?" Ellen cut a forkful of pie and slid it into her mouth as Mona shook her head.

"He doesn't want a cent, and if you try to make this about money, he'll withdraw the offer."

"That doesn't make any sense. Nobody does something for nothing. Is he trying to impress you or is he looking for brownie points with God? I know he's one of your religious friends."

Was there curiosity in her sister's questions? Mona couldn't read the tone or the expression on Ellen's face as she scooped nibbles from the edges of her pie. Where had God taken her in those hours in a coma? Into the pit of fear? Futility? Desperation?

"Harold knows he can't possibly impress God with anything he does, that Jesus lived a perfect life and died to do that for him. Harold loves God by loving people. It's how he does life."

Ellen laid down her spoon and looked at her sister. "You're telling me he just goes around loving people and doing good things for them because they need it?"

"He does it because God made people in His image, so loving them is like loving part of Him. Maybe like if Stacy had left a child behind and you'd want to pour your life into loving a bit of Stacy through that child."

Mona knew better than to speak Stacy's name. She waited for the rage. Ellen looked down at her empty hands, then finally toward the window.

"That's the stupidest thing I've ever heard you say. God could never love us like a mother loves a child. Why do you spew that ridiculous crap? I'm a *drunk*, Mona, on my way to rehab. The one whose kid walked out on her. My own kid can't love me. My husband can't love me. You work your fool head off to try to do it every day, but some days you'd probably like to flush me with my own vomit. So don't sit there and tell me God loves me the way I love Stacy. I would have died for her. I'd still do it if I had the chance. Maybe I'm still trying to."

Ellen's fists gripped the blanket that lay across her lap as she slowly began to rock. Mona watched as her sister's hands worked the fabric, gripping and releasing in a steady rhythm.

"You understand what it's like to love your child so much you'd die for her, Ellen. It's part of God's heart He's letting you see in yourself. He loves us so much He doesn't want to leave us on our own to be flushed away in our vomit. With more love than every mother's and father's heart, He died to give us an escape from the brokenness we bring to the world."

"Love? In a father's heart? You have the nerve to even speak those words to me?" Ellen's eyes had gone cold.

Mona stood. "I'll be back in the morning. I'll be ready to drive you to whatever rehab center you choose, if that's what you decide to do." She moved toward the door. "You've been given a second chance, Ellen. No matter what you decide to do with it, it's God's gift to you. But there's nothing He wants more than to stand beside you in the struggle. It will be your choice if you push Him away." She turned and walked into the hallway.

Adam leaned against the wall next to Ellen's door. His arms were folded across his chest. She knew he'd heard every word.

He eased himself away from the wall and reached for her hand.

"I just heard a wonderful woman speak wise words to someone she loves. In fact, she took the words right out of my mouth."

He looked into Mona's eyes. "You've been given a second chance, Mona. No matter what you choose to do with it, it's God's gift to you. But there's nothing I want more than to stand beside you in the struggle. It will be your choice if you push me away."

Adam took her hand in his, and she felt his warmth as he walked her through the hospital door and out into the night.

᠖

The semidarkness of the shop enveloped them as they sat side-by-side on a blue velvet settee. Mona's brown leather jacket nestled around her shoulders. Adam had slipped it from her arms and gently tucked it around her before sitting beside her and taking her hand in his. Her fingers were icy. They'd been cold all day, and she tucked her free hand beneath her thigh as she stared at a display of antique quilts on a rack across from her. Already the words were sticking in her throat, and she hadn't even begun. From the corner of her eye she could see his blue sport coat was unbuttoned, and one arm rested on his leg as he angled toward her.

"There's no easy way for me to lead into this discussion, Adam. For the past three months, you've been amazing. You've supported me and encouraged me. I don't know what I would have done without you."

"You don't know what you would have done without me—that's a familiar phrase, a polite phrase. But how about a little honesty. I think the real question is whether or not your life has been different because of me, Mona."

"I . . . I don't know what you mean."

Adam leaned forward. "I think you do. It's not a difficult question. For the past three months, I've driven two hours one way to spend every Saturday with you. I changed cell phone plans to keep from going broke. A florist in Greenville is vacationing in Cozumel this winter because I met you. But it's not about flowers and phone calls. I've started planning my life around you. My life turned inside out the day Mona VanderMolen walked into my uncle's furniture store looking for her mother's rocking chair.

"But I know what's going on in my head. What I'd like to know is whether or not your life is different because you met Adam Dean last summer. Based on the things you said today at Elsie's,

I'm afraid the answer isn't what I would have thought it to be a week ago."

Mona felt his eyes drilling into her face, and her breathing quickened, but she kept her gaze fixed on a pink and lavender wedding ring quilt.

I can't tell him I'm losing my heart to him, Lord. Not when I've got to ask him to leave.

"You're my good friend, Adam. I don't know where I'd be in my rehab if you hadn't forced me to do laps around John Ball Park Zoo or made me walk the malls. You've helped me keep pushing forward."

"So I've been a good physical therapist, that's it? But not someone you'd open up to with the deep stuff—your warts and flaws, your fears, especially fears about something as serious as your health."

In the distance, she heard the sound of whining and scratching. Oscar. She leaned forward, and Adam gently pushed her back down onto the couch.

"I'll let him out. You chew on that a minute." He headed up the open steps to the loft in easy strides, opened the door to Mona's apartment, and gathered the squirming dachshund in his arms. Then he turned and headed back down and toward the rear of the shop and the back door.

She didn't know where to begin. She'd never heard this tone before—not angry, but indignant, challenging. She barely knew where to begin. She decided to choose the tangible list that floated into her brain and to push aside the part about fears. Ellen and Hallie had given her enough fear to deal with in the past forty-eight hours without having to take on a major discussion of her own.

How is my life different?

She stared at the quilt as a list of the easy things formed in her mind, memories that had stacked up over the past three months.

She knew that little things that used to mean nothing now meant more than she cared to admit—the sight of his number on her phone or his Suburban headed toward the shop. The warmth of his skin when he took her hand.

His friendship had divided her life into *before* and *after*. She could barely remember the *before*.

She knew that, above everything else, Adam had given her glimmers of hope that one day she would be cherished and loved, prayed for and nourished, in body, soul, and spirit. She wondered if her mother had hoped for those gifts and if her heart had broken waiting for what had never been given.

If he's the man you believe him to be, then why were you afraid to tell him about a routine MRI? And why can't you tell him about the headaches and the lights?

She shivered as a chill ran down her back, and she pulled her jacket closer about her shoulders.

The back door slammed, and Mona heard the sound of the office door open and a scuffling of toenails on the hardwood floor.

"I put him down in the office where he could get to his supper." Adam's footsteps drew closer, and then he was sitting beside her again, her hand in his, his eyes looking into hers.

"Mona, we've been seeing each other for three months. Every Saturday I've driven over here, I've dug myself a little bit deeper into your life, but maybe that's not what you want. Before this weekend, I would have thought that if a crisis hit your life, I'd have been on speed dial. It looks like I may have been wrong.

"I also would have thought that if you were even slightly worried about your health that you would have mentioned it, and we could have talked about it. But I seem to have made a lot of false assumptions about our relationship."

"Adam . . ."

"Let me finish." There was tightness in his voice. "I also wouldn't have thought you'd have deceived me. Or if you had for some reason, you at least would have tried to make it right as soon as possible. But the whole day passed today, and I never heard a word from you.

"And I'm not sure I can even tell you how frustrated I am about the MRI, about your unwillingness to make your own health a priority. I'm not willing to watch you take your body for granted the way your sister does. I almost lost you once."

Mona could feel the pulsations of a headache forming behind her eyes, and a shimmer of light cascaded through her peripheral vision. She drew her eyes away from the quilt display and glared at him.

"How dare you compare me to my sister and suggest I'm abusing my health! That's insulting."

"But is it true?"

"It is *not* true!"

"Then why have you cancelled twice?"

"Because it's medically unnecessary. It's simply a follow-up."

Adam cocked his head to one side, and Mona closed her eyes. She couldn't stand the look on his face—questioning and seeing through to the bones of her at the same time.

"And is it so easy to lie to yourself about what you're afraid of?"

"Stop it."

"Is it why it was so easy to lie to yourself about why you didn't want me with you when Ellen and Hallie ended up here? Did you lie to yourself about that, too, because you're afraid of me?"

"Stop it. I didn't take the time to call you because what was happening was too important, and I was sitting at my sister's bedside with visitors and doctors coming and going. I wanted to wait until we could be alone and have time together, but I should have at least been honest enough to have told you that."

She pulled her hand from Adam's and tucked it under her other leg. "I'm not afraid—of you or an MRI or anything else you've got going on in that crazy head of yours. I answered Ellen's phone when you called yesterday. You were talking so fast I couldn't get a word in, and I was so shocked it was you, I didn't have time to think. Then you hung up, and I didn't know what to do. You sounded so secretive and excited, and I was embarrassed because I hadn't called and told you about Ellen. And I was embarrassed because you were sharing secrets about me with my sister, and you just blurted it all out. Suddenly I felt like I was in junior high again, and I just wanted to forget about how uncomfortable it all felt until I had to face it."

Mona could feel the tension in her shoulders, and her quickening pulse. She willed herself to focus on long, slow breaths. It was all coming out in one giant wad of excuses, and even as she said it, she realized how fearful she truly sounded.

"I understand embarrassment, Mona. I understand wanting to wait to talk. But my question is bigger than that. I'm asking you to think about why after months of our being together, when your life hit a wall, your first instinct was to cut me out of the crisis. Because you've really been cutting me out slowly for a long time, whether you're ready to admit it or not."

The silence pressed in. There were so many truths, and Adam was asking for the most difficult ones, ones she'd barely put into words even to herself. How had she gotten here? A week ago things had seemed so much simpler.

"I was making a choice for you, Adam. My family is a mess, and it's going to take every ounce of strength in my body and mind to try and get them through this. And helping them won't mean three months—it will mean a lifetime. I can't pull you into the middle of that. It's too complicated."

He smiled, and Mona saw relief and humor there. "First, let me relieve you of the heavy task of making choices on my behalf. I'm actually willing to take responsibility for that myself. I have to admit, your family is a bit of a mess. But then, mine has its challenges. And it's going to take every ounce of your strength to try and help Ellen and Hallie. I agree.

"But life is complicated, Mona. The first day I drove to Stewartville and showed up with a car full of hyacinths, I committed myself to the complications of your life, whether you knew that or not, and I've recommitted every day since then. So you can't hide behind Ellen and Hallie."

"Hide?"

"From me, from yourself, from whatever's scaring you about that MRI, from God."

"I don't know what you're talking about."

Skittering toenails clattered across the shop floor, and a black body heaved its girth into Mona's lap. Oscar pawed lightly at Mona's khakis, and she leaned forward and pulled the quilt from the rack and spread it over the dog as she felt him nuzzle into the wedge of space between her body and Adam's. The silence slid between them once again.

"So I'm back to my original question. Is your life different because of me, Mona?"

She was suddenly overwhelmed with a desire to stand and run from the room. She'd met a man who deluged her with flowers, fixed her favorite Velveeta and strawberry jam sandwiches, prayed as easily as he breathed, demanded nothing from her, and tended her body and spirit with grace. She knew the answer. It terrified her.

Mona stared at the rise and fall of the blanket between them as Oscar's gentle snores rose from beneath the quilt. Adam took her hand, and Mona fought not to pull it away.

"Is it that you don't have answers, Mona, or that you're afraid of the answers you do have?"

She focused on the rhythm of the quilt, suddenly embarrassed at how hard it was to look at him as she gave voice to words she knew she had to say.

"Yes, these three months have changed me—you've changed me, my body has changed me—everything about me has changed, and I haven't had a vote on most of it. I can't do what I used to be able to do. I have Elsie balancing my books and Harold moving my furniture. My seventy-five-year-old friends are taking care of me when I should be taking care of them.

"There are moments when I can't remember my own phone number or how to count change or walk down stairs. Just thinking can be so much work that some mornings I want to curl up in a ball and quit. But I have a business to run and a niece to take care of and an alcoholic sister to keep track of . . ." The edges of her voice shook as a flush of anger surged through her. Adam's hand moved to her shoulder, and she fought the impulse to push it away.

"Do you see what you're saying, Mona? You're really sick, and you can barely talk about it. So you've decided to hide it from the people who really care about you, to not show up for your MRI, to ignore your pain and headaches—to shove them into some closet inside you and slam the door shut. We're all worried about you. How can you be responsible for taking care of Ellen and Hallie when you're acting just like them?"

Mona's head snapped back. "Stop comparing me to a frightened child and a drunk." She shoved Adam's hand from her shoulder. For a moment he looked startled, then his expression eased into a slow smile.

"People who care say and do tough things for the people they love. It's what you do for Ellen and Hallie. People who care don't just stand on the edges of other people's lives and send Hallmark cards when a crisis hits. I'm ready to be done with the Hallmark stage with you, Mona, and on to something more. I just need to know if you are, too. This isn't some kind of game for me."

"So you're telling me while I sat waiting to hear if my sister was going to live or die, what I was really doing was playing a game to shut you out?

"And what about your games? How did you know about Ellen? Who told you? You came and left the hospital in the morning like you were ashamed of us. Why not stay when you left my breakfast? And where did you go, anyway?"

She watched Adam absorb her sarcasm. His eyes told her that her words had stung, but she couldn't stop the stream. Her voice broke, and her final sentence came as a whisper.

"You knew I was there alone, and you left me."

Adam slowly smoothed the quilt around her legs, then stood.

"I was with you the whole time, Mona, in the chapel praying. I figured it would be best not to come until I was asked, and you didn't seem to be interested in asking, so I didn't intrude.

"I knew your sister was in the hospital because I was worried sick about you, and I'd called Harold. He gave me the details, so I came over early this morning. I figured you weren't taking care of yourself, and I thought your favorite breakfast would brighten your morning. I didn't leave because I was ashamed—of the circumstances or of your sister. She knows I was there because I spoke to her and prayed with her."

"You prayed with Ellen . . . she let you do that? She never said a word to me." Shame and disbelief coursed through her, and she fought the desire to pull the quilt over her head and hide beneath it.

"I'm not sure you trust me, Mona, or that you trust yourself. I'm a guy with a pretty basic plan. I just keep showing up and praying that as you get to know me, you'll come to trust me and eventually love me. But at some point, you'll have to decide if that's what you want—a relationship with a flesh-and-blood flawed man who loves you, or whether you want to be a Hallmark card kind of a woman."

He reached into the pocket of his jacket and pulled out his keys.

"I need to be going. Harold's invited me to spend the night at his place again. I think he likes the company and enjoys humiliating me at chess. I have some business with your sister early in the morning. Just thought I'd let you know in case it comes up later and I'm accused of being a sneak."

He leaned down and hitched the quilt up around Mona's shoulders.

"If I were you, I'd head up to the safety and security of that apartment of yours before the warmth of that comforter gets the best of you. Next thing you know, you'll doze off down here and that will be the end of you."

Adam leaned over, and she felt the quick pressure of his lips as he kissed the top of her hair, then headed toward the back door and out into the night.

Mona was sure the room felt colder after Adam left. Perhaps it was the draft from the opening and closing of the door. But in the end, the stairs seemed too daunting. In the morning she awoke on the couch in the shop with Oscar at her side, still huddled beneath the warmth of the wedding ring quilt.

Chapter Eleven

The cold, hard tile of the bathroom floor bit into Ellen's shins as she clutched the toilet. Droplets of bile dripped from her mouth as she clenched her eyes shut and waited for the retching to pass. She rocked slowly, her head bent low as the spasms rose and fell and finally receded.

She slumped back into a corner, the cold green walls cupping her thin body engulfed in an oversized hospital gown. On the floor beside her, a fresh towel lay in a heap where she'd thrown it as she'd staggered into the room. She reached for it and drew it across her sweaty face and lips, then dropped her head to her knees.

It was the fourth time that night. In two hours, the morning shift would come on duty, and Mona would be coming. She had two hours to decide.

For the fourth time, she leaned forward, grabbed the sink, and pulled herself to her feet. For the first time, she faced herself in the mirror.

Large gray eyes stared back from sunken holes, and her cheeks were gaunt and pale. The creamy complexion that she prized reflected a sickly green from the bathroom tiles, and crusts of a scab showed at one corner of her mouth where the ventilator had pulled at her lips. The bruise on her forehead had feathered out at the edges and crept into her eyebrow and over the bridge of her nose. Her blonde hair was sweaty and matted to her head.

Ellen's hand drifted to the mirror and hovered before the reflection. Her mother's face stared back at her, ravaged by drugs and emaciated by disease. The sunken gray eyes held the heartbreak of a sixty-year-old woman.

She turned on the faucet and slowly rinsed the sweat and filth from her face as memories streamed through her mind.

Music lessons at the piano as her mother's fingers had gently guided hers.

The rich harmonies of her mother's alto as they'd sat side-by-side in church.

The shielding curve of her mother's arms in the presence of her father's rage.

The eyes of quiet grace in the grip of cancer.

Ellen stared at her face as water dripped from her chin. Another face reflected back—the face of an eight-year-old girl, water coursing down her face as a pastor lifted her from a baptismal tank and her mother and sister looked on.

A wave of nausea rose and subsided as she looked into the sunken eyes. "You've finally left me, too, Mom. There's nothing left to give to Hallie. I can't hear your voice anymore." She reached for the towel hanging on a rod beside her and slowly dried her face. Then she turned from the room and shut off the light.

Every bone in her body ached as Ellen made her way back to her bed. She eased her body between the rumpled sheets and pulled the tray table close. Her nurse had promised to buy her a robe and a few toiletries from the hospital gift shop before Mona came, but the pen and paper with her list had been pushed aside, and an envelope bearing the words *To Ellen* sat in its place.

She glanced at the clock. It was barely five in the morning. She couldn't think of a soul who would have brought her a note at that hour. Hallie would have addressed it to Mom. Mona would have stayed, and Elsie wouldn't give her the time of day from nine to five, much less get up before sunrise to do something for her.

She ripped open the envelope and scanned the familiar writing. The penmanship matched the notes she'd been receiving for months. Simple, unembellished. But this was the first to not come through the mail. The postmarks of all the others had told her from the beginning that they'd come from Stewartville—she'd always imagined from Mona or a close friend. Just another way of preaching at her, another way to press her guilt button. But she hadn't let them get to her. Once she'd gotten used to them, it actually felt nice to think someone prayed for her. Now one had landed on her hospital tray in the dead of night.

Like the others, it was short:

> *Dear Ellen,*
>
> *When we leave our loved ones behind, it's easy to think we're abandoning them. But even though you'll be separated from Hallie, you'll be in her thoughts and her heart every day. Deep inside, she knows that by going away, you're doing your best to stay with her. A mother doesn't need to be beside her daughter to guide her in what's right. Sometimes just living what's true is our greatest act of love.*
>
> *The prayers of family are going with you. You won't be alone. God will be with you in the days*

*ahead, in every hard moment, even when you're
certain that it can't possibly be true.*

*God is renewing you. His gifts and His song are
yours for the taking.*

*"Those living far away fear your wonders; where
morning dawns and evening fades you call forth songs
of joy" (Ps. 65:8).*

Ellen read over the note three times before she reached for her
purse in the drawer of her bedside stand. She folded the lined paper neatly, then zipped it into an inside compartment of her purse
beside a creased and faded picture of her mother.

Mona stood hunched over her dinette table, rummaging through
wrinkled M&M's wrappers, scraps of paper, assorted mini note-
books, and dozens of pens. She was fuming. For the third time
that week, the keys to the truck had walked off. Or maybe they
hadn't. Her biggest frustration was knowing that her keys could
be sitting under her nose and her brain might be telling her they
were a Tootsie Roll. She scrabbled through the pile, laying aside
the items one by one.

When her cell phone rang, she knew it would be Ellen. She
was already ten minutes late to pick her up, and she braced herself for screams. But instead of an angry outburst, her sister simply
launched into a litany of details, briefly explaining the importance
of each as though she were checking off items on a prearranged list.

Mona nearly fainted as she listened.

There was no time to talk. Ellen had an appointment to check into Fairhaven Life Center in Grand Rapids at 11:00 AM. No, she didn't need Mona to take her after all. Everything was arranged. Hallie would enroll in Stewartville High School on Monday. All the necessary papers had been signed and were in the hands of the social worker, who would be waiting for Mona's call on Monday. Could she find a way to get some of hers and Hallie's clothes and personal items from the house in Bloomfield Hills? Give her love to Hallie. She'd call from Fairhaven as soon as she could, and she'd be sending necessary paperwork back.

In the background, Mona heard a voice reminding Ellen of the time.

"I'm sorry about the rush, Mona, but Fairhaven said they could get me into a program that's starting this morning if I could come right away. It's not that I don't want you taking me down, but I need to do this on my own. I want you to know that I'm giving this my best shot. And even though I've never said it before, I want to say thanks for the cards and the support. Tell Hallie I love her, and I'm doing this for her."

Then she was gone.

Mona stared at the scattered mess on her table as realities settled in, one by one.

Her sister was on her way to rehab, and Hallie would be moving into the loft. Today.

And one final realization: the voice in the background—the person with Ellen—had been Adam.

Harold slid the second plastic storage container under the yellow canopy bed and made a mental calculation of the remaining space as he knelt on the hardwood floor. For a moment, he felt dizzy, and he settled back on his haunches to let the feeling pass as he eased the tension between his shirt collar and his neck with a long, skinny finger. Hauling and toting seemed to take more than he had to give lately. It was good that Adam had helped pull the boxes from the closet shelves in the two spare bedrooms last night so he could sort their contents into the rolling storage cartons.

Two weeks wasn't much time to get ready for two women. But God had painted the picture pretty clear. Open the door, and the Lord would nudge them through. Harold just hadn't thought that opening a door would mean cleaning closets.

And hiding memories. He gazed at the shadowed shapes and colors obscured by the plastic of the one remaining container. Through the side, he could make out the graceful script on a familiar sheet of paper. A fragment of melody floated through his head, then a picture of Lynn's face, and he pushed the memories aside. Even after thirty-two years, it still hurt like it was yesterday. Today, he didn't have time to think about it.

Hallie was due to arrive at noon. He had ten minutes. He leaned forward, reached beneath the bed, and gave the boxes a shove. Then he lined up the third storage container with the remaining empty space and pushed it into place.

Some hurts would always be there. Life didn't erase pain or memories. Ellen was learning that. Hallie, too. But there were other things they could learn if they didn't let anger and bitterness scar over the wounds. There were gifts in the pain, if they could look beyond the now and unclench their hands to receive them.

Harold gripped the yellow bedspread and slowly pulled himself upright as the room spun and swayed around him. He eased himself to the edge of the bed and sat, drawing in slow, easy breaths as waves of nausea washed over him. It would take a minute or two to get his bearings back. He was learning that, but sitting time was prayer time, and the prayers came easily for Hallie and Ellen, Mona and Adam.

A knock sounded at the back door, and Hallie's voice called through the kitchen. Harold glanced across the room and at Lynn's oak library desk, the deep drawers neatly shut and hiding the files and documents inside. The paperwork would have to wait until later. No one knew what was there, anyway. He had two weeks to sort through it all and put it where it would be safe from prying eyes.

He reached for his cane, rose slowly, and headed toward the kitchen.

Adam pulled his Suburban into a space beside the wide sidewalk that led to the front entrance of Fairhaven Life Center and put the vehicle in park while he let the engine idle.

"Would you like me to walk you in?"

"No, but thanks. I'll be fine on my own."

A dusting of snow eddied and swirled in front of the oak double doors beneath a pillared portico. He rested his hands on the wheel as he took in Ellen's expression. She stared out the window to the three-story brick building beyond. Somehow, she'd managed to get her hands on makeup before he'd arrived, and it appeared she'd taken great care to disguise the dark circles under her eyes. Her hair had been neatly twisted into a series of knots at the nape of her neck, and someone had brought her a beautiful scarf that drew a glint of blue from her gray eyes. He saw her eyes trace the outline of the building, and he read her apprehension. Perhaps she wouldn't be offended if he asked. She'd been open and friendly on the ride down—different than what he'd expected.

"Why Fairhaven? Grand Rapids has lots of programs. Lansing, too, for that matter."

Ellen shrugged. "It's supposed to be the best, and I'm sure you've heard of my taste for the best. Mona's certainly mentioned it." She turned and smiled brightly. "Among other things."

"If you're asking if I've ever heard Mona run you down behind your back, the answer would be never."

"Never? Then I imagine she doesn't mention me at all. Probably easier for my religious sister to act like I don't exist. That way she can tell herself she's being spiritual. Has she said anything, then?" Ellen focused her attention on retying the scarf at her neck.

"Not a lot, really. I know you and Phil have split up. I know you were a cheerleader in high school, went to State and studied music—piano performance, I think—then met Phil, had Stacy and Hallie. I know you love decorating and you're good at it. She really admires your creativity. And I know Stacy drowned while the girls were at Mona's beach house and you and Phil were away on vacation. And she told me you took care of her while she was in the hospital after her accident last summer."

Ellen finished off the scarf knot with a final tug and glared at Adam. "I took care of her? She told you that? I don't think there's a soul in the world who can take care of Mona VanderMolen. The woman will give you a run for your money if you plan on trying.

"And you're telling me she's never trashed me? In the three months you and she have been dating or whatever you want to call it, you haven't heard her criticize the way I raise Hallie or spend my money or treat my so-called husband? You've never heard her make sarcastic innuendos or tell embarrassing stories or roll her eyes like every other sister in the world?"

"Never."

"You wouldn't lie to a drunk, would you?"

Adam laughed. "If it will make you feel any better, she told me that you once made a marble cake for a college boyfriend and confused baking powder for baking soda and it came out as flat as a pancake, but the marble cake story is as ugly as it gets."

Ellen reached for the phone that lay on the seat between them, disconnected a battery charger that had been plugged into the Suburban's cigarette lighter, and stuffed it into a small gym bag on the floor at her feet.

"Well, there's something else I can hate her for, too. Mona—the do-gooder with the sister who's the lost cause. She's my mother, down to the Bible, and I'm my father, down to the bottle. But then, maybe she never told you that part, either." She zipped the bag closed with a jerk. "Thanks for stopping so I could pick up some clothes and a few other things. And thanks for not preaching. I heard it all when I was a kid, and believe it or not, a lot of it's still in my head, even though I've tried to wash it away with a few thousand bottles of liquor."

Adam angled his body toward hers as he struggled to read her face. If he pressed too hard, he knew he'd lose her. "I've only asked you one question, and you still haven't answered it. Why Fairhaven?"

Ellen pulled her bag into her lap and zipped up her black leather jacket. "It's easy, really. Because I was told they do more than help drunks stop drinking. They're into that whole 'give people hope' thing. Funny little word, *hope*. I guess if I don't find it soon, the drinking won't matter, will it?"

She ran her fingers over a picture of Hallie on the front of her cell phone, and her face tightened. "Maybe Hallie's right. Maybe she'd be better off if I just gave up and walked away. I don't suppose you know what that feels like, a nice church guy like you?"

The window behind Ellen's face had glazed over in clumpy, moist flakes of snow. He looked beyond her, and scenes rose and fell in gentle swells of memory, one blurring into the other.

Julie lying in a box of quilted satin in her favorite heather green jacket, a jade and rose Chinese silk scarf tied at her neck and held in place with the Celtic knot pin he'd bought her for their first anniversary.

Their empty bed and silent home.

The agony of loneliness that had almost swallowed him.

He remembered despair so deep that everything else in his life had faded to blackness. He remembered walking hand-in-hand with the pain and not knowing how to tear his hand from its grip. He remembered the void of believing he would never come back.

Ellen's face drew him back, and he cleared his throat and rubbed a hand quickly across his cheek. He saw the questions in her eyes as he reached beneath his seat, pulled out a spiral notebook, and placed it on the seat between the two of them.

"Use it for whatever you want—collect recipes from the other residents, take notes in your sessions, whatever. But the answer to your question is yes, that I did walk away for a while. From God, from my family, from life. The only thing that brought me back was getting honest with God and with myself. He let me suffer, so I gave myself permission to become a victim. Then one day, I realized that anger is its own slow death, and I started pouring it all out to Him."

Ellen turned toward the window. "Don't patronize me. God

stopped listening to anything I had to say years ago when He took Stacy, and all Mona's little notes with verses just prove to me that if He's really God, He's trite and all He cares about is taking. The only thing I ever had worth giving was my daughters, and He's already taken the two of them."

Ellen's hands suddenly felt cold, and she clasped them together for warmth. Beyond the window, flakes of snow zigzagged from the sky and clumped on the shrouded form of a juniper bush.

"So is this where I get my sermon—the final send-off before I go in?"

Her shoulders were hunched against the cold, and Adam sensed the tension in her words.

"Is your question an invitation or a door slamming?"

Ellen laughed and glanced toward the window as a black mini-van pulled into the parking space beside them and a teenage girl in a navy peacoat, blue jeans, and sneakers emerged and sprinted up the sidewalk and through the front doors.

"I like a man who doesn't consider me a captive audience because he gave me a ride. But why don't I throw caution to the wind and give you your chance to make it a religious one-two punch. After all, Mona hit me with her final shot this morning—a flowery little note with a verse, just like all her other ones these past three months. After months of being ticked about them, I've decided she means well. I only wish she'd admit they're from her rather than trying to make them sound like some voice from heaven or our mother or something. So go for it, Adam, and send me off with deep words of spiritual wisdom."

Ellen tipped her head forward and closed her eyes, and Adam saw Mona's face in her profile—in the curve of the cheek, the angle of the nose, the shape of the lips—bent over her office desk with the noise of the shop muffled by her closed door as she prayed for her sister. He knew at that moment that Ellen's words were a door flung open, in spite of anything she might say.

"All I can give you is the truth, Ellen. It's pretty simple. Everything was God's fault after my wife, Julie, died. I made myself the judge of all things, put myself in charge, and messed things up royally. By the time I joined my uncle in his business, I could barely function. You and I are more alike than you think. I kept my anger on the inside and went dead. You just wear yours on the outside and invite the fight."

"Invite the fight?"

"With God. Taunting Him, screaming in His face, daring Him. The same things Hallie was so good at until last summer."

"So that's what you think this is all about? Daring God?"

She was facing him dead-on. Her question was real, but Adam knew it was a question she'd have to answer herself.

"Doesn't really matter what I think. But ask yourself if picking Fairhaven might have been you stepping into the ring. I guess you'll have to decide if you're willing to pick up the gloves or if you're afraid to go head-to-head."

Ellen tugged her black leather jacket up under her neck as she pushed open the door and pulled her purse to her shoulder. "I guess two weeks will show both of us if I'm a fighter and whether or not those prayers my sister talks about all the time or the God behind them are worth anything.

"You're a little strange, Adam, but I think I like you. You can count me in to help with the Christmas thing. I'm glad Mona has someone watching out for her."

She grabbed her gym bag and stepped into the cold, then paused and looked back. "Tell Hallie I love her. Who knows? Maybe she'll listen to you." Then she slammed the door as the wind tossed a blast of cold air into the Suburban.

Adam watched as Ellen walked through the growing storm and into the dim glow of light on the far side of the oak double doors.

Chapter Twelve

At the stroke of two, Mona collapsed on a steamer trunk behind a coat tree hung with vintage dresses. Her head was pounding, and her legs felt as though they had turned to rubber.

Elsie stood six-deep in customers at the front of the store, directing yet another Black Friday sale drama. Her lavender puff of hair was barely visible above the heads of four women who were haggling over Adam's only remaining reproduction piecrust table. From Mona's vantage point, it appeared that a buxom woman in a sable fur coat and dramatic, fake eyelashes had beaten down her competitors for rights of ownership. Mona ventured that the librarians across the street at the Stewartville Public Library wished they could shush the woman as she announced she'd driven from East Grand Rapids specifically for one of Adam Dean's pieces.

Mona settled back on the trunk and screened the woman's voice from her thoughts. Even with Elsie and Jessica coming in at eight to cover the sale crowd, the shop had been slammed beyond her wildest dreams. Adam's new line of furniture seemed to be at the top of everyone's Christmas list. More and more people had been stopping in to request his growing collection over the past three months. When she and Adam had discussed bringing a few Arts and Crafts pieces into the shop in September, neither had guessed how quickly his furniture would fly out the door. And she'd been shocked when she'd tallied the books at the end of October and discovered that a third of the shop's profits had come from Adam's reproduction furniture line.

Floor space had quickly become a nightmare, and the aisles were crammed with Adam's nightstands, armoires, chifforobes, dining-room tables, sewing tables, sideboards, and occasional tables. By October it became obvious that the usual holiday decor would have to be cut back. The eight-foot Christmas tree and antique children's sleigh that had made their annual appearance since Mona had owned the store had been reduced to a table-top tree and a few wreaths and candles. Business had never been better, but customers were also complaining that they could barely move and that it was getting difficult to find true antiques among so many reproductions.

The woman's voice rose again, and Mona noted the look of victory on her face as she and Elsie turned and headed toward the cash register that sat on the narrow plywood counter at the back of the store adjacent to the stairs leading to the loft. Elsie glanced in Mona's direction and winked as she passed, calling out over her shoulder to the three remaining women.

"Ladies, now don't you be disappointed. Mr. Adam Dean himself was in yesterday and promised he'll have several new piecrust tables in before December third. They'll be a lot like this here table, but with some special inlay he's copied from a piece in the Smithsonian that's one of his favorites. I can have him call you personally to describe them to you, if you'd like."

Mona smiled. The woman could talk Michelangelo into art lessons.

A gentle vibration registered in Mona's pocket, and she reached for her cell phone and flipped it open as she watched the women scurry to the back of the store.

"Mona, I only have a few minutes. The director at Fairhaven has given me permission to call you while they finish processing my paperwork. Is Adam there yet?"

"No, should he be?"

"Any minute, I expect. He's coming for Hallie."

Mona's heart dropped. "Hallie? What for?" She stood and headed toward the front of the shop, her eyes scanning Main Street through the beveled glass of the oak front door. She couldn't imagine a reason Adam would be showing up to take Hallie anywhere.

"It's a favor, really, a pretty big one, and he was brave enough to agree. He doesn't seem to be intimidated by much of anything. Got that religious thing going on, but I imagine you find that charming. I imagine you're planning on holding on to him."

Mona ignored her irritation. "Ellen, why is Adam coming for Hallie? She's not even here. She spent the night at Elsie's and then went to Harold's to work on some project they've cooked up. He's supposed to bring her by at three."

"Well, there's been a little change in plans. Adam's driving her to Bloomfield Hills to get her things so she can start school on Monday—clothes, her computer, personal stuff. I knew today was your big sale and there was no way you could spend six hours driving there and back, plus two or three hours collecting clothes for her and for me and letting her see Abby and a few friends. Your brain would melt to oatmeal. So Adam's agreed to do it.

"I've also given Adam permission to pull a few files on Phil's and my investments. I'm expecting to make some decisions in the next few months. I guess it's time for me to start figuring out a few things. So all that said, once they get on the road, I wouldn't expect them back until after midnight. And when it's all over, you're going to owe that boyfriend of yours big time for agreeing to be held hostage for twelve hours with your niece and some girl named Cara Cunningham that he suggested they take along. He said you know her—she's your pastor's daughter. Her mom and dad stopped by the hospital yesterday, and they seemed like decent enough people. They're already on your special pray-for-Ellen squad. They had a lot of nice things to say about Adam. I didn't know he spent Saturday nights with your friend Harold to go to church with you. Sounds like even your pastor likes this man."

Mona stared at the grandfather clock as the pendulum swayed back and forth. Adam and Hallie alone for twelve hours with her pastor's daughter. She could hardly imagine what Hallie might possibly think up to say or do. She wondered where her duct tape might be as she ran her fingers through her hair.

"Ellen, I'm sure this could wait a day or two until I can take Hallie down. Why today? And who's going to supervise what she brings back—Adam? I can't wait to see what the two of you could end up wearing if he's in charge. And by the way, he is not my boyfriend. What am I—in tenth grade?" She began a slow pace from the clock to the front door and back again.

"You know, Mona, I've got people standing around me who can hear what I'm saying, but I'm still going to tell you to shut up and do the listening for once, because I'm really trying to do this because it's what's best for you. I know it's hard for you to wrap your brain around that, but just try. When I first laid my eyes on you when I was crawling out of my coma, I thought you might have been on a binge with me. You look like you've got one foot in the grave and you're ready to fall apart. You've got a man who's willing to help you, and you'd be stupid not to let him."

The jingle bells on the shop door rang. Behind her, Mona heard the sound of feet stomping on the rag rug. She turned and waved a free hand as Adam closed the door behind him. Through the door, she caught a glimpse of his Suburban parked along the curb in front of the library across the street. He brushed the snow from the shoulders of his brown leather jacket as he waved at Elsie.

"He's here, Ellen. I've got to go."

Elsie's voice rang out from the back of the shop. "Well, if it isn't Mr. Adam Dean himself. If you could just step back here for a moment, these ladies would like to have a word with you about your furniture."

Adam smiled in Mona's direction and headed toward the cluster of women as she turned back to the phone.

"Mona, I need to say one more thing before things get crazy for me here." The line went silent for a moment. "When I get out of here, I want you and me to get away—just the two of us, some place special, some place you'll really like. We'll both need a little indulgence by then. I know this is your holiday season and you're going to have to contend with Hallie for the next few weeks. But I think I'm going to need a few days to get my bearings when this is over. I'm smart enough to know rehab is going to be tough. Will you let me plan something that will help us . . . talk a little?"

Mona tried to remember how many times she'd reached to open a door to Ellen, only to have the bolt slid back into place. She felt suspicion hovering over her heart, and she struggled to shrug it off.

"Why?"

"If you want the truth, I'm being forced to ask you. Someone's asked me to take a step now that will help me build bridges when I'm done with the program. Who knows—maybe I won't even want

to do it when I get out. But right now, I'm saying I'm going to finish what I start, and I'm trying to believe that's where I'll be then.
I'm trying to do the next thing I'm supposed to do, even if I don't
fully believe it now. There's a part of me that wants to believe that
when I get there I'll still want to do it."

Mona swallowed. It seemed honest enough. "That's faith, Ellen.
Taking a step today, even when you're unsure about tomorrow."
She felt a throb of pressure behind her eyes. "Plan it, Ellen. I'll be
there."

They hung up, and Mona slid the phone back into the pocket
of her slacks.

*Please, God, I'm asking for Your gift of faith for my sister. Faith to
trust You again.*

She turned and watched Adam's head bowed low over his
piecrust table as he pointed out the detailed edging beneath the
eyes of admiring fans.

What had he and Ellen managed to talk about for more than
an hour? And what would he think of her house, her furniture,
her clothes? She envisioned him walking up the sweeping stairs of
the Bloomfield Hills house and into Ellen's massive bedroom with
its country French furniture as Hallie and Cara ran ahead into
the walk-in closet and pull Armani and Nina Ricci willy-nilly from
the hangers.

The thought sickened her. Not the thought of chaos and wrinkles and jumbled clothes crammed thoughtlessly into Ellen's sleek,
black luggage. But the thought of Adam in Ellen's home and the
awareness of jealousy, fresh and raw, unleashed from the dark
spaces of her heart.

Mona sat chin-in-hand behind the office desk, the door pulled closed to screen out the noise of Elsie negotiating a deal for a claw-foot dining-room table. Adam had run across the street to grab take-out meals from Trina's. She faced the bare stud walls and wondered for the umpteenth time how the months could pass so quickly. She'd meant to put up drywall last summer, but then the accident had changed her priorities, had changed everything.

She stared at the cell phone that lay on the desk in front of her. She'd known before she'd even dialed that no one would answer at Dr. Bailey's office, that the staff would be off for the holiday weekend. But at least she could say she'd called and made an honest attempt to schedule the MRI. Or had she? She picked up the phone and slid it into her pocket.

Adam would be back in moments. And then what?

And then what, Mona? Keep ignoring the pain, keep working to prove it's no one's responsibility to take care of you? Keep trying to convince yourself you're all you need?

She heard the distant jingle of the bells on the front door.

What about Adam—who never demands, who isn't frightened by your shaved head or deranged relatives, who keeps coming back, even when you act like a fool? He's lost one wife. Why would he stick around to watch another woman shrivel up and wither away? When are you finally going to end it for his sake and get this whole mess over with?

A quiet knock sounded, and Adam stepped inside, closing the door behind him. He set two large brown bags on the floor and eased himself into an oak swivel chair facing her.

She struggled to look him in the eyes as she searched for the words to begin.

"The first time I met you, we were in this office. I made an

143

absolute idiot of myself. Something I do rather often." She glanced up. The warmth she sought reassured her as he smiled.

"I found you totally charming."

"Something I found amazing, but then, you're an amazing man, Adam, in so many small ways that have been startling to me and in so many significant ways that seem so rare in people I've known. I know you truly care about me, and I want you to know that I called today to schedule my MRI."

His eyebrows rose. "Oh?"

"Yes . . . but they were off for the holiday."

"That didn't surprise you?"

"Well . . . not totally, I guess. But I left a message on the machine. I'm sure they'll call me back next week."

"And if they don't?"

She felt herself bristling, and once again, the question *why* drifted to the surface of her thoughts.

"I need to ask you a question. Did you bring me lunch?"

"You're changing the subject, but of course I brought you lunch."

"No, I'm not. Just listen and try to hear me out. You brought me lunch today like you always do, and I didn't ask for anything."

"Why should you have to ask?"

"It's not about the *should* of anything; it's just about who you are. And what did you bring me?"

Adam crossed his arms, and Mona saw the furrow come across his brow as he studied her face. "Since the weather's turned cold, you've been avoiding salads. Yesterday, you had a big turkey dinner, so you're probably interested in something a little lighter. I went with the spinach quiche with a multi-grain dinner roll and a slice of Trina's blueberry pie because it's your favorite. I also got split pea soup for Elsie and Harold and cheeseburgers for Hallie and Cara so they can eat on the road."

"Do you realize this isn't exactly a natural instinct for most men? How did you know exactly what everyone would want—for instance, that Elsie and Harold love split pea?"

"It's nothing special. I pay attention."

"That's where you're wrong. It is special. You care about people. You notice details. It's second nature to you, and it can be a little . . . unnerving."

"Unnerving?"

"Yes . . . no. I mean, you don't understand. I've managed to live almost half a century without being noticed by men, much less being taken care of by one, and suddenly a man is noticing every detail of my life. It's unnerving. And then there's the nice factor. The more I know you, the more painfully aware I am that I've got more in common with Ellen than I'd like to admit. I'm headstrong, and yes, I don't want to crawl back into that MRI tube again and give the doctor a chance to tell me that something else is wrong with me. In the past three months, I've realized that Ellen and I are both rather messed up. We just wear it differently."

"I see." Adam settled back in his chair. "I'm listening if you want to tell me about that."

Mona waited for a look of condescension, but it didn't come. Fear pulled at the corners of her thoughts, and she braced herself for the first shadows of indifference as she pushed ahead.

"Our home was a mess. We grew up breathing shame like most people breathe air. We were never good enough for my dad—no one ever was. So I became the good daughter, and Ellen became the rebel. Life became one big effort to earn Dad's approval. I failed, of course, but worshipping success and perfectionism were approved addictions in the church where my mother took us. Those became my drugs. And once I knew Jesus, Satan convinced me that I had to keep working for God's love. So I chose all the things that brought me acceptance from people in my church."

The words were suddenly excruciating, and Mona looked away. She didn't want to talk about the struggle and what had taken so long to understand herself.

"Adam, I'm trying to tell you how hard it is for me to trust and not to control everything and everyone in my world. I've been on my own for forty-five years, trying to prove something to the world. You've helped me see that there are a lot of things about me God needs to change. In the past three months, all kinds of insecurities and needs have been churning inside of me, and I can't expect you to fix them. I just want you to know I realize they're there, and God's working on me."

Mona drew her eyes away as she pulled a pencil and legal pad toward her. Her heart was pounding as she stared at the paper and began to trace circles into the margins. Again, she braced herself for indifference and the first hint of withdrawal. But Adam's tone was warm and even.

"I know I can't make you trust me, and I'm not on a special Nice Guy Campaign to win you over. I was glad to drive Ellen today, and I'm glad to take Hallie. I want to help in any way I can, if that means praying or talking or showing up or not showing up, if that's what you need. But you're right. Only God can change those things in you. You're in control of your own life, Mona. You're not obligated to report in to me about your decisions."

Mona had hoped there would be more, but Adam had stopped. Her pencil paused briefly. The silence grew uncomfortable, and she began to jot a list of items for Hallie to gather from the house.

"How did it go—the drive down? And what about Fairhaven?" Her tone lightened, and she hoped he'd notice and draw her back to questions about their relationship. He paused and seemed to be considering his answer, then spoke.

"Interesting. We had a good talk, actually. I was surprised she didn't seem more resistant about the place, but I figured you'd had a social worker try to convince her it was the best choice. And then she made a couple of comments about the notes you've been sending her and the one you left today—said she wished you'd just signed them instead of making them sound like your mother. That kind of caught me off guard."

Mona's head snapped up. "What are you talking about—Fairhaven was totally Ellen's decision, not mine. And what notes? I haven't sent my sister any notes, this morning or for as long as I can remember."

"So you're telling me . . . Ellen chose Fairhaven of her own free will?"

Mona put down the pencil and pushed the list away. "Nobody ever chooses anything for my sister, Adam. She picked this place herself, I assumed because it had a great spa or something, and I don't know a thing about it. She told me the social worker gave her a list of suggested residential treatment centers and outpatient programs. She said this one was near Stewartville, and she thought it would offer her the kind of help she needed. Why on earth would you think I chose it?"

His eyebrows raised. "I thought everybody within two hours of Grand Rapids knew about Fairhaven. It's known for being the best Christian counseling center in the Midwest." He leaned toward the bag on the floor beside him, pulled out a lidded Styrofoam cup, and set it on the desk in front of her. "Cinnamon spice tea. In case you need something bracing right about now."

Mona silently repeated the words. A Christian counseling center. It was impossible. She blinked as she felt her eyes grow hot. She stared at the cup of tea in front of her and the man who smiled so easily from the other side of the desk.

"And what notes are you talking about? This is just crazy."

"Well, she referred to a note you'd given her before she left this morning and notes she'd been getting from you for the past couple of months."

None of it made any sense. She hadn't been able to get her sister to darken the door of a church with her since she'd married Phil, and now Ellen had picked a Christian rehab center. And who on earth had been writing her sister notes for the past three months, and had Adam said they sounded like they'd been written by her mother?

"The tea is perfect, thank you. I should probably tell you that it's quite possible that I might cry a bit right now. I thought I'd warn you. I just never expected this from Ellen. I can't figure out what's going on."

Adam leaned forward in his chair, reached across the desk, and took her hands in his own. "Dance, if you're feeling joy. Run and give Elsie a hug. Stick your head out the window and scream if you need to. But don't apologize over tears because you see good things happening for your sister. It could even be God answering those prayers of yours, you know." He squeezed her hands, then flipped to a fresh sheet in the legal pad. "Now write down what you're afraid of. Work on it while you eat lunch."

By the time Hallie arrived thirty minutes later, one sheet had been filled, and the cinnamon tea had been drained. Mona's lunch sat beside her, untouched. Adam's empty chair faced her across the room, a reminder of the words he'd spoken.

Write down what you're afraid of.

She bowed her head over the paper that lay on the desk before her.

Mona sat cross-legged on her loveseat with Oscar nestled in the crook of her legs. The silence of the apartment embraced her after the chaos of the day. A file sat on her lap, and she flipped it open.

The first document was a hand-written notarized letter granting her temporary rights of guardianship for a period of two weeks while Ellen was in treatment at Fairhaven. Hallie was to be enrolled in Stewartville High School. The letter included contact information for Hallie's guidance counselor at Bloomfield Hills High School. A fifteen-hundred-dollar check made out in Mona's name was paper-clipped to the top, with the notation *For room, board, and expenses* on the memo line.

On a second document, Ellen had copied her insurance and dental cards, along with a handwritten notation of the name and phone number of Ellen's lawyer.

On a third sheet of paper, Ellen had listed contact information for Fairhaven Life Center, as well as contact information for the Stewartville social workers and police officers who had spoken to her. That sheet included one additional name and number: Katrina Newberry, Realtor, specializing in central Michigan residential and commercial properties.

The final item was a sealed envelope bearing Hallie's name.

Mona pulled a folded sheet of legal paper from her pocket and smoothed it on the arm of the couch. The whole night lay before her. She figured she had plenty of time to pray as she waited for Adam and Hallie's return.

"Yes, Lord, what I'm feeling here is flat-out fear. I believe I'm about to become the mother of a teenager."

"Were you thinking, maybe, you were moving into a private suite at the Amway Grand?"

"Aunt Mona, sarcasm is a way of putting down other people to make yourself feel good. I believe you were the one who taught me that. And I didn't have time to be picky. Besides, I only brought the important stuff."

Mona surveyed eighteen lumpy garbage bags, in addition to suitcases and assorted piles of sports gear and gym bags, strewn across Harold's workroom floor at the back of the shop.

Hallie leaned on the doorframe leading to the front of the store, her arms folded across her chest. She was wearing the plaid pajama pants and hooded sweatshirt she'd been wearing when she'd collapsed onto Mona's couch a few hours past midnight. Her red hair stuck out as though a strong northwesterly had just blown through the room. Mona now knew how wise Adam had been to drop her off in the wee hours, then to come back to deliver her things after he'd caught a few hours' sleep at Harold's. He sat on a stool at the workbench behind the pile, trying not to smile.

Mona moaned. "Hallie, I have *one* closet in my apartment. Where do you think I'm going to put this stuff? How many pairs of jeans did you bring?"

"I really wasn't counting."

"I did all a man could do. I made her stop at eighteen."

Mona rolled her eyes.

"And now eye-rolling, Aunt Mona. Really, I'm quite disappointed in you."

"Girl, you are so treading on thin ice the whole room can hear it cracking under your feet. You have a letter from your mother on the counter in the shop. You may go read it while Adam and I discuss which dresser I can beg him to haul up to my apartment for you. Whatever you can fit into that one dresser is all that goes upstairs. The rest we'll have to figure out."

Hallie's hands flew to her hips. "No way!"

"My way or the highway. You can always go to school for two weeks in the outfit you're wearing."

The alley door opened, and a draft of cold air and snow bellowed through as Harold stepped into the room, wearing a red and black buffalo plaid coat and black wool cap with earflaps. He was moving slowly and leaning heavily on his cane, and Mona saw his eyes shut briefly as he paused for a moment before he closed the door. *The pain from the gout must be bad today. Last year when it flared, he could barely walk for weeks.*

"Harold would never do anything so horrible to me, would you, Harold?" Hallie smiled sweetly and tipped her head, her red hair cascading to her waist.

Harold surveyed the piles in the middle of his workroom as he pulled his cap from his head and hung it from a nail in the wall. He slowly unbuttoned his coat, revealing his bib overalls and a plaid flannel shirt buttoned clear to the top. He slid a finger inside his collar and gave a tug.

"Sounds like one of them trick teenager questions. Now what

do we have here? Looks to me like you have my work space tied up a bit. These Hallie's things you went down for last night, Adam?" He poked at a bag with his cane.

Adam slid off the stool. "You can see why I didn't have the strength to make it any farther than your couch. Besides, I didn't want to wake you. We made it back at three. Thanks for the hospitality, as usual."

Harold sized up the piles. "Got a little space issue, seems to me."

Hallie sighed, and her arms fell to her sides. "This isn't my fault. I didn't know what to bring. Plus, half of this is my mother's junk."

Harold tugged his collar again. "Hallie, would you bring me a glass of water?" She threw up her hands and marched off as he lowered himself onto a bench near the door.

"Mona, if you don't mind, I can take a lot of this stuff to my house. I've already been making space for Ellen and Hallie, and it only makes sense if she starts moving her things into her room now. Might make things a little awkward for a while with her clothes in two places, but I don't think you've got a lot of options. And it would give her an excuse to drop by and see an old man and start getting used to the house."

Mona looked at the chaos at her feet and Harold quietly tugging at his collar and the cane at his side. It seemed a simple enough answer.

Hallie reappeared, a glass in her hand, walked around the mounded piles, and handed the water to Harold.

"Harold's graciously offered us a solution, Hallie. He's suggested we take your extra clothes to his house and move them into your new room. You can keep the really important things you'll need for the next two weeks here. If you need your other stuff, it will just mean hanging out with him. In the meantime, Adam's going to take a dresser up to my apartment, and I've already cleared out closet space for you. There's also storage for your sports things in the chifferobe here in the back room. How does that sound?"

Hallie gave a lumpy bag a kick. "Do I get to pick the biggest dresser?"

"You can have the pick of the shop. Lucky for Adam, all but four sold at the Black Friday sale yesterday, and they're small ones."

Hallie rolled her eyes, and for once Mona chose not to say anything. She glanced through the doors and to the counter where Ellen's letter to her daughter lay on the counter in the same spot where Mona had placed it. Hallie hadn't touched it.

Something in Mona's heart told her it would lie there all day.

Chapter Thirteen

Hallie stared through the darkness at the orange florescent numbers: 6:22.

For fifty-seven minutes, the clock had taunted her.

The bar from the sleeper sofa dug into her back, and she flung herself to her side and threw the heavy blanket off her shoulders. Stupid quilt—a person had to be a sumo wrestler just to roll over in bed under one of those things. No wonder she'd woken up. Whoever had made this one must have been trying to kill somebody. The idiotic thing shoved the air right out of her lungs.

She glanced across the room. Aunt Mona lay facedown like a rag doll tossed on her four-poster bed. At least she was sleeping. For the past two days, she'd looked like she'd lost a game of chicken with a steamroller. Serious old-lady lines around her eyes hadn't been there a few months ago. And her walking had slowed way down, even though she tried to pretend everything was the same. At times, Hallie was sure she saw her aunt dragging her hand along a wall or holding onto furniture for balance. And then there was her speech—the words that frayed out along the edges when she was tired, or blurred into one another late into the evening, or that didn't come at all. But the hardest thing was to know what to do about the long silences, to know if Aunt Mona was still inside her head somewhere, or if she'd spaced out and floated away.

It was all too weird. There was no way for Hallie to tell if she should be scared or if things were just going to be different since the accident. Was she supposed to talk about the changes or just pretend they weren't really there? It wasn't as if Aunt Mona walked around talking about how she felt. Was she afraid of not being the same? Was a person supposed to walk up to someone they loved and tell them they were acting kind of strange? After all, life handed out a lot of scary things that adults never seemed to want to talk about. Maybe this was just another one.

A car door slammed in the alley below, and Oscar growled from beneath a lump of blankets near the small of Aunt Mona's back. The clock glowed an orange 6:24.

Hallie shifted her weight to her elbow and slid a hand beneath her pillow. Her fingers felt for the paper, and she pulled out a white envelope. She leaned back and traced the script of her name with one finger in the dim glow of the streetlight that filtered through the window above her head. The thinness of the envelope told her the contents held a single sheet of paper, maybe two. Nothing too long. An emotional pile of garbage with some guilt slathered on the side. The condemning voice rang in her head.

She'll never change. She's said it all before, made promises she won't keep, begged for forgiveness, and asked to start over. You're only setting yourself up to be hurt again.

A pain shot through Hallie's side as the bar dug into a rib. A second voice whispered, *And what made you worth God's forgiveness when He came running after you?*

Scenes flashed through her memory.

Stacy diving beneath the waters of Lake Michigan to find the necklace that had slipped through her fingers—the necklace she'd torn from Hallie's neck, the necklace Hallie had taken from

Stacy's dresser and worn swimming just to make her sister jealous. Then the agonizing minutes as she'd held her breath and waited for Stacy's head to reemerge from the water, and the memory of being carried away as a silent crowd waited for the emergency squad to arrive and search for her sister's limp and lifeless body.

Then a separate scene two years later, standing beside Aunt Mona on the breakwater at Pere Marquette Park as the waves swept her aunt onto the rocks and into the pummeling surf.

Hallie slammed a fist into the wadded blankets. "Please take them away," she whispered.

She reached for her neck, felt for the chain, and traced the shape of the heart that had hung there once—Stacy's necklace that had been found and given back to her. It had grown heavy in the days after she'd returned home with her mother after Aunt Mona's accident. When they'd come to Stewartville, she'd taken it off. No telling if someone might ask about something she didn't want to explain. Ever.

The room was silent except for the sound of Oscar's low growl from beneath the blankets. Hallie flipped the envelope over in her left hand and eyed the still-smooth seal.

Do you know how many times I've cleaned up her messes and listened to her lies?

Again, the whisper.

And what about your messes and your lies? She's broken, just like you.

A fresh scene washed over her. She and her mother wedged in a vinyl recliner beside Aunt Mona's bed as the sound of a ventilator filled the room. Her mother's arm resting across her shoulders, and Hallie's head cradled on her chest.

Hallie opened her eyes and slid the envelope back beneath her pillow. "Ask me anything, but don't ask me to forgive her again. I can't."

The whisper came again.

This isn't about how many times your mom's failed or you've failed. It's about how much I've forgiven both of you. Once you see that, it's all you'll ever need.

Ellen stared at the piece of paper in front of her and rolled the Bic pen between the palms of her hands.

The paper stared back, the blank page mocking her.

There's nothing you can say she'll ever hear.

She lowered the gooseneck lamp toward the desk in an attempt to block the light drifting to her roommate's side of the room.

The voices battled in her head.

Write—even if you don't know what to say.

What could she possibly say that would mean anything at all? That she was sorry she'd screwed up her daughter's life? That she lay awake every night haunted by the memory of the first drink she'd ever taken? That she was sorry she wasn't strong like her sister and couldn't crawl out of the hole she'd fallen into after Stacy had died? That she agonized over the pain of knowing Hallie's father only showed up as a caller ID number every couple of months?

She gripped the pen and began to write.

> *Dear Hallie,*
>> *I don't know if you'll ever read these letters, but I've decided to write to you every day.*

The words stopped.

Then what? Ask her to forgive you, like that will ever happen. Pretend she doesn't hate you? Say the same things you've already said a hundred times?

She stared at the cinderblock wall. Why even try?

Ellen glanced at her watch. Six twenty. In ten minutes, Gloria would be getting up to head to the kitchen for breakfast duty. Ten minutes to get something written, anything.

How do I tell her I've always wanted to be a mother, but I've never known how?

She scrawled a paragraph, like blood rushing from a wound, then folded the paper and tucked it into the Gideon Bible on the desk.

By the time Gloria woke up, the gooseneck lamp had been turned off, and Ellen was sitting in the dark, crying.

Harold Rawlings sat before an open Bible and a notebook at his kitchen table, a cup of black coffee in his right hand. The pot on the counter was still nearly full so Adam could sit and share a cup, then fill his travel mug on his way out the door to the early service with Mona and Hallie. Before he'd gotten out of bed, Harold had known it would be a second-service Sunday. He tried to excuse it in an old man, but it was hard. Second services had never set right with him. Somehow it seemed that the least he could do was meet God first thing on the Lord's Day. But lately, the headaches had been slowing him down. Some days, they'd brought him to a dead stop.

He pulled a three-by-five card from the pocket of his freshly pressed shirt and ran his eyes down the list:

Move files from front bedroom to attic room

Move Lynne's boxes to attic room

Call Doc Bailey
Call Katrina Newberry
Bake snickerdoodles for Hallie

He drummed his long fingers on the table, but the thought wouldn't come. Something important. Something he should have gotten on the list yesterday, if only his dad-blamed headache hadn't gotten in the way.

He slid the card back into his pocket. It would pop up later, and he didn't want to cut into his prayer time. He needed a long stretch for every one of them, and already it was almost five thirty. If God kept sending him these needy ones, the day might come when he wouldn't get any sleep at all.

He opened the spiral notebook and ran his fingers over the pages that had curled from the pressure of a hand bearing down to write. He flipped to the middle to a page bearing Ellen's name. Then he opened the pages of his Bible to Psalm 50:15 and lowered his head. The words drifted slowly into two hazy lines of text, and he blinked to clear his vision. A wave of nausea gripped his stomach, and he closed his eyes. He knew this verse by heart, anyway. He didn't need to read it. He willed away the growing knot in his stomach and focused his thoughts.

"This is my prayer for Mona's dear sister today, Lord. That she call upon You in her day of trouble, and that You will deliver her and she will glorify Your name for Your goodness to her."

The prayers continued and the nausea passed. Once again, he picked up the pen and began to write. By the time Adam appeared in the doorway, Harold had made his way through half his names. But as the taillights of the Suburban disappeared around the corner in the early morning darkness thirty minutes later, his head was bowed once again over fresh ink.

The clock on First Federal Bank read 6:17 AM as Adam made a left and pulled into the alley behind the antique shop. His goal had been to be on the road by six, and if Harold hadn't been sitting at the kitchen table with a notebook, his Bible, and a pot of coffee when he got up, he would have made it on schedule. But Harold had let him off easy. Not a single question about his early morning exodus. Just a few encouraging words and a cup of coffee to go.

"Always a pleasure to have your company when you come, Adam. Looks like we'll miss you at church today. We ran you ragged these last few days, and I thank you for all you've done for Mona and her family. I hope you find a little breathing space before work on Monday."

A little breathing space. Harold knew. He always seemed to know.

Adam pulled the Suburban beside an aging green F-150 pickup truck parked in a halo of streetlight and put the vehicle in park while he thought about the woman who'd taken over his life. He'd come to know a lot of things about Mona VanderMolen in the past three months.

She couldn't cook, and he didn't care.

She ate stray, fuzzy chocolate from the bottom of her purse, and he thought it was charming.

She was strangely frightened of Glenda Simpson's cat, Miss Emily, and didn't like being asked why.

And she never locked the doors to her truck, even when rational, caring men told her it was dangerous.

Adam slid out of the Suburban, walked to the driver's side of the truck, and tried the door. It swung open, and he smiled. He slid in and pulled an envelope from his pocket.

As he'd driven the long stretch of M-57 back to Stewartville with Hallie napping on the seat beside him, he'd come to his decision. In the early morning hours at Harold's kitchen table, it hadn't taken long to write his note explaining his reasons.

He needed to leave Stewartville. Since Ellen's hospitalization, his life and Mona's had pressed together in a tightening spiral. She needed the freedom to walk into church with Hallie at her side and to focus on Ellen. And she needed time to look across a room and not see him. The past two days had pressed deeply on his spirit, and a heaviness had settled over him. He knew what he needed most—to sit in silence and pray.

Adam reached beneath the front seat of the truck and pulled out a worn red leather Bible, the one Mona carried to church on Sundays. If anyone would understand where he was headed this morning and why, she would.

He tucked his note between the pages of her Bible and placed it on the seat of the truck. Then he walked back to the Suburban and headed west out of town and toward the beckoning silence.

Mona held the workroom door as Hallie squeezed through and headed across the alley to the truck, dragging three garbage bags stuffed with clothes.

"Try to cram any more in the front with us, we'll have to hang out the windows to drive to church."

Mona shook her head and watched as Hallie opened the door and wrestled the bags onto the front seat. Harold couldn't possibly imagine what he'd gotten himself into inviting two women to live in his home, each who had closets the size of Cleveland.

Mona pulled her leather jacket from a coat hook near the back door and felt in the pocket for her keys as she stepped into the alley, then pulled the shop door closed behind her and locked it. She hurried to the truck through the brisk morning air, opened the driver's door, and wedged her body into the sliver of space that remained in the cab. She could barely see Hallie's fluff of red curls above the pile of bags between them as she slid her right hand beneath the mound in search of the seat belt.

"Pray that Joe Spencer is having a cup of coffee at Trina's right now, Hal. Then see if you can find my Bible buried under this mess."

She turned the key in the ignition and headed up the alley. Two turns later, Mona made a final right turn down Cedar Street toward the church as she craned her neck around the pile of bags.

"This isn't good, Aunt Mona. That cop who dragged me into town is parked in front of the church. But maybe he has a family plan for traffic violations. And this is probably another good way for us to get put on the prayer chain."

"Not funny, Hallie."

By the time Joe Spencer followed the truck into the parking lot, greeted a dozen friends and acquaintances, and delivered a friendly warning about the dangers of obstructed fields of vision, Mona was not only mortified but was ten minutes late for the morning service. She and Hallie slipped into the back row as friends and neighbors turned in their pews and smiled patronizingly.

It wasn't until Pastor Cunningham announced the annual all-church Christmas concert that Mona realized she'd forgotten to bring in her Bible. But the thought didn't stay with her long. It was replaced by a jarring awareness that more than her Bible was missing. Adam, who'd promised to meet her at church in their usual spot in the seventh row on the left side, was nowhere to be seen.

Joe Spencer pulled the last two garbage bags from the front seat of the truck and sat them among the heap at his feet. A collection of CDs, DVDs, and books had spilled across the green vinyl bench seat. He leaned in and gathered them in his arms, then turned and shoved them deep into a bag and tied it tightly with its yellow plastic drawstring. He pulled his notebook and pen from his chest pocket and scribbled a note:

> *Your tax dollars at work. You'll find your bags*
> *delivered to Mr. Rawlings' house and placed on his*
> *back porch. Drive safely. Joe Spencer*

He tucked the note under the windshield wiper of the truck and hefted two of the bags to his shoulder as he headed toward his cruiser.

The westerly wind cut through Adam's jacket as he made his way up the familiar wooden stairs, and he drew his head close to his chest. A dusting of sand lay in swirls and hardened curls of crust across the surface of the snow. The pounding of the Lake Michigan surf meeting the barren shore swelled over the row of condos that lined the half-mile stretch of Gilead Bible Conference shoreline. By the time he reached the top of the dune and the Prayer

Tower, the condo rooflines would drop away, and the view would give way to the lake beyond.

He hadn't been back since summer, when he had come alone to pray and had found Mona weeping—the day she'd hijacked his prayers and, weeks later, his life. Too often after that day, his thoughts had traveled to her, her tears, her angry niece, and so he had prayed. He'd told himself it was what he was meant to do with thoughts of a woman who had captured too much of his attention.

When word came of the accident, of Mona's struggle for life, he faced his own struggle—how to keep his distance from a dying woman he barely knew, how to explain to himself why he so desperately wanted to be at her side.

The wooden stairs gave way to a straight expanse of boardwalk as Adam made his way toward the Prayer Tower. He knew the door would be unlocked. Families living in the condos on the Gilead grounds often used the tower, even in winter.

He paused, his hand on the door, and remembered his first sight of her there. Mona, barefooted and crying for her niece in the shadow of the trees outside the tower.

Adam turned the knob and walked inside, the view of the lake and the crashing waves drawing him to the front of the room. He stopped as his eyes swept the horizon and traced the line where the sky met the waves, and he jammed his hands into his pockets for warmth. He looked to the south, where her beach house lay obscured just beyond the curve of a dune. She'd spoken of it so often he felt as if he could see it.

He'd come to pray and to be alone, but she was there. Her presence had followed him. Or perhaps he had followed her even here.

He turned to a side bench and dropped to his knees in front of it as the tower swayed gently in the winter gale.

"Father God, I'm here to talk to You about the woman I love."

Chapter Fourteen

Mona glanced at the grandfather clock near the front of the store. Two forty-five. Only fifteen minutes before Ginny Mae was due to stop by to look at one of Adam's escritoire desks. For the fifth time that hour, she slipped her cell phone from the pocket of her jeans and flipped it open, then snapped it shut again.

"For heaven's sake, swallow your pride and call the man," Elsie's voice bellowed from inside Mona's office. "You've been drivin' me nuts for the past three days with that phone of yours, openin' it and slappin' it shut, openin' it and slappin' it shut. You're givin' me the jitters."

Mona slid the phone back into her pocket and ran her fingers through her hair, then reached below the counter, pulled out a three-ring binder, flipped it open, and leafed through the pages.

"I don't know what you're talking about."

"'Course you do, child. The man hurt your feelings by not showin' up to church Sunday. He's got a pretty heavy job description—comin' through for you, livin' up to your expectations, and keepin' you happy."

In Mona's peripheral vision, a figure with a fluff of lavender hair moved into the office doorway. She turned the pages faster.

"You got a customer with deep pockets comin' in here in ten minutes lookin' to buy one of Adam's desks, and you don't have one in the shop to show her or an answer for when one will be available. So why haven't you called him to ask him about your inventory, missy?"

"I'm looking through his order book right now." Mona leaned on the narrow ledge of counter and scrutinized a page.

The fluff of hair disappeared back into the office as the front bells jangled. Mona glanced up. Ginny Mae Francis came through the doorway and headed straight toward the back counter. She was wearing a maroon suede jacket with a dyed-to-match rabbit fur collar, and her chin-length, straight-cropped, gray hair bounced as she walked.

Elsie's voice rose. "Don't waste my time with nonsense, woman. I don't see no arthur-i-tus keepin' your fingers from dialin'. Plain and simple pride's holdin' you back. Maybe some other woman's snatched him up. You got some learnin' to do when it comes to men."

Mona snapped the book shut and stared across the counter into the widening steel-gray eyes of Ginny Mae Francis.

"Why, hello, Mona. It seems I've interrupted a fascinating conversation about men." She smiled sweetly.

Mona considered choking Elsie. If there was anything Ginny Mae liked more than showing off her money, it was passing on gossip.

"Ethan and I couldn't help but notice that your friend Adam wasn't with you in church yesterday. I hope he's not ill."

Mona forced a smile. "Not at all. He had another commitment."

Elsie's voice called from the office. "Adam has many, many responsibilities."

Ginny Mae turned and surveyed the shop. "Yes, I can imagine. I heard he was helping your family this weekend. I understand your sister and niece were here for the holiday. How are they?"

Mona recognized the glint of the predator in the gray eyes. "I'm blessed to have Hallie here to help me with the holiday rush. She'll be coming through the door any minute, as a matter of fact. Her mother is taking a few weeks away, so the timing is perfect."

Mona stood stone still as the gray eyes raked her face. "Blessed, I'm sure. Isn't it a bit unconventional for a mother to take her child out of her own school in the middle of the year? And where is Ellen enjoying her time away?"

A hot rage surged through Mona.

You don't even know how transparent you are, you ravenous wolf.

"Ginny Mae, I'm sorry to inform you that we sold the last of Adam's escritoire desks last week, but he's scheduled to be in on Saturday with some new pieces."

Ginny Mae's eyes bored into Mona's, and her eyebrows lifted. "I see. New pieces. What type and design? I imagine you can answer *those* questions."

A fluff of lavender reappeared in Mona's peripheral vision, and she turned to face Elsie. She was wearing a pair of red polyester slacks and a white cardigan sweatshirt with Christmas bulbs quilted from ribbon scattered over the front. If it hadn't been for a quick narrowing of her eyes, everything about Elsie's holiday appearance would have appeared welcoming, but Mona knew better.

"Why, hello, Ginny Mae. I'm pretty sure Adam was hoping to show you some of his one-of-a-kind pieces personally before anyone else got a look at them. His things are flyin' out the door these days. We can't get them for just everyone, and he has a couple of special items that are just callin' your name."

Mona didn't know whether to gag or burst into laughter as she watched Ginny Mae's chest swell.

"Special items? Such as?"

Elsie surveyed her red fingernails carefully. "Adam's very protective about his exclusive clients and doesn't share all his information with Mona and me. But I'll have him give you a call just as soon as he's available to set up a private appointment. May take a day or two. He's in high demand these days."

Ginny Mae narrowed her eyes and looked at Mona. "A busy man who's building his own client base and keeping valuable information from the shop owner who provides the outlet for his merchandise. Sounds to me like the news is true."

"What news?" Mona shot back, furious at herself for even taking the bait.

Ginny Mae rolled her eyes. "Oh, please. As if you don't know."

Mona stepped around the side of the counter, crossed her arms, and stared into the gray eyes. Ginny Mae blinked and took a step backward.

"I . . . I'm sure you've heard. Everyone at Trina's was talking about it this morning. It's nothing, really. Adam's just been here so much on weekends, and with the storefront next door for sale and your sister and niece showing up and Hallie enrolling in school, people thought . . . it was natural for them to assume . . ."

"To assume what, Ginny, Mae? That it was okay to stick their noses into my life? To speculate and gossip? To start a few rumors?" With each question Mona's voice rose, and she watched Ginny Mae's lips set into a hard, firm line.

"Mona, your niece suddenly appeared out of nowhere, moved in with you, and she's telling everyone at the high school that she and her mother, who could buy the entire town of Stewartville, are moving in with Harold Rawlings. Her mother was admitted to the hospital in an alcohol-induced coma, and now she's disappeared.

"You've been dating a man for the past three months who sells his furniture out of your store. The empty storefront next door is for sale, and someone seems to have expressed an interest in buying it, although nobody in town seems to be able to find out who that person is.

"And you're going to stand there and tell me it's not natural for people to be curious, to try to fill in the blanks and figure this out? You must be plumb out of your mind. People in this town don't have so much as a daily paper or a stoplight. We grab our excitement where we can get it, and you and your family seem to be doling it out in spades right now.

"Not to mention that people really like you, Mona. People who are happily married like Ethan and me would be tickled to see you finally get married. Adam Dean is a fine-looking Christian man who looks like he could give you a good life. The whole town would show up for your wedding. You'd probably be unwrapping gifts until you're fifty. So you might want to think about the fact that a lot of people are looking on right now because they're hoping and praying for something good for you from all of this."

Ginny Mae was one of the few people Mona knew who could spit out compliments and insults in the same breath. She hardly knew what to think, except that she didn't want all of Stewartville peering through the windows of her life for an inside view. She counted to ten before she allowed herself to speak.

"And I."

"Pardon me?"

"Ethan and I. You should have chosen a nominative case pronoun when you were speaking."

Ginny Mae looked bewildered. "Am I supposed to understand what on earth you are talking about?"

"Probably not. But it seems obvious to me that even though you and I both speak English, Ginny Mae, we don't actually communicate much of the time, but let me try to clear that up.

"It's apparent that you have a deep interest in me and my family, and I'd like to assure you that in the future if I ever have a need to share personal information, I will negotiate a deal with the Dairy Delight for use of their street sign. I think this is the only way to be fair to the community and disseminate personal information to everyone in an accurate and equal fashion. Perhaps we should all consider renting signs in the future rather than relying on gossip, which can be somewhat unreliable. Now if you'll excuse me, I have some bookwork to complete."

With those words, Mona turned her back, walked into the office, and closed the door behind her.

Mona dropped into the scarred leather chair behind a desk piled with manila folders, catalogs, mail, and a copy of *Kovel's Antiques and Collectibles Price List*. Her heart pounded in her chest as Elsie's voice drifted through the door, bidding Ginny Mae good-bye in her most polite tone.

Has my life become a community soap opera? And what are people saying to Hallie? She's been in school three days, and she hardly speaks a word when she comes home. Maybe this is why.

The front door slammed, and staccato steps approached the office door. It opened, and Elsie stepped through and closed it firmly behind her.

"The woman's a fool, but lucky for us, a rich one with pride enough for the whole town. If she hadn't had a hair appointment at the Curl Up and Dye, I could have talked her into a houseful of furniture to feed that ego of hers." She folded her arms. "Now for you, missy. You're probably sittin' here stewin', and that would be a sorry waste of your time. People talk—and it's not your job to change them, so you're stuck with the job of lovin' 'em anyway."

Elsie folded her arms, and one toe began to tap. Mona sighed inwardly. The toe tap was always a bad sign.

"The bigger question is whether or not you're makin' room for Adam in your life for good or you're willin' to let him walk away. Whether it's today or tomorrow, you've got to decide which you want—unless, of course, he's already doin' it for both of you."

Mona felt the vibrations of the hardwood floor beneath her feet as the workroom door slammed at the rear of the shop.

"I can't talk about this now, Elsie. Hallie's home from school."

"Don't matter if you want to talk about it. The questions are already borin' into your brain like little worms. Is Ginny Mae right? Is Adam tryin' to buy the property next door, and why would he do that? And why hasn't he called you for three days after disappearin' into nowhere? Has he had enough of your crazy family? Is somethin' takin' up his time back in Aplington, or maybe somebody? Kind of like tiny little worms in your brain. Watch out or they'll make you crazy." Elsie winked as she stepped aside, opened the office door, and called toward the front of the store.

"Miss Hallie Bowen, come show your shinin' face to us and tell us about your day. And I believe your aunt has somethin' for you."

Mona shook her head. The woman was going to drive her nuts. Little worms in her brain? As if she didn't have brain problems enough. She picked up a letter addressed in Ellen's graceful script from the top of the mail pile—the second envelope in two days—as Hallie appeared in the doorway. Her backpack was flung over one shoulder, and she was wearing a hooded sweatshirt and jeans. She scowled as she shifted her bag to the floor.

"This school stinks. Some teacher who must have forgotten we live in the twenty-first century has assigned A Tale of Two Cities, so I'll be upstairs reading. You'd think she could show a DVD. And if the surprise is another letter from my mother, you can keep it. Her sudden interest in communicating with me is too little too late, not that anyone seems to be interested in my opinion these days."

She turned and stomped toward the stairs.

"You know, geeky English teachers can be totally cool people," Mona called after her.

"Not when they assign twenty-eight pages of reading a night, hate city girls, and don't grade on a curve." Feet pounded up the stairs, and the door to the apartment slammed.

Elsie raised her eyebrows. "Needs prayer, that one. And a slice of french silk pie from Trina's. Want me to bring you anything?"

Mona sighed. "Serenity. I don't suppose Trina's got the secret recipe for that." She dropped the letter back to the pile.

Elsie put one hand on her hips and the other on the doorknob. "Serenity's just mumbo-jumbo in a world livin' inside out and up-side down. But peace? We can all have that, and it ain't no secret Who's got the recipe and where He wrote it down."

Two minutes later, Hallie thundered down the stairs and headed out the front door with Elsie, lured by promises of pie. Mona sat alone in the office, staring at the familiar disarray of her desk. A draft eddied around her shoulders, and she reached to the floor behind her desk and pulled the familiar Stewart-ville centennial afghan around her shoulders—the afghan she'd thrown over her nightgown the first day she'd met Adam and he'd walked into her office with an early morning delivery. She settled the blanket around her neck as Elsie's questions bored into her brain.

Why hasn't he called you for three days, and why did he leave in the first place? Did Ellen say something to him, or Hallie? Or is someone taking up his time back in Aplington?

Make room for him or lose him. Decide which one you want. Unless, of course, he's already deciding for both of you.

Mona pulled her cell phone from the pocket of her jeans and set it on the desk in front of her as the questions replayed through her thoughts.

When Hallie and Elsie came through the door of the shop an hour later, the questions still lingered, but Mona's hands lay quietly folded on an open Bible as she prayed over the jumbled knots of life.

But the flow of her thoughts was interrupted by the sound of her cell phone and the voice of a receptionist at the imaging center in Grand Rapids. A cancellation had opened up an appointment. Could she possibly come in for her MRI that afternoon?

When she hung up, Mona sat frozen, her finger poised over Adam's speed dial number for three full minutes before she closed her phone, slipped it into her pocket, and headed toward the door.

Mona squeezed her eyes shut as her mind painted a picture of herself tucked snugly beneath the red, yellow, and blue Dresden Plate quilt of her walnut four-poster bed, Oscar sleeping soundly beside her. For the twentieth time, as quickly as the image came, it disappeared.

The hammering echoed in her ears as she lay encased in the

tube. First the Gatling gun, then the jackhammer. The familiar rhythms came in staccatos and bursts that ricocheted through her body. She clutched the panic ball in her hand and tried to forget she was wedged into a cold cylinder with no means of escape.

A flutter of cool air drifted around her shoulders, and she felt a sudden surge of frustration. She'd forgotten to ask for a warm blanket to be cocooned around her arms and legs. Her left hand fingered the thin cotton of the hospital gown. Stripping off her favorite jeans and slipping into the loose-fitting gray fabric again had felt like surrendering herself to the arms of death for a return visit.

Her mind had become a battlefield. Her mental list of pleasant memories and serene retreats had been devoured by the narrow mouth of the tube. One moment, she was lying in the sun at the beach house, the waves lapping at her feet—then in an instant, the water was surging as her body was dragged beneath the surface and her head was slammed against the rocks along the breakwater. Hallie was watching in horror as Dan Evans struggled to free Mona's limp form from the pounding surf as her blood swirled through the water.

No matter where she willed her mind to take her, the tube dragged Mona back beneath the waves. Over and over again, she willed her thoughts back to the serenity of the shore, binding each image in threads of truth.

"You will keep in perfect peace him whose mind is steadfast, because he trusts in you."

"Be strong and courageous. Do not be terrified; do not be discouraged, for the Lord your God will be with you wherever you go."

The sounds of the beach washed over her. She sat beside Hallie in the silence of a sunset, where God's voice had whispered in the beauty. She'd always heard Him there, and the voice had spoken of comfort and power and presence. But in the tube, God pressed in, and she could feel His hands on the raw spots in her soul, probing the pain.

"My flesh and my heart may fail, but God is the strength of my heart and my portion forever."

She lay isolated and alone, her arms folded across her chest as if in death, face upward, as the machine echoed about her. With each clatter a confession broke free.

Pride.

Self-sufficiency.

Fear.

The panic ball slipped from her hand to her side as her fingers released their grip.

Father, forgive me for forgetting who You are and how much You love me. Help me look into Your eyes and find confidence in Your perfect love and know that it's more than I'll ever need, that You're more than I'll ever need.

She envisioned the brick that lay on the front floor of her car. Her memorial.

You're my strength and portion, Lord. You alone.

"Just three more minutes, Miss VanderMolen. You're doing great."

Again, the sounds of the water washed over her. She was back on the beach, the sun warm against her skin, the waves lapping at her feet. The water no longer surged, and her eyes were shut, this time in prayer as the quiet crescendos of the surf swept through her thoughts, stroking her soul with a Father's quiet caress.

Chapter Fifteen

Mona sat cross-legged on the bed, sorting through a mound of underwear as she listened to groans emanating from the floor at the end of the bed. She grabbed a wadded pair of athletic socks and lobbed them in the direction of Hallie, who lay facedown atop a pile of garbage bags.

"Get moving, child. We've been here twenty minutes, and you haven't finished one bag. Harold can hear your sorry whining all the way in the kitchen, and I don't care if he's baking cinnamon rolls: you're not getting a bite until this job is done. So start separating the things we need to wash, and put away the rest of it. And by the way, do you happen to own two matching socks, or should I just give up now?"

Hallie moaned and covered her head with her arms. "Leave me alone! It's Saturday, and teenagers all over the world are sleeping in. The only reason you dragged me over here is because Adam's coming today, and you're avoiding him. Middle-aged women are so transparent. Didn't anybody ever teach you to play the guy game better than this?"

The words stopped Mona short, and a pair of gray sports socks dropped to the bed. Of all the smart-mouthed statements! The past few days with a teenager had tempted her more than once to begin pulling out her already sparse hair.

"I am going to say this just once, Hallie. I don't play guy games, do you understand? I'm too busy trying to remember which foot is my left one or what my phone number is. My brain is hardly up to anything as complicated as games.

"The facts are really very simple. The man called me every day for three months straight, and I got used to it. I even liked it. He seems to have stopped. He didn't bother telling me why, and it hurts. It's also making me a little crazy. I'm sure I'm not supposed to be telling this to a fifteen-year-old, but like I said, I'm no good at games. I have no clue if he's showing up today or not, and it's unsettling. I'm occupying my time with useful tasks. So here we are, unpacking your mess so Harold can walk through this bedroom without tying a rope around his waist so someone can pull him to safety if he gets lost in the rubble."

Mona caught her reflection in the oak dresser mirror across the room as she slid to the side of the bed and stood. The dark circles under her eyes showed the exhaustion she felt. She zipped her russet sweater higher over her brown turtleneck and tried to ignore the chill that had settled into her bones.

Hallie groaned as she rolled to her back and flung her hair from her face. "Guilt—it's an adult conspiracy to make kids work. Old people have been using it for generations." She sat up and gathered the Handle-Tie from the trash bag in front of her.

Mona took a playful swat at Hallie's head and knelt beside her. It had been hard to say the words out loud, to admit that Adam had stopped calling, even if she was admitting the obvious. What she hadn't said was how much she'd missed his calls. She'd barely been able to admit it to herself. The *why* of her silent phone had kept her awake for three nights. She knew with certainty that Adam wasn't a game player, either, that if he'd stopped talking, he had a good reason. And chances were if he showed up today, it would be with an explanation.

Together, she and Hallie dug into the bag and began disgorging piles of jeans, T-shirts, and sweaters interspersed with CDs, videos, and books. Hallie sorted and folded until neat piles lay stacked in front of them like a department store display. Mona smoothed the wrinkles from a red Tommy Hilfiger sweater as Hallie tore open the second bag and dumped it to its side.

With a quiet thump, a red leather book slid onto the blue braided rug between them. Mona reached for it, flipped it over, and ran her hands over the cover. Recognition flashed through her mind, then the questions. Then a dawning realization as she felt the blood rush to her face.

"This doesn't make any sense. It's my Bible. I've been looking for it since Sunday. I'd decided it must have fallen out of the truck with all the bags we dragged in and out. I always leave it on the front seat. So how on earth did it get inside a bag with your stuff . . . unless . . . unless Joe Spencer thought it was one of your books and put it in a bag when he moved your stuff over here?"

Mona's thumb smoothed her name embossed in gold on the cover. Just beneath it, a white envelope was slid between the pages. She pulled it out and scanned the familiar block letters. She shook her head as she felt a knot form in her stomach.

"What is it?" Hallie's eyes were on her as Mona quickly tucked the envelope back between the pages.

"Nothing."

"Then let me see it."

Mona felt her face flush. "No! I'll read it later. It's from Adam. I imagine he must have put it there late Saturday night or Sunday morning. I guess he wanted me to find it when I was going to church. He knows I always use this Bible on Sundays."

Hope pulled at her, but she didn't want to open the note with Hallie peering over her shoulder. Whatever it said, he'd cared enough to tell her. He hadn't just walked away and left her without an explanation. There still had been six days of silence, but he'd left her with a reason.

Hallie snatched the envelope from the pages of the book. "So we're going to read it, right?"

Mona grabbed the envelope back. "*We* are not going to read it. *I'm* going to read it." Her mind was racing. "It's important for me to know if he's going to show up today or not. I have customers who are expecting stock."

"Stock, right. Give me a break. Do you think I'm a ten-year-old?"

Mona gripped the envelope.

Dear God, I wrote off his integrity because of my wounded pride and fears. I judged him without knowing the facts and let my mind fill in the blanks with every accusing scenario that drifted through my thoughts. Please, I need wisdom to know what to do whether he comes today or not and to know what to say if he does.

Her finger hovered over the flap. Something deep inside her told her to leave the room, to read the note in private, yet she knew she had to stay. Hallie had been shut out too many times.

"Okay, here's the deal. I'll open it and read it here if you promise there'll be no peeking. I'll summarize it for you, like a book report. Adam trusts you. He knows you would have been with me in the truck and I would have read it with you rubbernecking over my shoulder, so here goes."

Hallie nodded and giggled. "You know, I invented or bought

most of my book reports until this past summer, so no making it up as you go along."

Mona swatted at her head again, then tore through the envelope and unfolded the single sheet of lined paper. She leaned back, holding the paper close to her chest, and read silently.

> *Dear Mona,*
>
> *Please forgive me for leaving without letting you know first. I only decided this morning that it would be best if I left early. I believe you need time in these next important days to focus on Hallie and her adjustment, on Ellen, and on what your own heart needs during all of these changes.*
>
> *I realize I need this time for a break, too. I'll be there Saturday, as usual, with new inventory. But I'll leave it up to you to call me during the week if you need me for anything.*
>
> *You and your family will be in my prayers every day.*
> *Adam*

Mona folded the paper slowly. He'd made himself perfectly clear. He was backing away, and he didn't plan to call anymore. She swallowed.

And he was coming today.

It had to happen eventually, with all the mess and complications of life. What was I expecting? Did I think he'd be content driving over on weekends forever?

"Well?"

Mona opened her Bible, shoved the note inside, and placed it on the floor in front of her.

"Nothing, really. He thought you and I needed time to settle in, so he drove home early. He'll be here today as usual. Poor guy, we half killed him, what with taking your mom to Grand Rapids and driving you to Bloomfield Hills and back. Besides, I'm sure he'd had enough of women for one weekend. Between your mother, me, you, and Cara, we must have driven him half out of his mind." Mona grabbed a pair of jeans from a nearby pile and began folding furiously.

Hallie's eyes narrowed. "Really? Because the Adam I know doesn't treat us like we're a hassle. That description would belong to my father, and Adam Dean is about as different from my father as anyone I've ever met. And that's the highest compliment I could give any guy."

The sound of voices drifted into the bedroom from the kitchen, then faded away with the sound of approaching footsteps. Before she recognized a single word, Mona knew it was him, and she felt her throat beginning to close. Seconds later, Adam stood in the doorway as she busied herself refolding the pair of jeans for the third time. She told herself it shouldn't be hard to look up into his eyes just to say a simple hello, but she was wrong.

Trina's was jammed. The Saturday morning crowd packed out the small dining room until well past two on weekends. If Trina could bake it or fry it or make it from a cow or a pig, it was on the steam table, and most of Stewartville was there to get their $6.95 worth of it.

Adam and Mona sat in the corner booth farthest away from the buffet table. Railroad crossing signs hung from the rough-sawn

cedar walls, and the tables were decorated in red and white gingham tablecloths with red lanterns. A model train mounted on a
track near the ceiling chugged its way around the room. During
the week, Trina saved electricity and the train sat silently, but on
Saturdays, it ran nonstop from 6 AM until 9 PM to help draw in the
weekend crowds. In a town that only claimed bragging rights to a
red flashing traffic signal, the train was Stewartville's own scaled-
down, locomotive version of the Indy 500 and maybe better, since
it came with Trina's sausage gravy and biscuits.

Mona stared at the table and carefully folded one corner of
a paper placemat bearing the names and addresses of Stewartville businesses as she ran her finger across the crease with her
thumbnail. Her Bible lay on the wooden bench seat beside her.
The noise of the crowd made it hard for her to think, and she
tried to focus through the jumble of conversations. She felt the
strain in her shoulders and neck, and she focused on relaxing
her face. She wondered if Adam noticed the tension she felt, or
if he even cared.

Did he know how hard this was for her after a week of silence?
Did he suspect she'd expended every ounce of her emotional energy trying not to notice the silence of her phone?

And what about the MRI Wednesday afternoon? Should she
even bother to tell him she'd gone ahead and had it—that she'd
forced herself to lie stiff and straight like an entombed corpse
while the outside world had dissipated behind the pulsating throbs
of the machine? That she'd forced her breathing to the shallowest
of cool sips so that she could feel each one, steady and slow? That
God had taken her hand, and one breath at a time, she'd faced the
broken places in her that had festered into fear?

Adam broke the silence.

"How's Hallie doing?"

"She's settling in, complaining about homework, but she wouldn't be Hallie if she wasn't complaining about something." She forced her eyes away from the lantern in the center of the table and to him. He'd slipped off his jacket and laid it on the seat beside him, revealing a chambray shirt under a navy sweater. He leaned easily into the table, his hands folded across an envelope that lay upside down on his placemat. His expression was open, and his brown eyes searched her face.

"Are you okay? You're looking tired. Are you sure you haven't overdone it this week?"

Mona forced a smile. "Tired, I guess. Holiday season. Hallie. Ellen. And Harold's asked for some afternoons off, so we've been a bit shorthanded at the shop this week. Just a little worn down."

"And what's your plan for dealing with that?"

"I don't know. I don't really have much of a plan. But I took a little time to myself and took a relaxing break in an MRI tube for half an hour or so. I went whole hog and treated myself to the deluxe package. I was even offered a lovely headset with my choice of music, but I declined. I prefer my claustrophobia without musical accompaniment."

"You're not kidding me? You went?"

"I went."

"And when do you get the results?"

Mona averted her eyes for an instant. She wasn't sure. But somehow she felt that saying it would sound as though she didn't want to tell him the truth.

"I'm not sure. I really don't remember anything the tech said to me when it was over." She looked at her placemat and began a new line of creases. "Anyway, it's done. I just wanted you to know I'm a person of my word, and I'm sure they'll let me know the results as soon as they have them."

She was suddenly aware that she wanted him to ask what it had been like during the test, if she'd been okay, how she felt about it now that it was over. But it was a stupid thing to want, after all, from a man who had suddenly decided it would be best to stop calling, to stop checking on her, to stop asking about the details of her life. She cleared her throat and took a long drink of water. She wished the waitress had brought a straw to swirl through her glass and give her something to look at.

Adam fingered the envelope that lay on the table between them. "You've got a lot on your plate, Mona. Are you taking care of yourself?"

"Of course."

"From the looks of you, I'd say you're being less than truthful. But then, from the looks of you, I'd say you'd like me to change the subject. So have you heard from Ellen?"

Mona took another drink. The only thing she knew was that, sitting here with Adam, she didn't know what she thought she'd known. "Not exactly. Hallie's gotten a letter from her every day since Tuesday. She won't open them—just shoves them into her book bag. I thought I'd call her today and see how she's doing."

Adam shoved the envelope across the table. "She asked me to give you this after her first week. You might want to read it before you call. I'm just the delivery guy. I don't have a clue what it says." He folded his hands. "I don't know your sister real well, but I want you to know she said some encouraging things when I took her down, some things that might surprise you. I think that more than anything, she went to Fairhaven looking for hope."

Of all the things Mona had expected Adam to say, she hadn't

expected this. The word shocked her. *Hope*. Ellen and hope. It was everything she'd been praying for.

She knew even one tear would doom her to the rumor mill. Mona VanderMolen crying in Trina's with Adam Dean just inches away and all of Stewartville looking on over plates piled high with biscuits and sausage gravy. She took the envelope and slid it quickly into her purse. She fought to keep her voice even.

"My sister looking for hope. I'd say that's an astounding change for a woman who's been furious at God and the world in general for the past few years."

A teenage girl in jeans and a Trina's T-shirt slapped two plastic-covered menus on the table and headed off again. Mona shifted her weight. She needed to order. Even the smallest silence could lead to questions and places she didn't feel ready to go.

"That must have been some drive. I'm afraid to imagine what she could accomplish in one short hour."

Adam smiled. "I was like a lamb being led to the slaughter in the Greenville Meijer store. We had fifteen minutes, and she'd made a list. I was in charge of the Water Pik, shampoo, creme rinse, and more lotions and gels than I knew existed, while she shopped for clothes and a gym bag. We looked like a couple on one of those television game shows. I've never spent money so fast in my life."

Mona could see them—laughing and flying through the Meijer store, heaving toiletries and clothes into a cart while people looked on. She decided to change the subject.

"How are things at home?" The moment she asked it, she regretted the question. It came too close to asking how he was getting along without her. She felt as if she'd entered a minefield.

"Interesting. Chaotic. My cousin Steph's gotten engaged. Tony's a great guy. He treats her like a queen, and he has a good job—he's a teacher in North Muskegon. But Sadie's having a fit. She's got a boyfriend in Aplington and doesn't want to move with her mom. She doesn't want a stepdad. There's lots of drama and acting-out going on. Aunt Florence and Uncle Elmer are talking about selling the shop and retiring to Arizona to be near Aunt Florence's sister. There's going to be a lot of change in the next few months."

"Change. Not an easy word, but where we all are, I guess."

Mona pushed aside her menu and creased a new line into her placemat. She had to just say it, no matter how awkward it might feel. The only way out of this mess would be straight through it. She slid her Bible onto the table and looked straight into Adam's brown eyes.

"This hasn't been my best week, Adam. I don't know how to do this any other way than to just explain it the way it happened. I went to church Sunday expecting you to meet me there like we'd planned, and I was pretty disappointed when you didn't show up. Then I didn't hear from you all week and wondered why the man who'd called me every day for months had suddenly just walked away one morning without an explanation. I wasn't even sure if you were going to come today, or if I'd ever have another delivery of stock again. I thought you'd just walked out on me with no explanation."

Adam's eyes widened. "Wow. I'd assume, then, that you never got my note, because I sure left you one, right where I was certain you'd find it. So if you didn't find it and you never called, I guess you made a lot of assumptions about me based on silence. And you never called to ask why? You never thought that behavior like that was out of character for me—cruel, even? You just assumed I was a jerk?" Mona saw a flicker of hurt in his eyes.

Straight through it. Be honest and say it.

She took a deep breath. "I'm sorry. It just seemed so . . . so logical at the time. I thought you'd had enough of me and my family and had headed for the hills. I told myself you were too good to be true anyway and I'd finally managed to push the self-protective and selfish side of you out of hiding. It made it less painful for me to be mad at a villain than to think I'd been dumped by the good guy I thought I knew."

His eyes held hers steady, and she tried to read his response. She knew her honesty meant exposing the child that cowered inside her, the part of her that was afraid to trust him to be a good man.

His head drew back slowly. "In the three months I've known you, have I ever betrayed your trust? And if I had, even in some small way, would it be possible for you to ever forgive me, Mona? Men can be good without being perfect. Men and women can have misunderstandings and still move forward. But I'm afraid you're looking for reasons to turn me into your father. I think you're waiting for disappointments so you'll have reasons to walk away."

Mona opened her mouth and then closed it again. Adam's words had fallen like a slap.

"You never called to ask why? You let me stand you up, to seemingly disrespect your feelings, and your feelings weren't worth a single call? Finding out if I was okay wasn't worth a single call? Three months of trust wasn't worth a single call? Was it pride or fear that kept you from dialing the phone and asking a simple question?"

He leaned across the table and reached for her hand, and she pulled it back. A pulsating throb pounded behind her eyes as she fought back angry tears.

"And what about you? You could have called. It was your choice to leave in the first place."

"I explained my reasons in the note. I only left because I felt it was important, for you and for me—to think and pray, to be alone, to figure out what we're doing and why."

To be alone—to figure out what we're doing and why.

He'd said it, this time to her face. He was leaving. And now she'd given him reason to make it for good. He knew she didn't trust him.

"You know, Mona, I'm not some jerk who walked out on you without a word. I'm not your father. I'm just an average guy, a pretty nice guy, who's going to disappoint you, make mistakes, act selfish, screw up. I'm looking for a woman strong enough to deal with that, to stand up for herself, who's willing to pursue the best things in me and for me, the way I pursue the best things in and for her, and to be the strong, beautiful woman God created her to be. I'm looking for a woman who knows that leaning on me isn't weakness and is willing to forgive my imperfections and her own. I'm looking for a fighter who's as willing to fight for me as I am for her."

Adam slid his arms into his jacket. "I'm sorry about the misunderstanding. I must have looked like a total idiot, and it must have stirred a lot of thoughts in you. I've got a lot on my plate right now, too. A lot of decisions are pressing on me. With all you have going on, I don't want to weigh you down any further, so maybe easing up on the calls and visits is a good idea after all."

Mona pulled the Bible from the table and placed it in her lap. She didn't want him to see her eyes. She reached into her purse and fumbled for her wallet.

"I have an appointment with Ginny Mae Francis in five minutes and deliveries in Greenville this afternoon. I'm sorry to run, but Uncle Elmer and Aunt Florence needed me back at the shop this afternoon to talk over some real estate matters.

"Get yourself a good breakfast. You really need to take better care of yourself. I'll be back next Saturday with more stock. I'll be praying about the results of that MRI. I've already paid for both of us." He slid out of the booth and to his feet, and Mona watched as he turned and walked out the front door.

Her eyes followed him as he crossed Main Street and entered the shop. Then she stood and exited the rear of Trina's Café and slipped into the alley. She let the door fall closed behind her and turned and collapsed on a bench near the back door. A movement to her right startled her, and she turned. Miss Emily sat to the right of the door atop a half-open Dumpster, perusing its contents.

It was a moment that reminded Mona that no matter how much she loved Stewartville, some days she downright hated it. Even in a back alley, there was no place to be alone for a good cry.

Chapter Sixteen

Mona dropped the mail onto her desk and collapsed into her leather chair. The morning's walk to the post office had done her in, but she'd compromised. Halfway there she'd decided that walking in twenty degree weather earned her the right to cut her usual walking distance of eight blocks to four. The way she had it figured, the colder the weather, the more bonus points, and by the time winter temperatures dropped to zero, she'd only have to walk to the curb to meet her exercise quota.

She slid out of her parka and flipped through the stack of mail. On top was a postcard from church saying they'd missed seeing her Sunday. She pitched it in the trash. Another week with questions about Adam had been more than she'd cared to face, so she and Hallie had packed themselves off to a country church in Orleans. The next envelope was addressed in Ellen's familiar handwriting. She placed it at the side of the desk for Hallie as a memory triggered in her thoughts—Adam slipping a white envelope across the table to her at Trina's.

"Good night, I totally forgot about it and never even read it."

She felt a wash of panic as she spoke. Too much had been forgotten in the chaos of the past few days and the agony of waiting for the call from Dr. Bailey's office with her MRI results. She dragged her huge leather purse from beneath her desk, pulled out the crumpled paper, and slit it open. The note was brief.

Dear Mona,

It's late, and I'm writing this from the hospital. Sleep comes hard in a bed where death has stared you in the face. I'm sure you know that feeling. Even though it's hard for me to admit, I woke up afraid. Then when Hallie walked out, I was afraid in a whole new way. It's hard to hear that your daughter thinks you're a lost cause. Then this morning when I found your note beside my bed, I realized that believing there's hope for me has been what I've been struggling against most of my life. I think you can understand that more than anyone. Maybe that's why you're the only person I can say these words to. I want to be more than a lost cause.

Thank you for being willing to hope, in spite of all I've ever said and done. Hating you for being the strong one was always easy because I never believed there was hope for me. And thank you for the other notes, even though they're preachy and cheesy, and I thought about ripping them up at first.

I know that rehab has to be a kind of death for me, and I don't have any real reason to think I'll make it through. I'm hoping I'll find some new kind of strength while I'm there. Don't call in case I'm messing up and losing the battle.

Take care of Hallie for me.

Love,

Ellen

Mona reread the letter twice, letting the words sink in slowly. With each reading, her confusion grew. She scanned the lines once again.

"Elsie!"

The door flew open, and Elsie raced through, her brow furrowed, a stray tendril at her temple dancing near her blue eyes. "What's wrong, child?"

Mona waved the paper. "Did you write Ellen a note and leave it at the hospital? Have you written her any letters in the past few months?"

Elsie rolled her eyes and placed her hands on her hips. "If I could deliver a message to your sister, I would duct tape a twenty-pound family Bible to her chest. Cover up a bit of that cleavage she flashes around."

"I will take that answer for a no. Then maybe it's Hallie or Harold. Somebody's been writing to her, and it sure hasn't been me."

"Well, you scared the pucker right outta my kisser with that hollerin' of yours, young lady. And was it you who gave these men out here permission to be doin' all this measurin'? They told me they had authorization, whatever that means."

Mona laid Ellen's note down. "What men?"

Elsie shoved her hands into the front pockets of a green and gold appliquéd cardigan.

"The two out here with measuring tapes mutterin' about load-bearin' walls. They say it has to do with renovations they're startin' next door. Say the whole project will take a couple of months."

Like a clap of thunder, a crash sounded overhead, and Mona and Elsie bolted for the door.

❧

Ellen sat at her desk, the notebook open in front of her and a pile of envelopes beside her. She'd read through Mona's notes slowly. By now they were familiar. She wasn't sure why she hadn't thrown all of them out as soon as they'd come. The first had arrived days after Phil had left her. The others had come periodically, every few weeks or so. At first, she'd resented them. She couldn't remember how many times she'd considered ripping them up. A few times, she'd even thrown them in the trash, but she'd always dragged them out again.

It had always come down to the verses. Most had been her mother's favorites, the ones underlined in her Bible or passages Ellen had heard prayed aloud from behind the closed door of her mother's bedroom. The familiar words had brought back her mother's voice, and so Ellen had stacked each note on its simple lined paper in a drawer in the French provincial desk in her bedroom, rereading them until they'd become part of the rhythm of her life and her mother's voice drifted through her days, whispering threads of phrases when she least expected it.

Of course, Mona would know that using their mother's verses was nothing short of emotional manipulation, and Ellen had seethed at the thought that she was being had. But in the end, her mother's voice had won out. Her voice was all Ellen had left. Still, she pretended the notes never existed and refused to give Mona the satisfaction of knowing she'd ever laid eyes on them.

After three months, she'd finally zipped the notes into a side pocket of her purse and decided to confront Mona with them at Thanksgiving face-to-face. Then priorities changed, and she'd found herself on a ventilator with a daughter who refused to claim her any longer.

Ellen flipped open Adam's three-subject notebook. In the first section only a half-dozen pages remained. The letters to Hallie had grown longer as the days had passed. In three days, she'd be back in Stewartville in the home of a stranger, facing the daughter who still saw her as hopeless. She couldn't imagine that anything she could write could possibly prepare Hallie for forging a new life in a new town with a new mother. No matter what Fairhaven may have taught her, learning to live in Stewartville would be like navigating a minefield.

She flipped through the second section—her business plan. The career counselors had helped her develop it, and in the past week it had grown from a simple concept to drawings, sketches, and a notebook of resources drawn from the Internet. She and Gloria had sat up late into the night, discussing business locations, marketing strategies, and inventory options. As a fifty-five-year-old businesswoman who'd come to Fairhaven three times and who owned three profitable gift shops, Gloria's experience and perspective were a gold mine. By the end of her second day, Ellen felt as though having Gloria as a roommate would be one of Fairhaven's greatest gifts.

A yellow plastic divider marked the beginning of the third section, and Ellen folded it back. She leafed slowly through page after page of script as her eyes scanned the entries, some brief and hastily scrawled, others bold and heavy.

She flipped back to the first page and began reading: *Dear God, I'm angry, and I'm going to tell You why.*

The door opened. It was Gloria.

"I can come back. I know you're writing again, probably to that daughter of yours in Stewartville."

"No, I can finish up after group. Come on in."

Gloria closed the door and settled on her bed. Her salt-and-pepper, chin-length hair highlighted an angular jaw and deep brown eyes. "I'm glad someone's sending you letters. Not everyone who struggles the way we do gets support. I know we're responsible for our choices, but it still hurts when people walk away."

Ellen forced herself to look interested, but she wished Gloria would leave. Then again, a few minutes here and there wasn't asking much from someone who was helping her launch her business.

"We've all got our baggage. You know, I shouldn't say anything because I've been here enough times to know the rules better than most, but I met a woman from Stewartville here a long time ago. I don't suppose the confidentiality thing matters much anymore because she died a long time ago. I'm pretty sure her first name was Lynn, and I think her last name was Rawlings. I don't suppose you know anyone from Stewartville by the name of Rawlings, do you?"

Ellen closed her notebook. Perhaps she would listen after all.

Hallie barreled through Harold's front door, through the living room, and into the front bedroom. She flung open the closet door and began excavating a pile of shoes and boots that lay in a heap on the floor.

"I can't find them!" She lobbed a pair of running shoes toward the bed.

"Slow it down, missy!" Elsie's voice followed her into the room, and Hallie heard the front door close, followed by the sound of footsteps approaching the bedroom across the hardwood floor.

"And try to make less noise than a herd of stampeding buffalos. Harold's trying to take a nap in his room. The snow will still be on the hill in twenty minutes, and Cara and her friends said they'd wait until you get there before they leave." Hallie could hear the swoosh of the zipper on Elsie's pink nylon parka as she made her way into the bedroom.

Hallie made a dive beneath the bed and pulled out a plastic storage box. She pulled off the lid and began piling the contents on the floor beside her.

"Those are *not* your things, Hallie Bowen, so put them back this instant!"

Hallie pulled back on her heels and looked up. Elsie was glaring at her, anger radiating from her face.

"All right, so my boots aren't in here, but what's the big deal? Some music and old pictures, hey there's a dress in here, and . . . whose stuff is this anyway?"

Elsie knelt to the floor and began stacking items back in the box.

"They're Lynn's." She snapped the green plastic lid back in place. "She's Harold's daughter, and if he'd wanted to tell you about her, he'd have told you himself."

Hallie spotted the toe of a furry Ugg beneath the bed and grabbed it as she began pulling her shoes off her feet. "So why doesn't she keep her stuff at her own house? And don't get so snippy. It wasn't like I was going to violate her sacred possessions or something." She slid her feet into the boots as Elsie slid the box back in place under the bed, then turned to look at her.

"Hallie, Lynn died before she ever saw thirty-five. It's probably good you know this before you and your mama move in. Harold's wife died of cancer when Lynn was a teenager. She was smart as a whip and could play the piano beautiful like her mama. But Harold had a hard time raisin' her on his own. She kicked up her heels, and he never was a hard hand at discipline. She got into drinkin' pretty heavy, ran off to Grand Rapids before she gradu-ated high school, and lived a pretty hard life. They never did work things out in the end. Broke his heart. She died a while back. He don't talk about her much, and I wouldn't bring her up unless he brings it up first, do you understand?"

"Of course."

"It's just her pictures and her memories, child. Things that are special to Harold. Let them be, do you hear me?"

Hallie stood and promised. But even as she spoke, she could see the edge of the box poking out beneath the yellow gingham dust ruffle, and she knew it would be hard to keep her word.

Chapter Seventeen

Adam slammed the door of the Suburban and turned his key in the ignition. He pulled a notebook and pencil from his jacket pocket and scanned a neatly numbered list, then checked off the first item. Mona's counter was finally done. But the long hours at the Artisans' Center had been the easy part. Delivering it would be the real challenge, and he'd worked too hard on figuring out how to surprise her to give up on his plan now.

The trick would be keeping people's mouths shut. His friends from the Artisans' Center who'd volunteered to help load the counter into Uncle Elmer's delivery truck weren't the problem. None of them knew Mona or anyone in Stewartville. But once he hit the city limit, everything would be up for grabs. Pastor Cunningham had agreed to rustle up a few teenagers to help unload. He just prayed that none of them had mothers who had a love for antiques or other people's business. It was impossible to believe he'd be able to keep this a secret from Mona. All it would take would be one slip of the lip in church or at Trina's to spoil the surprise. But the more he'd thought it through in the past few days, the more he'd realized he wanted it to be a surprise. A total and complete surprise.

His eyes drifted down the list—people to call and details to confirm—all ways to distract himself from the thousand thoughts that pulled him toward Mona.

His finger hovered over her speed-dial number a dozen times a day, indecision tearing at him as he told himself she needed time to focus on family, to be alone with God. He worried about her headaches, about her MRI, about whether she was sleeping enough. He wondered how Hallie was adjusting to school, if her anger at her mother was still raging, and if she and Cara were spending time together. He prayed for Ellen, for her to dare God to speak to her and to be willing to listen.

But his thoughts always returned to Mona and the emptiness he felt as he'd stood in Trina's and walked away. As the days had passed, he'd prayed more and spoken less, until Aunt Florence had finally faced him and asked if something was wrong. He'd found he didn't have an answer.

Adam tucked the notebook back into his pocket. Ellen had promised she'd cover the rest of the details. Of course, he could give himself an ulcer thinking about where trusting her could leave him, but he refused to let his thoughts go there. All he had to do was rip out the old counter and install the new one in twenty-four hours. That part would be a piece of cake.

What would be hard would be first deciding if, after pouring his heart and soul into the woman he loved, he could ever bear the sight of watching her walk away.

The sounds of the shop rose and fell around him as Harold's hands glided over the smooth walnut dresser. Elsie's voice drifted back from the front room. She was showing Wilma Delmers the Edwardian Gorham teapot Mona had snatched up from the Wilson estate sale. Above her voice, Hallie's and Cara's laughter mingled as they downed lemon bars at the trestle table. The strains of Vivaldi drifted from beneath the closed door of Mona's office where she'd fled to escape the sound of pounding hammers that resonated through the floorboards above their heads.

Renovation had begun next door. Workmen had invaded not only the storefront next to the antique shop but the attic space above it adjacent to Mona's loft. A crew of six men had arrived from a Grand Rapids construction firm on Monday and begun demolition on the former pizza parlor. A Dumpster had been moved into the back alley, and mountains of debris began making their way out the door. Two days later, the space stood stripped to the brick walls, exposing the massive rear workroom and the stairway leading to the second floor.

Harold's eyes drifted over the grain of the wood as he listened to the pounding overhead. He imagined the men had begun stripping the upstairs, a full sixteen hundred square feet, down to the studs. It would seem that Mona would be needing a whole lot of Vivaldi.

Harold had to admit the dresser looked good. The Bible boxes on top were perfect. He'd already planned the note he'd slip inside. And even though he hadn't been sure he'd finish on time, he'd managed just fine. God was in the details.

He turned slowly toward the display room and Mona's office, gripping the dresser top for balance and maneuvering slowly toward the office door without his cane. He'd let the girl off the hook long enough. It was time to find out if she was willing to put her money where her mouth was, even if it meant he might have to risk a question or two. He knocked twice, opened the door, and leaned into the frame.

Mona sat behind her desk wearing a Stewartville Antiques

sweatshirt and white turtleneck. Her feet were propped on an oak swivel chair at the side of her desk, and a blanket was thrown over her long legs. A paint-spattered CD player sat in the middle of her desk.

"Have you ever just wanted to throw up your hands and go home, Harold?"

"We all have those days, I'm afraid. Some of us more than others."

"Well, I want to go home, Harold, to escape the pounding chaos of this place, except that this is my home, and there is no escape. I can't stand much more of this. Has anyone been able to figure out yet who the new owner is and what the heck they're doing besides forcing me to eat Excedrin like candy?" She lowered her legs to the floor and dropped her head to her desk.

Harold ignored the question. "You know, you don't have to stay. You could go to my house and lie down. Plenty of peace and quiet there until Hallie comes home. I'm sure all this pounding isn't good for your head, and as long as we're on the subject of headaches, I need to follow through on our conversation the other day. Have you called Dr. Bailey and scheduled your MRI?"

The voice came back, muffled. "Yes."

"And when is it scheduled?"

She lifted her head, and he saw that her eyes were weary. "I've already had it, Harold. They stuffed me into a tube like a pimento in an olive and pointed a machine gun at my head. Now I get to wait for the results during the holiday rush while coping with a hormonal teenager and the sound of air hammers ringing in my ears."

"You know, you've got choices, Mona. Stop telling yourself you're a victim like your sister. Get out of here. Go to my house. Or better yet, go to the beach house for a few nights."

He saw her eyes widen. He couldn't remember ever directly telling Mona to do anything before, and a flush of warmth flooded over him. His neck and face suddenly burned fire-hot, and the room began to spin. He slid one hand to the doorframe and gripped it.

"Don't be crazy. It's almost Christmas. I can't leave the shop or Hallie."

"Of course you can. You're not the glue that holds the world together."

She straightened in her chair, and he saw her eyes narrow. "What's gotten into you, Harold?"

He ignored the question and focused on holding himself straight. His knees were weakening, and he knew he had to speak fast. "Ask yourself what's best for you, Mona. What do you need right now? Rest? Obviously. Time to yourself? Obviously."

He saw her shoulders relax. "You know, maybe I could . . . take a day to myself before Ellen comes. Hallie could stay with Cara. She loves being with her, and I think Cara's really helping her right now. And I wouldn't have to contend with customers and pounding and whining. An entire day would be heavenly."

Harold smiled. "Go wild, Mona. Give yourself two days."

She pulled the blanket from her legs and stood to fold it. "That's impossible. I have to pick Ellen up on Saturday." He saw the resolve in the set of her shoulders, but he'd prepared for it.

"No, you don't. Someone does, and it will be best if it's me."

Mona looked up, then squared the corners of the blanket and placed it on the seat of the oak swivel chair. "That's asking too much. You don't know her. She can be a little . . . unpredictable."

"I think Elsie and you have trained me pretty good in dealing with unpredictable women. She's going to be living with me,

Mona. We need time to get to know each other before we're living under the same roof with Hallie pulled into the mix with us. It makes good sense, and it would give you two nights at the beach house. You could do some Christmas shopping. I'll bet you haven't bought a thing yet. What are you getting for Adam?"

"Don't try to distract me, Harold."

"Okay, then, I'll stick to the simple truth. It's a good idea, Mona. It gives Hallie something to look forward to, gives you a chance to rest, and it gives me and Ellen time to get to know one another a bit. Now stop arguing about the idea of doing something for yourself, and mind your elders."

He took a deep breath and smiled as she walked around the desk. In an instant her arms were around his shoulders as she hugged him, then stepped back. "Don't think I don't know what's really going on in that mind of yours."

He raised his eyebrows and willed his legs to hold him steady. "So you've got me figured out? Then I guess that's a yes, and I'm picking up Ellen on Saturday. I've made the arrangements. I'm having Debbi Cunningham drive me down to Grand Rapids. Her sister works at Fairhaven, and I'm going to drop her off for a few days. Adam told me Ellen would be ready at nine o'clock." He turned slowly to go, his hand firm on the doorframe as he paused. "I guess I should tell you the truth after all. It's a gift to me to have your sister and Hallie coming. That's the part you don't see. They can't get here too soon, as far as I'm concerned."

Harold closed the door and leaned against the wall for a moment before he shuffled back to his workroom and leaned heavily on the smooth walnut of the highboy chest. The room was once again spinning out of control, but it didn't matter. He'd gotten what he wanted, and it had been easier than he'd thought. Mona hadn't remembered the words at Elsie's that had almost cost him. He didn't want her or anyone else suspecting he'd seen Dr. Bailey except as an old friend. Except for John Curtis, of course. But the appointment had come and gone, and he didn't have to worry about people's suspicions anymore. No one suspected anything, and he'd gotten his answers.

The sounds of pounding echoed above his head, and he smiled.

Chapter Eighteen

The idea had come as Mona hovered on the edge of sleep, drifting in and out of the spaces between thought and dream. She stood once again on the pier, the waves lashing about her, but this time she spoke into the wind, her words whispered soundlessly into the tempest.

Her lips moved, and words poured out, streaming and rushing into the torrent of the storm. Before her face, the wind slackened, and the rise of the surf sagged upon the rocks along the pier. Then her mind slowly drifted toward the surface of consciousness, and the sound of Oscar's steady breathing pulled her awake. She was in her bed in her apartment, but the dream had caught her up and left her breathless. She threw back the covers and slipped out of her pajamas and into a pair of sweatpants. Then as quickly as the idea had come, she rushed from the apartment into the early morning cold and straight to Glenda's. The brick had almost claimed her once, but today it would have her for good.

Today she'd return, alone, to the pier that had almost taken her.

Her feet scuffled through a dusting of freshly fallen snow as she made her way through the dark streets to the Simpson's driveway. For a moment she paused and glanced through the darkness toward the bay window before she knelt and carefully selected a stray brick that had been kicked loose near the street. It would never be missed. This time the brick nested easily in the palms of the Isotoners before she slid the chunk into her jacket pocket and headed home through the cold and the darkness. The weight of the brick slapped heavily against her side, and she smiled. If she hurried, she could slip back into bed before Hallie realized she'd been gone.

The loft door closed softly, and footsteps receded down the stairs as Hallie waited for the familiar sound of the truck engine turning over. The clock read five thirty.

The alley below was silent.

She glanced at her aunt's bed. Oscar's form lay burrowed beneath the blankets.

"I'm giving her fifteen minutes, dog, then I'm going after her." She pulled the quilt over her face. "This entire family is crazy, and it appears I'm stuck with them for the rest of my life."

Hallie rolled onto her stomach, slid her hand beneath her pillow, and pulled out a rumpled envelope. She gripped it in her hand.

"Okay, God, I said I'm only giving her fifteen minutes, and I meant it. So this will have to be short. I figure it's Your fault I'm awake, so You were probably hoping to hear from me.

"I'd tell You how messed up my family is, except I know You know. You watch us mess up Your world every day and know what we're going to do before we even do it, but You love us anyway. Learning You were that kind of God kind of blew my mind—knowing You know how much I hurt inside and actually care about me. Mostly I'd thought You were like my dad, in some far off place, occasionally pretending to listen when You were really more interested in everything else in the universe.

"So for the past few days, You've locked me in a stare-down, and I guess You've won. Pastor Cunningham tells me I'm learning early what it means to love like You—to keep giving to imperfect people when they break your heart. I thought forgiveness was something I was going to do once, but I guess the truth is that it means that every day I have to die to a thousand things in myself. I don't get to live my own life anymore.

"So here I am, lying down and giving up. Today, forgiving my mother means I'm willing to uncrumple this paper in my hand and start working on the mess inside of me. Forgive me for my anger. Help me do what I know I can't do myself. And help me be willing to die all over again in an hour, because I know that's what living for You is going to take."

Hallie smoothed the lines of the envelope between her palms and held it there.

Mona sat in the truck as the late-afternoon sun settled on the horizon, an open Bible in her lap and a permanent marker nestled in its spine. She'd dressed in layers, but her toes had already begun to prickle icy-hot through two pairs of socks and her leather snow boots. Shards of cold cut through the cracks in the doors of the truck as the wind battered the shoreline from the west, and her breath turned to a swirling frost and hovered before her face in a crystalline cloud.

She'd told Elsie she'd need two days. Two days to sort out her heart. Two days to calm the pounding in her head. Two days to sift through her feelings toward Adam. Two days to face her fear over the growing gap of silence from Dr. Bailey's office and the MRI results that never came.

The silver-gray ice mountains stretched into the frigid waters of Lake Michigan on the western horizon. The formations lay in rolling hummocks of translucent ice scarred by deep crevasses. Some expanses lay rounded and sloped, like the gentle curves of the dunes. Others had frozen and formed jagged, rock-like clusters. It was a rolling, heaving moonscape that quietly undulated with the movement of the water beneath, growing and receding with the crashing of the waves and the caprice of the wind and the temperatures.

The sounds of the wind pummeled against the truck, and Mona listened for the winter sounds of the lake, of ice grinding upon ice, sometimes in low, guttural groans, sometimes in cracks that resonated below the surface.

In the winter months, the shoreline expanse of Pere Marquette Park could be desolate and barren. Few people visited the quarter-mile-long breakwater, and only the foolish, drunk, or suicidal attempted the ice-covered walk to the lighthouse at the end.

Mona stared through the swirling snow at the spot where she and Hallie had first spotted Dan Evans playing volleyball the day of her accident. He'd been in exactly the right spot at the moment they'd needed him on the pier. But what if he hadn't come to check on them after his game? She knew the answer everyone always gave, the answer she gave—that God wasn't finished with her yet, that He'd led Dan to them. But why had God let her live and taken Stacy, a child? It was a question that had exhausted Mona's thoughts on sleepless nights and had stalked her in waking hours, overtaking her at the sight of a mother and daughter or at the sound of a child's laughter.

From deep within, words welled up. "I don't pretend to know I have the answers to all the pain and to all the 'whys,' Father. After all these months and losing Stacy, my suffering hasn't given me a list of answers. I guess that puts me in good company with Job. It's brought me here—to my knees, to a wrenching awareness of how desperate I am without You. The pain has shown me who I am when You tear away the trappings of my self-sufficiency, and it's ugly, Father. You knew it was ugly all along, and maybe that's why You loved me enough to bring me here."

Her words poured out as the cold cubicle of the truck became a confessional.

She was sorry her pain had stripped her naked and wrestled her to the ground. She hadn't known it would show how weak she really was, how willing to doubt, to accuse, and to blame.

She was sorry she'd let it shrink her soul—make her angry, want to quit, and believe that life wasn't fair—even when she wasn't brave enough to say it out loud.

She was sorry that for so many years she'd been willing for others to be broken and dependent but she'd been unwilling to be broken and dependent herself.

She was sorry she struggled to be thankful, to embrace the good things she'd overlooked in the pain and the gift of the pain itself.

She was sorry she'd forgotten to worship and that she'd doubted His love for her and His desire to give her good things, to bless her, and to give her hope even in silence and suffering and the barren places of her heart.

In the distance, the surf pounded against the icy walls of the shoreline as she sat in the silence. She struggled to give shape to her grief—to find words for the sorrow that had driven her there.

You saved me, and I wanted more. I walked away from You in my pain instead of into Your arms.

You brought me to the edge of death and meant for it to be the beginning of a new life for me, and I never saw it. My brokenness was a gift, but I saw it as a burden. You've been trying to make me like Jesus, and some-where along the way, I decided I wanted an easier assignment.

Her breath swirled in milky puffs and drifted toward the windshield.

I'm here, Lord, broken, asking for forgiveness, and I'm laying myself down. I'm giving it all to You—the pathetic way I've held on to my life, my fears, my doubts, my anger. I'm exchanging it for whatever You've chosen for me, as hard as that may be.

She pulled the pen from her Bible and pulled the brick from the seat beside her into her lap. Her lips formed the words as she wrote:

My Bethel, my altar to God, who answered me in the day
of my distress and who has been with me wherever I have
gone.

Mona double-wrapped her red, hand-knitted scarf around her head and neck, then pulled her leather gloves onto her hands. She slipped the brick deep into her right pocket and her cell phone into her left, then pressed the door open against the wind and stepped out into the buffeting blast.

The force of the gale slammed the door shut as she set out toward the pier, her head bowed against the force of the wind. The cold cut through her leather jacket. The light was beginning to fade, and she knew she didn't have much time. Ten minutes, maybe, to finish. The fringed knots of her red scarf beat against her shoulders as she leaned into the wind, her head bent into her chest, focusing on her path as the brick weighted her course to the right. Her boots fought against the icy crust, then broke through the surface with each step, throwing her weight first to the right, then to the left as she fanned her arms to her sides like a tightrope walker.

She'd barely conquered five yards before her left leg was throbbing. Her balance had always been unsteady, and her left leg was working against the pressure of the wind and the drag of the brick in her right pocket. She battled to remain upright, knowing that if she fell, the struggle to stand again would diminish her strength even further. By the time she'd reached fifteen yards, both thighs burned and her left leg felt as if it would give way beneath her.

She peered at the concrete walkway in front of her through layers of crimson. The breakwater where her body had been pummeled and crushed lay crusted in ice. The long expanse was barely visible in the dusk. The corner where she and Hallie had stood was obscured by the deepening darkness and swirling snow. A blast of wind pounded her, and she staggered, nearly falling as her boot caught on a lip of ice.

Her hand felt for the brick in her pocket as she turned and looked back toward the truck. This was insanity. What had she been thinking? Not another soul was visible anywhere on the beachfront, and in minutes, it would be dark. It had seemed like a good idea in the early morning hours as she'd plucked a stray brick from the edge of Glenda Simpson's driveway. Now her goal seemed absurd for a woman who could barely limp a few blocks to the Stewartville post office in an inch of snow. She didn't want to envision the price she'd pay if she ended up in Mercy General and Elsie got another emergency medical call.

Mona stood, reeling in the wind, and considered her options. The ritual had only been symbolic, after all. God knew her heart, and the heart was what mattered, wasn't it? The wind would be to her advantage if she chose to walk back.

She looked at her tracks through the swirling snow as they slowly filled in beneath eddies of white. God had brought her this far. She was standing, surrounded by the force of His breath, encompassed by the beauty of His creation, with a hunger so strong to simply touch Him, to know Him, that the struggle faded and all that remained was desire. Suddenly, she knew that an altar was calling her—her body leaning into the decision, forcing its way through the struggle, locked in combat against doubt and reservation. God would take her the remaining few yards.

She placed her right foot on the glazed crust and pressed down. Her foot slipped to the right, and she threw her arms wide.

You know I can't do this on my own. I need You to take me there one step at a time, Lord, no matter how long it takes.

She set out again, each step breaking through the icy crust and threatening to send her crashing to the ground. She focused on each breath and the position of her arms, forcing herself to count each stride until she reached twenty. Then she stopped and looked up.

Where the curve of the dune met the apron of ice leading to the pier, she pulled the brick from her pocket. She carefully knelt and clawed at the crust until she'd dug a small hole in the snow. Then she laid the brick inside and covered it over.

"My Bethel, Lord. You answered me in my distress, and now I'm here to give myself back to You. Like a kernel of wheat, dead to myself, grow me into something new." Her red scarf snapped against the pummeling wind as she spoke the words.

When she was finished, she rose slowly and turned, carefully planting her feet in the faint boot tracks that remained, each step back to the truck weighted with victory.

Chapter Nineteen

"I came up here for peace and quiet, as if that's possible around here, you miserable, whiney dog."

Oscar pawed at her thighs, and Hallie pulled the afghan from the back of the loveseat and threw it over the black form wedged between her crossed legs. For the past two days, she'd come home from school to the dog's whining, Elsie's irritation, and the workmen's pounding. Since the renovations had started, Elsie had gone on the warpath and threatened to call the National Guard to have the work crew dragged off at gunpoint for driving customers away. The continual thumping and bashing had even gotten to Harold, who'd stopped coming in to the shop.

A pile of letters lay on the loveseat beside Hallie, and she held a small, leather-bound book in her hand. She glanced at the door. Elsie was alone downstairs. Hallie doubted she'd come up, but the woman had a sixth sense when it came to guilt.

Hallie glanced at the cover of the book.

"That's the year, Oscar: 1966."

Aunt Mona had never told Hallie her grandpa's diaries were off-limits, but then, she'd never invited her to read them, either. The way she figured it, this was a perfect time to sit down and get a peek. One look certainly couldn't hurt. And how cool would it be to read what her grandfather had written on the day her mother was born?

She glanced at the door again, then back to the book, and quickly flipped to February. The writing was small and boxy, written in precise letters that looked almost like a printed page. Some days were blank, followed by days where the pages were filled in. She wondered if all the books on the shelf were like that—with days and weeks missing—and why someone who'd take the time to keep a diary for so many years would forget to fill in so much. Were those days the boring ones or the ones where so much happened that it slipped away before he could get it all written down?

She flipped to the sixteenth, the seventeenth, then the eighteenth, her mother's birthday. Her eyes fell on the page, and the breath went slowly out of her.

It was blank.

The following two pages were blank. Her hand went to Oscar's head beneath the blanket, and she let it rest on the warmth of his fur.

Her breathing came faster as her fingers flipped the pages and her eyes scanned the cramped words.

The truth hit, in phrases and images and in the things not written as much as in the words she read. The words that had been too painful for her mother to ever speak. She'd never heard her say them. Yet the truth was there.

Her grandfather had looked for strength at the bottom of a bottle. He'd never found it. Anger spilled off page after page—anger and emptiness.

Hallie sat alone with the truth and with her grandfather's diary for nearly an hour before her hands moved to her mother's letters. One by one, she read them.

🐚

Katrina Newberry was just finishing the last bite of a late lunch at Trina's when her cell phone rang. It wasn't an east-side area code on her caller ID, but then, investors from Lansing had been running her ragged checking out opportunities to build a retirement community in Stewartville. She never knew who might be on the other end of the line when investors were circling. She assumed her most professional tone.

"Katrina Newberry, specializing in central Michigan real estate."

"Hello, Katrina. My name is Ellen Bowen. I'm Mona Vander-Molen's sister—you may know her—she owns Stewartville Antiques on Main Street. I've been living in the Bloomfield Hills area, but I'm planning on making a move to Stewartville, and I'm looking for a business property. I understand that the building next to my sister's is vacant, and I'm interested in purchasing it."

Katrina reached into a large leather bag beside her and slapped a legal pad on the table. Then she pulled a pen from a leather planner that sat on the table in front of her and began to write feverishly.

"Ellen, I'm sorry to disappoint you, but that property has already been purchased by an investor and is currently being renovated, but I'm sure we can find something suitable for you. What kind of business are you involved in?"

There was silence.

"Ellen?"

"You've got to be kidding. That building's sat empty for as long as Mona's lived there, and now somebody's bought it? Who? Maybe I can buy it from them. I'll make them a great deal—I've got the money."

Katrina scrawled out several words in capital letters and underlined them. "I'm so sorry, Ellen. I'm not at liberty to disclose the name of the investor. They purchased that property for a very specific purpose, and I can assure you they wouldn't be interested in your offer. If I thought they had the slightest interest, I'd encourage you to make one, but I'm afraid that's just not the case. But we can look for something else on Main. What kind of business are you hoping to open?" The pen hovered as Katrina waited.

"It's going to be . . . well, I guess my plans were somewhat contingent upon my getting that specific building. I may have to do some rethinking, but it will be a specialty gift shop."

Katrina laid down her pen and slipped the legal pad back into the leather bag. "Ellen, I'd encourage you to schedule an appointment with me. There's nothing special about that particular storefront, and I'm certain we can find you something similar in a great location. There are other Main Street locations that may be available if you give me time to check. When do you plan to actually arrive in Stewartville?"

"Tomorrow."

"And where will you be staying?"

"With Harold Rawlings."

Katrina made a quick mental note. "I know Harold well. How about if I get together a few ideas for you and give you a call next week? That will give you time to settle in. You have my number. I have yours in my cell now, and of course, I know where you'll be staying. In the meantime, you focus on what's bringing you to Stewartville. Consider the rest taken care of."

Ellen thanked her and hung up.

Katrina shook her head as she picked up her fork and took a stab at the last bite of her Dutch apple pie. "Yes, my dear, consider the rest taken care of."

Mona sat in her truck on the lane that led to the shore at the base of the stairs to the Gilead Bible Conference Prayer Tower. She'd contemplated the climb for nearly an hour as the engine idled, telling herself it wasn't necessary to climb to the top. She had a better view of the lake from her beach house. But the presence of the tower always drew her. Today, it was calling her. She needed to be there, and she needed to pray.

A knock sounded on her window, and Mona turned. Dan Evans opened the door of the truck and slid in beside her.

"Going up?"

His simple question and the look in his eyes told Mona he understood why she was there.

"May I help you, Miss V? I'd love nothing more than to be your escort."

"Once again, my guardian angel comes to my rescue."

He laughed and glanced toward a car that slid slowly past on the narrow lane.

"I only did what anyone would have done. And it was a privilege to help my favorite English teacher who broke the hearts of all the students at West Shore High School by leaving teaching and becoming an entrepreneur. So how are you?"

"Now there's a question that will take a long answer."

"Then I don't want to keep you from what you came for. Maybe we can talk later. Are you ready to go?"

She nodded.

He opened his door and stepped back into the wind, then helped her from the truck. Together they climbed the series of stairs to the tower that overlooked the Lake Michigan shoreline, pausing occasionally for rest along the walkways. They stopped as they reached the door to the simple wooden structure nestled in the dunes among the trees.

"Will you need help down?"

Mona shook her head. "Down's the easy part, and I'm not staying long. I just couldn't go home until I'd been here to pray. You know this has always been my special place. Now what about you? When did you get home from college?"

His smile was easy. She hoped it never changed. "Late last night. I'd have been down to the beach house for a visit if I'd realized you were here. How is everyone? I lost track of Hallie about a week or so ago. We've been e-mailing. It sounded like things have been kind of rough for her with her mom."

Mona turned toward the door. "If you can give me ten minutes alone and walk me back to my truck, I'll buy you a cup of coffee and some onion rings at the Sardine Room before I head back to Stewartville. Our family could use another man of God praying for us right now."

Dan nodded. "I'll head back to the truck and be back up to get you in ten minutes. And whatever you're praying for here, I'll just double up on it down there." Mona watched as he headed back down the wooden walkway and disappeared. She couldn't help but think his mother was blessed.

Mona turned and entered the tower, closing the door behind her as a gust of wind swayed the surrounding pines. Her heart released with them as she felt her spirit rise. She was not alone. She was cared for. She was prayed for. Her portion had been assigned. The pines whispered around her, and her heart shouted back in praise.

Harold pulled a file from Lynn's desk drawer and laid it on the seat of the pressed-back swivel chair. John Curtis had been more than clear—he needed the paperwork in the mail as soon as possible. But then, John didn't have two women moving in with him and a splitting headache to boot. Maybe he should consider taking the prescriptions Fred Bailey had told him would help. Harold thumbed through a second file as he blinked. His dad-blamed eyes wouldn't focus. How in heaven's name was he supposed to find the right paperwork when every paper looked like it had been written in duplicate?

He pulled two more files from the drawer and picked up the one on the chair, then closed the drawer and headed to the kitchen. He'd already written out the address, and he slid the files into the oversized manila pouch he'd purchased from the post office. It was after business hours anyway. He'd have to mail it out to John in the morning. But there were other details that could be just as important. Things that needed mending. Things that needed giving. He turned and headed to the basement, gripping the rail tightly and flipping on a light as he descended the open stairs.

A few strides down a narrow, paneled hall brought him to a small workroom. He flipped on another light. A small wooden birdhouse rested in the center of the workbench in front of him. He smiled. She'd finished it. It remained to be seen if she'd actually give it away, but he could only do what he could do.

He turned off the light and headed slowly back up the stairs, gripping the railings firmly on both sides, then headed toward his bedroom. The papers were signed. John would receive everything by Monday.

He laid down on his bed and gave in to the pain.

Chapter Twenty

Ellen had made up her mind to be positive about going to Stewartville. Grateful, even. She knew real gratitude would be hard work. She was used to the other kind—superficial smiles and trivial phrases that rolled off her tongue. It had been a long time since she'd felt real gratitude. But fourteen days at Fairhaven had tweaked her perspective on a few things.

Some of the people she'd met were returning home for the third and fourth time, and some weren't returning home at all. Several had confessed that their jobs were on the line. A journalist from a community not far from Lansing admitted he'd written his own obituary. As the days had unfolded and other people's stories had surfaced, glimmers of gratitude had poked through to the surface of Ellen's soul. The counselors had fanned them, but they'd been blunt. As long as she saw herself as a victim, she'd continue to live life as a victim. It was the most honest thing Ellen had faced about herself since Stacy had died. Running from the truth had been destroying her. And the only way to face the truth would be to face her soul, change, or die trying.

She chose change in tiny steps—in each letter to Hallie, in each meeting she attended. With each step she took, she told herself she was walking into a new identity—*Mother*. She just wasn't sure if Hallie would walk beside her or abandon her for good along the way.

She'd chosen to wait for Harold alone in her room, where she could look down on the parking lot from the windows of the second floor. Mona had told her he was coming, that she and Hallie would meet her at the house. She'd tried to steel herself for the things a religious old man might ask an alcoholic woman coming out of rehab. Things Lynn's father might ask—a man whose daughter had fled Stewartville to hide in the city and a man who'd raised a woman who'd chosen never to go back home.

By the time the truck turned into the parking lot, Ellen had braced herself for the judgmental eyes and coldness of her father. She'd prepared herself for condescension and the veiled tolerance of a man hoping to prove his spirituality by taking in someone he could mold into an image of himself. She'd expected assessment and arrogance, but she was wrong. She was met by the shy smile of a gentle man as he briefly introduced her to a woman named Debbi, who shook her hand before heading into Fairhaven's administrative offices to find her sister. Then he handed Ellen the keys to the truck and asked if she'd drive the two of them home. He'd brought thick slices of freshly baked banana bread and steaming travel mugs of jasmine tea, and before they hit U.S. 131 north, Ellen was talking about college; her favorite composers, Debussy, Scarlatti, and Rachmaninoff; and her dream for a gift shop in Stewartville—a place that would sell eclectic creations made from antique remnants, repurposed decorative items, and mosaic artwork.

Harold hadn't looked at her at all as she'd found her way along the back roads toward Stewartville. He'd kept his eyes steady on the road in front of them, shaded behind a pair of massive, wraparound sunglasses, and listened as Ellen had rambled. It was only when she spotted Stewartville's orange water tower on the horizon that she realized she'd been talking for the entire trip, and he'd been quietly listening.

Ellen couldn't remember the last time she'd talked so much or felt she'd really been heard.

Mona stepped back and surveyed the tree. It was listing slightly to the left, and even though Jake Cunningham had chopped eight inches off the bottom, it barely cleared Harold's ten-foot living-room ceiling.

"There's no way we're getting an angel on the top of this thing, girls. And I'm not calling your dad back here, Cara. He was good enough to go cut it down and haul it in here. Besides, I think the rest of it looks terrific." Mona surveyed the collection of antique ornaments they'd brought from the shop, which hung in the sparse patches scattered over the branches. She turned and looked at the two girls sprawled on Harold's tan Herculon couch.

"It's pathetic. It's bald, like my Grandpa Clark," Cara pronounced as she swung her leg over the side. "But I don't think Harold will care. I don't think he's had a tree up since my dad's been pastor here. Maybe he doesn't believe in Christmas trees."

Hallie poked her in the ribs. "Harold's not like that, idiot. He just never went to the trouble to put up a tree for himself, so we're doing it for him. But we've gotta look for more decorations. I'm sure he's got some here somewhere." She stood up and jammed her hands into the pockets of her pink hoodie. "Cara and I will take the middle bedroom. I've already gone through all the boxes in mine."

"Hallie!"

"It's okay. Elsie was with me. She told me about Lynn and . . ."

The back door opened, and the sound of voices drifted into the living room. Mona glanced toward Cara.

"It's okay, Miss V. I can slip out the front door and head home."

"No! Don't leave. It's no big deal." Hallie turned toward Mona. "Tell her she doesn't have to go, please."

The sound of voices grew louder.

"Of course not, Cara. You're welcome to stay." Mona saw Hallie cross her arms and drop back onto the couch beside her friend.

Ellen stepped through the archway leading from the kitchen, and Harold followed a few feet behind, leaning on his cane, with one hand resting on top of the other for support. Ellen paused a few steps into the room, and Mona moved to her and drew her into a quick hug. She felt her sister's shoulders relax as she whispered into her ear, "Welcome home, Sis."

Ellen pulled slowly away. "Thank you." The dark circles beneath her eyes had faded, and the gaunt hollows of her cheeks had filled in. Her blonde hair fell simply to her shoulders and was tucked behind her ears. She turned toward the girls on the couch and stood quietly.

"Hi, Hallie." Her tone was even, not pressing, a tone Mona hadn't heard before. She sensed the effort not to beg, not to manipulate.

Hallie's eyes met her mother's. "Hi, Mom. I don't think you've met my friend Cara." Mona prayed for a flicker of movement, but Hallie remained seated.

"Hi, Mrs. Bowen. It's nice to meet you." Cara rose and moved to shake Ellen's hand. "We were just decorating the tree for Harold . . . and for you . . . for a surprise, but we kind of ran out of decorations. We were actually wondering if you had any more packed away anywhere, Harold, so we can fill in the bald spots." Cara tipped her head and smiled, her long brown hair cascading to one side like a chocolate waterfall. Mona wondered how many times the pose had been used on Cara's father.

Harold slid a long finger into the collar of his shirt and gave it a tug. He closed his eyes for a moment, as though he were deep in thought or drifting off to sleep. "I'm sure I have a few decorations packed away downstairs somewhere, but it would take me a pretty long time to—"

Cara clapped her hands. "This is perfect! Hallie, show your mother her room and help her unpack her things and show her all the stuff you brought her from home. Hallie and I worked all last night to get your room all fixed up for you, Mrs. Bowen. Harold, you find the ornaments, and I'll help you bring them up. Miss V, I think you should make hot chocolate for all of us and see if Harold has any pie left in the kitchen."

Hallie groaned. "Girl, you've watched *It's a Wonderful Life* one too many times."

Cara reached over and slapped Hallie's thigh. "Move it, city girl. Harold, I'll be down to help after I make sure Hallie's not slacking off."

Mona turned toward the kitchen, not sure what she'd just witnessed, but apparently the magic of a young woman capable of pulling Hallie off a sofa and setting her to work alongside her mother. Seconds later, Hallie and Ellen were headed dutifully toward the back bedroom, and Cara was dragging a scuffling and reluctant Harold toward the basement by the arm.

Mona forced herself to stay at the stove and focus on making five hot chocolates and pouring them into Harold's assortment of mismatched mugs. Everything inside her fought the desire to go to

Ellen's room and peek in. Was the room silent, or was real conversation being exchanged? Had Hallie even glanced at her mother, or was she choosing the torturous punishment of indifference?

A shriek echoed from the basement, then the pounding of footsteps on the stairs. Mona turned. Cara burst through the kitchen door, her eyes wide with excitement and her arms filled with papers and books she clutched to her chest.

"You will never, ever believe what Harold found down there!"

Ellen and Hallie careened down the back hallway and into the kitchen as Harold appeared in the basement doorway behind Cara, slowly pulling himself up the stairs.

The five of them stood in the kitchen, staring at each other in expectation. Cara's brown eyes were wide with the anticipation of her pronouncement as she dumped her pile on the kitchen table.

"We found the ornaments, but we also found books of Christmas carols and tons and tons of music—classical and jazz and church music. This is more than cool. Mrs. Bowen, Hallie told me you were this amazing pianist when you were in college, and you used to play when she was little, and she loved it. My dad would love it if you played in our church sometime. Mrs. Westra is our pianist, but she really only knows how to play by ear and not how to read notes, and her playing isn't really all that good but nobody has the heart to tell her. But now we have *you*, and you have a piano here at Harold's house to practice. Maybe you could even give lessons—how cool would that be? But for right now, would you play some carols for us?"

The room went dead. Mona's eyes went to Ellen's face, then to Harold's, then to Hallie's. Hallie stood behind her mom and stared at the back of her black sweater.

Ellen cleared her throat, and her words came out slowly. "Wow,

Cara. I don't know where to begin. I don't think I'd make much of a teacher, that's for sure. And I haven't played in a long time. I'm sure I'd have to work hard to play anything well, much less beautifully, but I'm willing to try. That's the reason I'm in Stewartville. I'm here to learn how to do things better after a long time of doing them lousy."

Ellen stopped, plucked an imaginary thread from her sweater, then went on, looking straight into Cara's eyes as she spoke. "You're right. I loved to play for Hallie when she was younger. I used to play one piece that she always adored. The music sounded like a story to me—hopeful at the beginning, sad in the middle, with a beautiful ending. I'm not sure she ever knew the name, but it was called, 'The Heart Knows.'"

The room was silent as Hallie's hand moved to her mother's shoulder. Harold cleared his throat, and Mona was certain his face went pale for a moment. For the briefest of seconds, she thought he looked as if he might pass out, then decided she was imagining things.

"If listening to me massacre Christmas carols is something you'd all enjoy, I'd be willing to try."

Harold's face eased into a smile, and the full force of Ellen's words hit Mona.

Thank you, Lord. I'm not sure what just happened here or how it happened, but I think we may have just seen a miracle.

Harold spoke. "It would be a blessing to me if you'd play, Ellen. There hasn't been music in my house for a good number of years, so my old Story and Clark is out of tune, but you'll find it in the front bedroom. Go through the music that Cara brought up and pick what you like. I'm going to settle down on my bed with the door open so I can listen while I rest. Music is just what I've been needing. It's a true gift to me. Having all of you here is a gift to me—especially you and Hallie."

Harold turned and headed slowly down the back hallway to his bedroom. Mona was certain that as he reached for his bedroom door, she saw his right hand tremble.

For the next hour, music drifted through the house as the two girls decorated the tree and Mona fixed a lunch of sandwiches and soup. Hallie edged in and out of her front bedroom, pausing briefly at her mother's side and flipping through a book of carols, then a book of classical pieces. By the time the tree was finished, they'd heard snippets of Chopin and Mozart, and Cara had placed a hymnal on the music stand.

When Mona went to check on Harold before lunch, he was sleeping soundly, and she didn't have the heart to wake him. By the time she came back to the kitchen, Cara had rounded up Ellen and Hallie, seated everyone, then pulled their hands together in a circle as she prayed over the meal.

When they raised their heads, Mona looked at Cara Cunningham in amazement. A fifteen-year-old child had somehow brought Hallie to the table beside her mother and drawn their hands together in prayer. She seemed to see the good in Hallie and draw it out, and see the weakness in her and call her to something higher. God had given Hallie a true friend, someone willing to stand shoulder-to-shoulder with her and help pull her through the hard times.

Mona lifted her water glass to her lips and drank quickly as a twinge of jealousy passed through her. Adam had been that kind of friend. But with Ellen finally in Stewartville, the days ahead were certain to get tough. Hallie and her mom would need her more than ever.

Mona battered down a rising swell of emotion.

She had to give him up. There wasn't room in her life for Adam Dean.

Chapter Twenty-one

By Sunday night, Mona was so confused by Ellen's behavior that the idea of sleep seemed as likely as Elsie taking a vow of silence. Mona lay in her bed and stared at the ceiling as she recounted the changes. Her angry sister had come back from Fairhaven quieter and more uncertain. The distant mother who'd lived behind closed doors was finding excuses to be in the same room with Hallie. Mona had even waited for an outpouring of disdain for Harold's house—for his bathroom, his linens, his taste in decor, even his clothing—but it had never come. Instead, there had been an occasional raised eyebrow and unexpected silences.

Ellen had gone to church without comment, not even insisting that they sit in the back row. Heads had turned and hands had waved as the three of them had slid into the eighth pew, left side. Cara had slipped into the empty space next to Hallie. After the morning service, Cara's father and mother had welcomed Ellen, and she had offered an actual smile and thanked them.

Mona thought she might faint right there in the center aisle of Stewartville Community Church.

Later that afternoon, she couldn't hold herself back. She began compiling a list of praises that kept her preoccupied for the rest of the day. God had stirred things while Ellen was at Fairhaven, and she could see the changes—changes in Ellen and changes in Hallie.

They were small things, really, like the effort she saw in Hallie's eyes as she made polite conversation with her mother across Harold's kitchen table. Or the sound of an untuned piano resonating from Harold's front bedroom and the fact that her sister's hands had willingly found their way to the keys. Or for the days or even the hours that passed without the smell of alcohol on Ellen's breath.

Mona stared at the glow of the streetlight beyond her window. As her list of praises grew, one question stood behind them all: what had happened to her sister?

Mona stood at the register, sorting the morning's cash into the till. In fifteen minutes, the shop would open, and she'd hoped to get the front sidewalk shoveled before Harold came in. In all the years she'd known him, she'd never heard the man complain, but lately, he'd been going home afternoons to rest, and Mona had noticed him slipping a few pills here and there. Then there seemed to be his growing unsteadiness, and she was certain that on a few occasions she'd noticed a tremor in his hands. She wondered about Parkinson's disease and how she could bring up a conversation about his health with a man who never wanted to talk about himself. Maybe having Hallie and Ellen with Harold would end up being as good for him as it seemed to be for them.

The back door slammed, and Mona heard the sound of voices. She counted the last of the tens into the drawer and closed it as Ellen walked through the doorway from the workroom, dropped onto the bench at the trestle table, and unzipped a gray leather jacket with a fur-trimmed collar. A few seconds later, Harold followed and leaned against the doorway dividing the workshop from the display room. Mona wished she could see his eyes, but he was wearing sunglasses and didn't seem to be interested in taking them off.

"I'll bet you never expected to see me before the crack of noon."

"Harold, what bribery did you come up with to get this woman in here so early?"

Harold tipped his head toward Ellen. "No bribery. Told me she had a busy day and needed a ride to the shop. I was glad to oblige and let her drive. She's got to learn her way around town sooner or later. Navigating through that one traffic light can be tricky." He motioned toward the workroom. "I'll leave you two ladies to discuss your plans."

"What plans?" Mona eyed her sister. "I wasn't aware we had plans."

Ellen pointed at the bench at the trestle table. "Sit down, and I'll remind you. First of all, where can I get a manicure in this town? I'm at least a week overdue."

"The Curl Up and Dye across the street. Now get to the point." Mona folded her arms and leaned against the counter.

Ellen cast a saccharine smile. "You'd think my sister would be thrilled that I'm not looking for a drink my first day back in the real world. Well, let me fill you in. I don't have long because I have an appointment at nine thirty. But we're scheduled for our girls' getaway starting Wednesday, so start packing."

"What are you talking about?"

"What do you mean, 'What am I talking about?' We talked about this on the phone just before I went to Fairhaven. You don't remember?" A shadow of disappointment fell over Ellen's face.

"Yes . . . yes, of course I remember." Mona forced her thoughts back. What on earth was she talking about—a girls' getaway? She vaguely remembered a phone conversation about going away somewhere.

"I've already made the reservations in Whitehall, your kind of place. We're going to eat chocolate until we burst and shop until we drop."

Mona leaned forward. "Say that again."

"What, the chocolate part or the shopping part?"

"No, the part where you said that you, Ellen Bowen from Bloomfield Hills, picked Whitehall, Michigan, for a getaway with your sister."

"It's *your* Christmas present, Mona," Ellen's tone was defensive. "I picked it for you, not for me. You'd think you'd be grateful." Ellen zipped her jacket and stood.

"Ellen, of course I'm—"

"Nope. I'm outta here. If I hurry, I can get my nails done before I meet Katrina Newberry." She headed toward the front door, the heels of her black leather boots smacking against the hardwood floor. Then she headed through the front doorway and down the street.

Mona uncrossed her arms and shook her head.

"I'm an idiot, Lord," she spoke into the silence of the shop. "I've blown it, already. She was trying to do something nice for me, and I threw it back in her face."

Mona walked to the front of the store and looked down the street toward the Curl Up and Dye, but Ellen had already disappeared.

The sign near the front gate said it all: Cocoa Cottage. Mona pulled her F-150 into the parking place at the side of the Arts and Crafts bungalow, slipped it into park, and turned off the engine.

"Ellen, where have you brought me?" Her eyes swept the exterior of the restored house as she drank in every detail.

"Isn't it just the coolest? Not really my style, but when I heard the name *Cocoa Cottage*, I knew you'd love it. Everything's been restored—the furnishings, the wall coverings, the fabrics, all the way down to the switch plates. But here's the best part. Every room has a chocolate theme. We're in the Godiva Room, so you owe me big time. They serve chocolate zucchini bread with hot fudge sauce, chocolate gnocchi cake, and chocolate strawberries, just to start. There's even a massage therapist. This trip is all about indulgence, shopping, and relaxation.

"Frankly, Mona, I don't think you've had any of those things for as long as I can remember. I've even scheduled a tour of a furniture restoration shop, just for you."

Mona turned toward her sister. For the first time in a long time, Ellen's expression was open, unguarded. Her gray eyes looked at Mona with a level gaze.

"Ellen, this is wonderful, but why now? We've never done anything together in our lives, much less something like this."

Ellen reached for the leather Gucci bag on the seat beside her. "I guess nobody gave you the script in my head and told you this is the part where you're supposed to get all giddy and excited and act like this was a good idea instead of telling me in your polite Christian way that you'd rather not be here with me."

"That's not—"

"Oh please. And why *would* you want to be with me? You've spent most of your life embarrassed that we're in the same family, while I've spent most of my life trying to be you, Mona. You were the smart one who did everything right. When I was little, I believed that if I could just talk like you talked and get better grades like you and dye my hair red like yours maybe Dad wouldn't hate me so much. I hated that I was the blonde one, the stupid one. Anyone could be blonde, but nobody had that crazy red hair but Mona VanderMolen."

Ellen looked toward the house. "At Fairhaven, they told me I've spent my life being a victim, but I've known that for a long time. I know I still am one, and I'm not sure I know how to be anything else. But the last few months have taught me that I want to stop, and that I have to try. Stacy is dead, and Phil has left me. Hallie has every reason in the world to leave me, too, because of the way I've treated her.

"We're here because I'm starting over, and I need to say that to people around me and draw a line in the sand. I need to make a fresh start somehow, and you're the first person I've chosen to do that with. I'm scared to death to walk back into my daughter's life and try to figure out how to start all over in a town where everybody knows your business. But I have to try, and I have to come home to do it, and the closest place I have to home right now is Stewartville.

"So even though this is your Christmas present, it's a gift to me, too—my new start. You're here because you're the only sister I have, and I'm asking you to help me."

Ellen turned and faced Mona. Her lips were pulled into a thin smile.

"Ellen, I—"

"No, let me finish this. I know how easy it will be for me to go down in flames at any minute, so I've done a few things, and you need to know. The owners of this place serve alcoholic beverages, and they've graciously agreed to remove it from our experience while we're here. When we get back to Stewartville, I need you to go down to Harold's basement and look inside an old green trunk near his furnace. You'll find a bottle of vodka there."

Mona struggled to keep the surprise from registering on her face. "Have you . . . ?"

"No. I can only tell you that right now, in this second, I'm strong enough to tell you it's there, and I don't know how long these seconds will last. I don't trust how long any of this will last, but I'm putting everything I have into reclaiming my life. I'm going to give everything I've got for Hallie, and I can't do it alone."

Mona reached across the seat and took Ellen's hand. "You won't be alone, and you haven't been. You know that, don't you? I've never stopped believing in you. And God's got plans for you."

Ellen shook her head. "Maybe we could work our way up to the God thing later, Mona. I can't go there now. We're going to be living in the same town, after all. Maybe we could start our conversation about my life with something smaller, less intimidating, like my business plan."

Mona caught the change in her tone and followed it. "Business plan? Sounds like you were busy at Fairhaven."

"Some friends there helped me, and I thought we could make this a research trip and talk to shop owners while we were bumming around Whitehall and Pentwater. I heard Pitkin's Pharmacy here in town has a bit of personality and would be a good place to start."

Mona saw movement at the kitchen window as figures moved about inside the house.

"Well, as long as this isn't some secret plot where Adam pops out of a cabinet with a Christmas present. I know he was in cahoots with you making secret plans, so I'm on my guard."

Ellen laughed as she slipped her purse straps over her shoulder. "No men on this trip, I promise. Just wild-eyed spending, some sisterly arguing, a little business planning, and as much chocolate as we can cram down our throats in forty-eight hours."

Hallie sat on the bed in her mother's room, her legs crossed beneath her on a white chenille spread. It was a small room, barely larger than her walk-in closet at home, and possibly the most disgusting room she'd ever seen in her life.

The green flocked wallpaper couldn't have been more hideous, like moss that grew from the walls, a furry fungus. Then there were the curtains, white, fluffy things with frilly edges and fuzzy pimples all over them. They were hung over windows that had been sealed with enormous sheets of something that looked like Saran Wrap stretched tight. The bedspread added the final touch—a white, furry bathrobe attempting to do an impression of a blanket.

The door of the tiny closet across the room stood ajar. Her mother's shoes were piled two-deep on the floor and spilling out onto the scarred, hardwood floor.

She must despise this room. Every square inch of it.

It seemed unimaginable: her mother, Ellen Bowen, here in Harold's house, sleeping on 200-count sheets, showering in an ancient, claw-foot tub, eating from chipped dishes.

Her mother walking on floors that had settled to the west and were battered and covered with scatter rugs, coming home to a house with mismatched siding.

Her mother reading books on a Herculon couch or kicking back in the crushed velvet Lane recliner.

Hallie swung her legs to the cold, hardwood floor and pressed them into the wood.

"She has to hate this house, this town. They're everything she's tried so hard to prove she isn't." Hallie stood and pulled open the closet door. Assorted shirts, sweaters, and slacks were jammed into the small space. "So why isn't she pitching fits? How can she just choose to not hate everything she's always detested?"

Her eyes fell on a white painted nightstand beside the bed. A spiral notebook and a Bible sat on the lower shelf. A pen had been slipped into the wire spine, and from where she stood, she could read the inscription on the pen: Fairhaven Life Center, Offering Health and Hope in Jesus Christ.

She remembered the day her mother had walked into the bedroom for the first time. Hallie had waited for her to curl her lip, roll her eyes, or turn and leave. But she'd simply sat on the bed and asked Hallie about school and her new friend Cara.

Hallie stared at the notebook and the Bible. Then she walked from the room, her feet cold against the wood floor, and closed the door softly behind her.

Mona found a stash of Godiva chocolates on the bedside stand and immediately devoured three, tossing one to her sister before they headed back down the stairs for a quick tour of the house. Thirty minutes later, Ellen was pouring out the details of her business plan as the two of them downed french-dipped sandwiches and club salads at Pekadill's, a restaurant down the street from the bed and breakfast. Mona could feel Ellen's excitement as she described the details.

She was going to open a gift shop on Main Street, and she'd already contacted a real estate agent about locations. She'd offer unique decorative items created from damaged antiques and renovation salvage, as well as artwork and jewelry, and she'd already created a list of items she'd planned to have in inventory before the shop opened.

By the time they'd finished off their lunches with ice cream and climbed back into the truck, Mona's head was spinning, but she was worried. Ellen's concepts were good, but marketing would be the trick. Her sister couldn't possibly understand the challenges of a small-town business where the population could barely support a grocery store. But she put on her most enthusiastic face and kept her reservations to herself.

Their next destination was Wild Flower Furniture Restoration and Antiques, where Ellen managed to chatter her way through a tour of the repair area, stripping, staining, and spraying rooms. No item of jewelry or artwork went unexamined as she made notes about stock, pricing, overhead, and customer preferences in a thick notebook she pulled from her purse. By the time the truck was headed back to town, Mona was thoroughly impressed. In their brief tour at Wild Flower, she'd heard Ellen's excitement build with the response to every question.

"You're like a Rottweiler with a bone. You can't lay this down, can you?"

"I've already designed prototypes, Mona. I've designed one-of-a-kind chandeliers and lamps from antique silver teapots that I've mixed with crystals and jewelry. I'm convinced I can draw a high-end clientele, but I'm planning to test market."

"My Internet presence will be the biggest element of my business. I know foot traffic will be limited in Stewartville, so I have numbers from my investment counselor that give me an idea about how I can leverage technology. I think even Phil might want to get in on the ground floor."

Mona had never expected this. It was obvious that someone at Fairhaven had been giving Ellen excellent advice. "You've put a lot of thought into this, Ellen. I underestimated you."

"Well, don't waste your time feeling guilty. I plan to work you to death in the next forty-eight hours. We start buying with our next stop—mismatched china, broken antiques, salvage pieces, anything we can find. If it looks like it needs to be trashed, I'll take it home and try to figure out what to make out of it. This isn't a total luxury getaway. From the very beginning, I've been planning to make you earn your chocolate, knowing I'll be giving you a reason to look forward to tonight's massage."

Once again, Ellen had deceived her, but this time Mona knew she didn't care. She was finally seeing the Ellen she'd prayed so long would emerge from the shadows.

Adam slid his hammer into the leather strap on his tool belt and stepped back from the counter. It looked even better than he'd hoped. The fit was perfect. It was obvious he'd set it into the exact position it had originally occupied.

Elsie leaned on the door to Mona's office, her arms crossed. She was wearing a red sweatshirt with gold jingle bells sewn all over it, and more than once that day, Adam had wished he'd remembered the earplugs he usually carried in his toolbox. Behind him, Hallie and Cara were seated across from one another at the trestle table, their books and laptop computers strewn across the surface.

"Mona never could stand that pile of plywood we've been usin'. Wasn't tall enough for her. Always gave her a backache. And when she figures out this is the original Hallet counter, I imagine she'll sit up and crow like a rooster. I don't s'pose you were plannin' on our bein' here when she first lays eyes on it?" Elsie's voice was laced with sweetness.

Adam leaned down and pulled a tack cloth from a red tool box on the floor. "No, Ellen agreed to bring Mona home in the evening when the shop is closed and no one's here. I'm sure you heard that last part, Elsie. You, too, girls. No one." Adam busied himself wiping down the front panel but could imagine the girls' eye rolling behind him.

"You know, you old guys have pretty strange ideas about presents, if you ask me. Her first one was a chair. Now after three months, you've finally worked your way up to a counter. I'd think you could come up with something better than hunks of wood. What's next—a hand-carved stump? Hasn't your generation ever heard of clothes, jewelry, maybe even diamonds?"

Adam heard giggling. He shook his head and leaned down to pick up his tool box.

"I'll be back at seven thirty after the shop closes, and none of you women had better be within six blocks of this place. I'm putting Harold in charge of all of you. He'll be directed to hog-tie and gag you if he so much as suspects any trouble." Adam gave the front of the counter a final flick of the rag.

But he knew he was the one in trouble. Harold hadn't been in the shop all day, and he didn't seem to be answering his phone. Adam only hoped that, when Mona came through the door later that night, three pairs of eyes wouldn't be peering through the front window.

The fire radiated deep into the living room, and it seeped into the cracks of Mona's exhaustion and warmed her. She sat on a red leather prairie settle, her legs tucked beneath her and a mug of steaming hot chocolate in her hands. The solitude of the room and fragrances drifting from the kitchen stroked her senses, and she felt her mind and body release to the comfort of the fire and the embrace of the house.

Ellen had run to Pitkin's Pharmacy for one final splurge at the store she'd fallen in love with. Even though they'd been there twice, she couldn't seem to get enough of the place. The store had caught Mona entirely off guard. Who would have thought that a small-town pharmacy would cater to the tastes of Chicago's summer yacht crowd and make a name for itself displaying evening dresses, Wilton silver, hemorrhoid cream, and Crayola crayons all in the same aisle? But Pitkin's Christmas decorations had been the best surprise of all—ten trees scattered throughout the store, all with different themes—everything from a Victorian tree to color-themed trees to an upside-down tree. It was possible that Ellen might be gone for hours and that they might have to strap boxes to the roof of the truck to get home.

And what if Ellen was gone for hours? Mona took a long slug of her hot chocolate. What if she started drinking again? Her sister had already confessed to one bottle stashed at Harold's. What if she was out buying a spare? What was Mona supposed to do if her sister decided to go on a binge? *When* her sister decided to go on a binge? Take the liquor away from her? Give her a lecture? Call in the National Guard? It would be naive to think that Ellen's walk into sobriety would be an easy one—for Ellen, for Hallie, for Harold, for any of them.

Mona leaned back and closed her eyes. The pit of her stomach was clenched tight. Too many conversations had ended in slammed doors and dial tones over the years. It was as if Ellen was standing in the middle of a frozen lake and trying to walk to safety, and no one could see the thickness of the ice or the unseen eddies swirling beneath her. At any moment, she could crash through the surface and carry them all into the icy depths with her.

Mona waited for the footfalls on the porch as the minutes ticked by. Moment by moment, the fire spread its warmth into the room as the stirrings of the house crept into her heart—light, comfort, peace.

Father, help me learn how to love her. Show me how to stand beside her day by day in the struggle. Show me how to pursue her when she runs away and to know when to let her go. Give me the vision to see who she is in You and to call out that vision in her life.

The warmth was seeping from her mug, and Mona took a long sip of her hot chocolate. It had been a long time since she'd thought about who God wanted Ellen to be instead of how frustrated she felt about who Ellen seemed to be. But there were things to be grateful for—things changing in her sister that she wouldn't have dared to hope for a month ago.

Ellen was talking to Hallie more and spouting her opinions less. The angry facade that had been there for years was crumbling. For the first time since Mona could remember, her sister seemed to be pushing toward goals. She was focused—on Hallie, on her own recovery, and on building a future. And for the first time since Mona could remember, Ellen had a dream that hadn't been handed to her by Phil or a girlfriend.

A quiet new force had been birthed in Ellen at Fairhaven, although she hadn't spoken a word about her time there. The only evidence that she'd even been away were Hallie's letters and a dark blue Gideon Bible Mona had spotted tucked away at the bottom of her sister's suitcase.

Laughter and conversation drifted from the direction of the kitchen. Fragments of banter rose and fell, interspersed among the sounds of baking. New guests were scheduled to arrive in the morning. By then, she and Ellen would be back in Stewartville, and they'd all be facing real life again.

Mona leaned forward and placed her mug on the octagonal coffee table in front of her, an intricately cast copper, brass, pewter, and bronze oriental piece that stood out in stark contrast to the Arts-and-Crafts furniture in the rest of the room. Yet it looked as if it had been created to fill its space in front of the leather settle. Mona ran her hand across the surface of the table, soaking in every detail of the scene. A Chinese bride and groom were being prepared for their wedding day. Blessings and gifts were being bestowed by family members in preparation for the ceremony.

Her fingertips traced the face of the bride, then the groom as the sound of laughter drifted from the kitchen. She thought of Harold, Elsie, Hallie, and Adam, even Miss Emily. Sometimes the things that never quite fit the spaces of life were the very things that made them home.

A quiet yearning swelled in her. More than anything, she needed Stewartville—to be in the place where she'd never quite fit, the place that had given her a home when she was broken. The place where Ellen and Hallie could find the same gifts.

The metal felt cold beneath her fingers as a phone call from Elsie earlier in the day replayed in her mind.

"Sad news. Glenda Simpson passed today. She'd been sick for months and laid up at home. Word at Trina's is that her husband plans to put down that crazy cat of hers now that she's finally gone. He always hated the thing."

Miss Emily. Another one of God's broken things.

Beyond the dining room, Mona heard the sound of the side door opening. Ellen was back.

It was time for both of them to begin the starting over and go home. It was time to see Adam.

Chapter Twenty-two

The mantle clock on the barrister bookcase near the front door sounded eight o'clock, and Harold counted the chimes one by one. In spite of the fact that they'd never had the luxury of a mantle, Minnie had given him the clock on their tenth anniversary. His wife had always been a woman of dreams, and Lynn had been just like her. They'd both believed God had hung the moon in the sky because people needed beauty beyond what they could touch to give them hope and dreams. Minnie had found that beauty in God, even after the cancer had come. Harold wasn't sure that Lynn had ever found it.

He pulled the cream afghan higher around his shoulders, then toyed with the top button of his navy buffalo plaid shirt as the pain pounded through his head. Perhaps just this once he could loosen it, but then everyone would be certain to sit up and take notice. No matter what happened in politics, religion, or world affairs, Harold's top button had always remained buttoned, and he wasn't about to stir the pot now.

But he knew he couldn't go on like this forever. So far, he'd seen a few questioning looks, the wheels turning in people's minds when he stumbled or when the words wouldn't come. But he'd always kept his thoughts and his feelings to himself, and his friends had always respected that. Old men get sick. They get Parkinson's.

They get tired and run out of steam. There were plenty of reasons he could be slowing down. And if he'd chosen to keep his affairs private, they were his reasons, held close to the chest like they'd always been.

Ellen would be arriving soon, and he'd probably have to chain her to the furnace to keep her from sneaking back to the shop to check on Mona. Just remembering her tone as she'd called from Pitkin's made him smile. She'd worked a scam on her sister, and she liked it. The woman was a pistol, he had to admit. She'd pulled one over on Mona with the excuse she was heading out one last time to shop, but she'd called Harold the minute she'd been out of Mona's sight. Had Adam arrived at the antique shop yet? Was everything in place, and were the decorations exactly the way she'd wanted them arranged?

Harold gave his collar one more tug and slid his hand under the blanket as he closed his eyes. He'd dutifully reported to Ellen that everything was on schedule. Elsie and Hallie had filled the shop with cinnamon-scented Christmas candles and strung garland just the way they'd been directed. They'd decorated the trestle table for dinner for two with the china, linens, candlesticks, and silver service Ellen had stowed in a box under Harold's workbench. And by the stroke of seven, Harold had shooed a reluctant Elsie and Hallie from the store with strict instructions that Hallie be delivered to Cara's for Bible study. Then he'd given the final warning before he'd headed home for a nap and two of Fred Bailey's pain pills.

"Leave 'em be, ladies. No sneaking back and peeking. I've already called Joe Spencer and told him if he sees so much as your shadows on Main Street, he's to pick you up and lock you in the clink for the night."

Harold waited for the arc of the headlights to fall across his closed lids as he lay in the silence of the room. It would be soon. The pain in his head was escalating. A file folder lay on the carpet at his side with John Curtis's name printed neatly along the tab. Ellen had promised she'd be on time. They'd need at least a full hour before Hallie returned from Cara's, if she agreed to everything he had planned.

And if she didn't?

He refused to think about the possibility. By the time Hallie came home, her mother would be playing the piano, and he'd be resting, right where he lay. It would be later, maybe days, maybe years, that Hallie would realize the evening had been a rehearsal and that he'd made her mother his partner in his plans. Ellen would be the first to know. He was asking her to bear it with him, as hard as it would be. He was asking her for a sacrifice, he knew, and he had no right to ask.

The afghan rose and fell with the rhythm of his breathing. It would be important to give her time to think. She'd be angry if she felt ambushed by any of it. He was asking her to bear another burden, and he knew what he was asking wasn't fair, but it was what would be best for all of them in the end. He could only ask, knowing she still might refuse and walk away.

His breathing came in shallow puffs. It had taken all his strength to pull the storage container from beneath the bed, to find the sheet music, then to slide the box back into place. He hadn't held Lynn's senior recital piece since the day he'd stored it away—the last music he'd heard her play before she'd left. He'd slid it into the file on top of the order of service before he'd laid down to rest. The sweeping font of the words stood out in bold black against the yellowed paper: "The Heart Knows."

Ellen's song for Hallie. The music Lynn had loved. God wasted nothing—a prayer, a word, a chord of melody.

Tires crunched against the brittle snow, and he opened his eyes. She was home. He sat up slowly and began folding the afghan in neat creases.

It was time.

It was obvious to Mona that Ellen's meltdown had finally arrived.

The moment they'd pulled away from Cocoa Cottage, the first signs had set in—glancing at her watch repeatedly, drumming her fingers on the steering wheel, refusing to stop for supper when Mona pleaded for food. The need for a drink had apparently caught up with her. She chattered on about everything and nothing—about where she could sign up for working out, how her lawyer could negotiate a deal to get the Corvette out of impound, about Katrina Newberry's ideas for a store location and her plans to rent the Bloomfield Hills house to one of Phil's lawyer friends for a few years while the real estate market rebounded.

By the time Mona recognized the faint glow of the Stewartville Regional Correctional Facility on the horizon, she was certain she'd survived a hostage experience in her own truck. But no matter how much she longed for the silence of her apartment, she knew she couldn't head home without making one final stop. Her greatest fear was that she might already be too late.

"Turn left at the bank. I've got to do one quick errand before you drop me off at the shop."

Ellen glanced at her watch. "Don't be ridiculous. Anything that needs to be done can wait until morning. Right now, you need to get home and rest." Her voice was irritated.

"It will only take a second. Less than five minutes."

Ellen tapped her manicured nails on the steering wheel. "What's so important that you have to do it this instant? It's nearly eight. This is ridiculous." She swung the wheel sharply to the left, and Mona motioned her down the street and into the driveway of a two-story house with a large bay window. Ellen slammed the truck into park and threw her arms across her chest.

Before she could catch herself, the words tumbled out of Mona. "What is your problem? Is it the bottle in Harold's basement? Because we can be there in three minutes, and I can pour it down the sink and that will take care of things for as long as I'm standing next to you. But I'll be out of the house in five minutes, and you'll be on your own. What's your plan going to be then?"

Ellen stared straight ahead.

"Is that what's bothering you, Ellen? Do you need a drink?"

"No, that is *not* what's bothering me, you idiot. For once in your life, you don't have a clue what you're talking about, so just shut up."

"Then tell me."

"I will not. And you're not going back to Harold's with me. I'll pour my own booze down the drain without your help, thank you. Tonight you're going your way and I'm going mine, and in the morning we'll see who owes who the apology."

Mona knew the tone and the wall behind it. She opened the door and stepped into the night. Then she pulled a large empty box from beneath a tarp in the bed of the truck and walked toward the front door of Glenda Simpson's house.

The red oak glowed with a soft burnish in the gleaming flicker of the candles Elsie and Hallie had strategically placed on the counter and throughout the shop. Adam surveyed it with pride from where he stood behind a large Victorian wardrobe near the stairs to the loft. It was one of the few pieces of furniture in the shop that would conceal his tall frame and still give him a view of Mona as she walked through the front door and caught her first glimpse of the counter.

He'd created and recreated the scene in his mind a hundred times over the past two days as he'd worked to install the piece. For months, he'd anticipated her reaction. He'd imagined her confusion at first, then recognition as he stepped from the shadows, and finally disbelief as he revealed the details—that her gift was the original counter from the Hallet Building and that he'd worked to make sure it found its way home.

She had to love it. He was counting on it.

Adam scanned the room one last time. The trestle table was set to Ellen's specifications. An arrangement of antique roses graced the center, interlaced with pearls, crystals, and ribbons of heritage lace and satin. She'd selected dinnerware in shades of burgundy and gold, each piece chosen from a different pattern and blending in a subtle burst of color. The table was draped in layers of gold and cream linen and lace, and antique rose and hyacinth petals had been scattered among the gold-plated serving dishes.

Dinner was warmed and waiting to be brought down from the apartment above—dishes he'd prepared himself earlier in the day and had brought over in the Suburban. Oscar was stashed at Jessica's, and Elsie and Hallie had been forced to swear upon a fifteen-pound, antique family Bible that they wouldn't come within a half mile of the shop until morning. The plan couldn't have come together more perfectly, and he couldn't possibly have pulled it off without Ellen's help.

Through the window, he spotted the glow of headlights. Ellen had been told to drop Mona off at the front door and explain that she needed the truck in the morning to run an errand. It was the only way he could be certain Mona would come through the front door and get the full impact of the counter. He slipped behind the wardrobe as he heard the sound of the front door opening, then the thud of a suitcase being dropped inside.

"I'll get the box, Ellen."

"You know you're a total idiot, don't you?"

"Of course. That's what you've always told me."

Ellen's voice dropped to a whisper amid the sound of rustling. "You know, you're just plain weird, and sooner or later, Adam's going to figure that out and you're going to scare him right into some other woman's arms.

"I'd help you drag your stuff up to your apartment, but according to you, I've got a date with a vodka bottle, so I've got to be running. I'll catch you tomorrow."

"That is *not* funny, Ellen!"

The bells on the door jingled as it thumped shut, and for a moment, Adam heard only silence. He counted to ten before he peered to one side of the wardrobe. Mona was kneeling on the floor with her back to him, her arms deep in a large box. He waited as she rose slowly and turned toward the back of the shop.

It was there, all he'd worked for—the look of confusion as she hurried toward the soft glow of the candles, then the sweep of her eyes across the length of the counter as she took in the carved detail of the acanthus leaves and the polished luster of the burnished wood, and finally the smile of delight.

He stepped out from behind the wardrobe and spoke softly. "It's been waiting to come home for a long time. It was made for that spot, designed for that exact location in the Hallet Building in 1891. She's beautiful, and now she's exactly where her creator always meant her to be. Merry Christmas, Mona."

She turned, and he saw a flush of color wash over her cheeks as she moved toward him. Her arms went around him to his shoulders, and she held him tightly as she buried her face in his neck, the soft spikes of her short hair teasing his face.

"I never could have dreamed of a more perfect gift. I can't imagine how you found it or even thought to do something like this for me. You always know exactly what I love."

She drew back and looked into his eyes. He saw the openness there he'd been praying for.

"Adam, why after all this time would you do this for me?"

He cradled her face in his hands, and he knew the time was right. "Because I love you fiercely, devotedly, totally, and I couldn't live another week without telling you."

"And you made Hallie and Ellen and Elsie and Harold a part of this?"

"They were all a part of it. Elsie and Hallie will never forgive me for not allowing them to be here right now. But Ellen understood. She fought for every detail to be perfect."

Mona shook her head as she pulled away. "Oh, no. I really blew it. The last thing I did tonight was insult her, and all she was doing was trying to help get me here." Adam's impulse was to reach out and draw her back, but her eyes told him she needed to speak.

"That's been my pattern lately. Messing things up, blaming

everyone else. Adam, I've been running away from my own brokenness and fears, my fear to love a man fiercely, devotedly, totally.

"Whether or not I wanted to admit it, I was angry and bitter after my accident. I let my battered body and my complicated life define who I was. I let myself believe I was damaged goods."

Mona turned away and stepped toward the counter. She rested her hands on the surface and stroked the grain of the wood. "From the day we spoke at the Prayer Tower, I felt a bond with you. I wanted to believe I was made for you, that God designed me to be in your arms. But I felt like my life and my body with all their complications and imperfections disqualified me."

Everything in Adam told him to move toward her, to pull her into his arms, but he stood his ground. "And what do you believe now?"

He waited as she walked to the front door and lifted the cardboard box from the floor, then walked back and set it on the counter between the two of them. The flush on her face had faded, and she gripped the box tightly.

"In the past three months, you've probably come to realize that there are things I clearly am and things I clearly am not. I walk a little crooked, and if you ask me to dance, I most likely will fall down. My skull looks like a roadmap, and some days I can't remember who's president. I can't cook, but I'm willing to try if you're brave enough to eat it. On the plus side, I'm a savvy business owner, a biker chick, and I'm passionately committed to becoming the woman God created me to be, even when I know I sometimes mess things up. But I need you to know that I'm fiercely, devotedly, totally in love with you, Adam Dean, even though I've messed that up, too."

She reached into the box, and Adam heard the sound of

scratching as Mona cooed soft sounds into the dark recess. The box tilted to one side, then righted itself, and Mona drew back. In her arms she held a cat, its tail and legs skewed as it struggled for freedom. She set it on the counter, and it leaped to the floor, scrabbled through the door, and disappeared into the back room.

"That," Mona announced, "is Miss Emily. She walks a little crooked, and her eyes occasionally point in opposite directions due to a brief and tragic tumble on permanent press in a Kenmore dryer. She can be a bit unpredictable at times, rather ornery, really. I think it's fair to say God gave her a second chance when she didn't deserve one."

Adam moved toward Mona and pulled her into his arms. "I suggest that the best possible future for Miss Emily is for me to take her home and love her, as wacky as she may be."

Mona drew herself further into his embrace, and he held her there.

"Will you be my wife, Mona?"

The words were muffled against his chest, and he felt her tears as he stroked her hair in the dim glow of the candlelight.

"Yes, Adam. What took you so long to ask?"

But even in that moment, he saw a shadow pass over her face, and he knew she was thinking of Ellen and of Hallie and how, together, they would weave the strands that would bind them to the future.

Chapter Twenty-three

Just when Ellen thought she might be finding the strength to stand on her own two feet again with the help of a God who seemed ready to listen and forgive stumblers and sinners, she'd been shoved back to her knees. If she'd predicted anyone's hand would have pushed her there, she would have guessed it to be Phil's or maybe Hallie's. But she would have been wrong.

She would never have expected Harold's gentle touch to have slammed her to the floor.

She pondered the thought as she sat in the darkness at his kitchen table in the predawn hours.

And who would have thought she would even have cared about an old man, other than a flash of obligatory sadness about the inevitabilities of life? But unexpected sorrow had flooded over her in a torrent with his request, and suddenly she had been standing like a child before her father again.

She'd tried pleading. He had no right to ask her. He was selfish, and she refused to help. She was hours out of rehab, and no one had a right to expect anything of her. She was on the verge of disintegration herself and had nothing to give to anyone. Nothing.

And then she'd collapsed in his arms, not knowing if she'd ever have the strength to stand again, ashamed to pour out her weakness on a man she barely knew and who needed her more than she needed him. But even as she thought the words, she knew she was wrong. She would find strength in his pain that would be her own and yet not her own, and Harold had known it.

When her tears came, they were tears for Stacy and Phil and her father and Lynn and Minnie and for all the pain she knew she'd never understand. But beneath the grief, peace beckoned in gentle whispers.

She'd repeated her refusal over and over until it became a mantra and the meaning had gone out of it and they both knew it. She'd asked why, and he'd said simply that he saw the spark of his daughter in her.

She never said yes, but her hand had moved to his, and she had felt the strength drain from his fingers and into hers, and she had known that in that instant he had given in to his fight and was moving on.

Somewhere in the haze of time before Hallie came home, she moved from his side to the piano and placed her hands upon the keys. She began with a favorite hymn of her mother's. Her fingers stumbled as the tears came with the memories of lessons and laughter and the sight of her mother's head bent in prayer over an open Bible. The memories drifted over her, one by one, as she played, and the words of the verses mingled with the letters of the past months pressed into her heart.

She'd carried his secret in the days that followed. He slept longer and asked more frequently for his pills. Her music became his lifeblood, and in the hours while Hallie was gone, Ellen returned to the piano again and again. In the blur of the late-night hours, she'd slipped to the basement to find release from the pain in the bottle she'd hidden there.

For the first three days, she'd risen early and tried to convince herself that if she stared at his door she had the power each day to wake him. But as his sleeping had increased, the kitchen clock had slowly worn her down, and by the fourth day, she'd turned her back to it. She didn't want to think about time. It had become her enemy, like the bottle or hours of silence or the night.

Ellen sat at the chipped Formica table and waited for the sounds of his waking. A draft stirred around her ankles, and she drew her feet to the rungs of the chair. The floor was cold. It was always cold in this house. The wind fairly billowed through her windows at night. She made a mental note to add slippers and thick socks to the list of gifts she planned to buy for him. An old man shouldn't have to live in a drafty house.

She ticked off the days on her fingers—just three days left to finish Christmas shopping, and she'd barely made a dent. One way or another, she had to find time to get to Grand Rapids. She could feel the panic rising in her chest. She knew she couldn't handle a road trip. Not now. Maybe Debbi Cunningham could help her. Debbi had called half a dozen times since she and her husband had visited Ellen in the hospital. Or maybe Elsie's daughter Jessica could help if she could just organize her thoughts long enough to make a list.

She reached for the notebook that sat in the center of the table beneath Harold's Bible and flipped it open. Her eyes scanned names and notations as she thumbed for an empty page. She spotted her name and her eyes froze. It was followed by a Bible verse, then Hallie's name and another verse.

Her finger traced the writing, then flipped ahead.

Dozens of entries and names filled the pages. She turned to the date of her hospital release.

For Ellen, Psalm 65:8: "Where morning dawns and evening fades you call forth songs of joy." *Precious child, my prayer is that you find the joy God longs for you to know and that you be restored in body, mind, and spirit.*

The penmanship was familiar, written in the neat, flowing script of the notes she'd been saving for nearly four months.

The sounds of movement stirred in the basement, and she quickly closed the notebook and shoved it back into the center of the table beneath the Bible. Stairs creaked, and the basement door suddenly flew open, and Hallie stepped into the room wearing a Stewartville Antiques T-shirt over gray sweatpants. In the dim kitchen light, Ellen could see that she was carrying a small boxy object that she quickly shoved behind her back.

"What are you doing up? Spying on me?"

Ellen pulled her hands away from the center of the table. "And what are you doing in the basement at this hour of the morning?"

"None of your business. But it looks to me like you've been snooping and reading Harold's prayer journal."

"How do you know it's Harold's prayer journal unless you've read it yourself?"

"You didn't answer my question. But, hey, I'm a teenager. I'm supposed to be nosy. You're an adult, and you're supposed to set the example. Put those two thoughts together and you might want to think about getting the bottle of vodka out of the basement." Hallie turned toward the living room.

"Stop! Please stop. Hallie, can we talk for just one minute? Go put down whatever you're trying to hide, just please don't walk away."

Ellen held her breath as Hallie stared into the living room, then turned and stepped back into the kitchen. She pulled a small wooden birdhouse from behind her back, set it on the table, then pulled out a chair across from her mother and sat down. The birdhouse had been painted the faintest wash of yellow, and tiny green shingles had been glued on the roof.

"It's your Christmas present. It was Harold's idea for me to make it myself. I guess it's pretty obvious that it's not exactly perfect—kind of like me . . . and you . . . and the way life has gone for us. At first it kind of looked like a box of chopsticks that got caught in a windstorm, and then Harold showed me I couldn't give up just because it was hard and wasn't going to turn out looking like something in a magazine.

"When I started building it, I thought it was just Harold's way of trying to keep me out of trouble, but after a few days, I realized he'd tricked me into thinking about you when I was trying so hard to forget about you. The day I drove you to Stewartville, I'd decided I was finished with you. I told myself I was done forgiving you for all the times you'd hurt me and were going to hurt me again. But a little at a time, God's changed my mind."

"Changed your mind . . . about me. How?"

"Nothing that would light up a movie screen. A lot of little things—people, prayers, letters."

Ellen hadn't been able to take her eyes off her daughter as she spoke. She searched for words that could somehow convey the enormity of the shame and failure that clawed at her—something profound or memorable or sincere enough to express the flood of remorse coursing through her, but she knew nothing she could say could measure up to the pain she'd inflicted on her daughter.

"I'm asking you to forgive me for my bitterness, Mom. If I can't forgive what I've been forgiven, I might as well grab a bottle of vodka, too. Either I'm in or I'm out with this faith thing. Either I figure out how to die to myself and live the life Jesus promised to give me, or I walk back into the mess I came from."

The words in Harold's journal echoed through Ellen's thoughts. Was this what it meant to know joy—to lose a sister and a father and to sit beneath a mother's steady gush of anger and yet speak of forgiveness?

The early morning light settled over them as they sat together and waited for Harold to stir. The hands of the clock moved to six thirty, then seven. With each passing moment, Ellen grew more fearful. At one minute past seven she forced herself to rise and slip quietly down the hallway and into the back bedroom.

In a moment she returned, choosing a seat beside Hallie and taking her hand in her own, the birdhouse resting beside them on Harold's Bible as she called 911. They sat alone in the kitchen, crying together for nearly an hour before they dialed Mona's number.

Later on, Mona decided that caller ID can be a cruel thing. She'd expected to hear Harold's voice when the phone rang at 8:05. She'd never thought it would be Ellen, quiet and in control, announcing that Harold had fallen into a coma and was being taken to the hospital.

"He has a brain tumor, Mona. He's had it for months and decided not to treat it. He didn't want anyone to know."

"A brain tumor? He didn't want anyone to know, and he told you?"

"I've been helping him."

"Helping him do what?"

"Helping him get ready. To die."

"What are you talking about? Harold has gout, he's old and takes pills, he walks with a cane, he . . . he . . . he . . ."

"Get your things together and get to the hospital, Mona. Hallie and I are leaving with the ambulance right now."

Mona hung up the phone. In seconds, her finger hit Adam's speed-dial number. She knew, as he answered and the sound of his voice enveloped her, that she did not want to walk through this or anything else in life without him at her side. Within two hours, he was there.

Somewhere between lunch and supper the first day, the second blow came—the call from Dr. Bailey's office with preliminary results of her MRI as she sat at Harold's side, her hand clasped in Adam's.

MRI normal, but suspicion of TIAs. Further testing and consultation requested as soon as possible. Concerns for risk of future stroke. The reality swirled through her head as she watched Harold's inert form on the bed in front of her.

For three days, she sat vigil in Harold's hospital room with the people she loved most—Adam, Ellen and Hallie, and Elsie and rotating members of the McFeeney family. For three days, she rehearsed the frailties of her body, mind, and spirit as she traced the lines in Harold's face, the frame she now recognized to be gaunt and wasting. How had she missed it? How had she been so blind to a loved one slipping away right before her eyes?

For three days, Harold clung to life, until, with an impeccable sense of timing, he left them all behind on Christmas Day.

Harold had demanded there be no funeral. For a man who'd lived his life holding his opinions close to the chest, he'd made a final rally at the end in a carefully worded letter that articulated his wishes.

His service was to be a graduation ceremony, because, dear brothers and sisters, he was not gone, simply gone ahead. There were to be no flowers, no casket, and no silly video presentation of him in his grain elevator cap or biting into a chicken leg at the last church picnic. If people couldn't come up with their own good memories of him, they were out of luck. There would be no carrying on with an open microphone and people giving emotional tributes. Pastor Cunningham would deliver the message, and Mona would read the Scripture. It would be a special favor to him if Elsie would speak a few words. And there would be music— lots of good old gospel hymns and the church youth band singing a few contemporary numbers with drums and guitars to get feet stomping and the old folks focusing on passing the baton to the next generation.

And the final piece in the service was to be Lynn's song, "The Heart Knows." He'd loved it best because it had been her favorite. Ellen was to play it, and Hallie was to sit beside her mother flipping pages, even if pages didn't need flipping. And when it was over, Ellen was to play her three favorite up-tempo pieces as people filed out to help hustle them down to the dinner in the basement. Jazz seemed like a good choice for foot-stompin' praise and maybe would take the heat off the praise band's choice of music and let folks talk about the wild ways of an old dead man for a few months.

Gilda McNally was to be asked to please take her pistachio pudding off the funeral dinner menu. He had always hated pistachio pudding and couldn't bear the thought of people chatting about his departure to Glory over green gooey plates.

His letter had apologized for all the pounding in the shop in recent weeks, but there had been no other way around it. John

Curtis had been advised to place all necessary calls within twenty-four hours of his service, and he would make certain that Harold's additional wishes would be communicated to everyone.

When Elsie had read her copy of the letter, she announced to her family that apparently brain tumors also put a little starch in your shorts, since it would have taken the Harold she knew twenty years to put together a list of orders like that. Then she'd walked up the stairs to her bedroom, slammed her door, and had not come down until the following morning.

Mona had asked Adam to take her to the church early so they could talk. She hadn't found time in the days of preparation for Harold's service to tell him how she felt about the call from Dr. Bailey's office, but she wanted to talk before the crowd arrived. She wanted Adam with her at the appointment, and she wanted to ask him in the quiet of the church, where they could pray together away from the busyness of the shop. He'd driven over early with home-baked muffins from Aunt Florence and a casserole for the dinner. They'd eaten the muffins together at the trestle table before driving to the church through a light powder of falling snow, then sat together in a puddle of light cascading from a southerly, stained-glass window.

The pews of Stewartville Community Church filled quickly for the mid-morning service, and Mona watched as people spilled out into the foyer and down the stairs into the basement as the crowd grew. Hallie and Ellen arrived fifteen minutes before the service began and chose seats on the front pew, left side, where they could slip easily to the bench of the piano as the service dismissed. Adam and Mona sat side-by-side in the pew behind them. Hallie's eyes were red and puffy, and Mona watched as Ellen slid her arm behind her daughter and gently stroked a shoulder.

Elsie stood ramrod straight as she delivered the eulogy, and not a soul stirred as her voice carried into the hallway and down the stairwell. She kept it brief. Harold had wanted little said of himself and much said of God. But the light in her eyes shone with something more than grief. Mona searched Elsie's face and saw devotion there, admiration, and love. Grief had cracked open a door and let something slip out that had been locked inside. Mona glanced around the room and wondered if others saw the passion that spilled out. Dear God, Elsie had loved him. All these years she'd worked beside Harold, and she'd loved him. Had he known it? She felt the warmth of Adam's hand clasped in her own, and tears came.

It was Mona's turn. Adam squeezed her hand, and she rose and moved toward the platform. Somehow she forced herself to focus through her tears. The Scripture passage Harold had chosen was from Psalm 65, about God's abundant provision for his people and gifts of joy.

The words resonated through her brain as she read them. *Gifts of joy.* From a simple man who'd never known wealth or influence or power but had poured gifts on everyone around him. Her legs shook as she moved back toward Adam.

Pastor Cunningham spoke, his words rising and falling as images of Harold's life scrolled through Mona's mind. Always working. Always stepping aside for others, even in death. A man after God's own heart.

With Pastor Cunningham's final words, Mona watched Hallie and Ellen move to the piano as one and settle themselves. Hallie sat quietly, not stirring the pages as her mother's hands hovered briefly, then dropped to the black and white keys, flowing from one movement to another. Mona knew what Hallie knew—the score wasn't needed. Ellen trusted what was in her heart, what had been given to her by her mother and Harold and Fairhaven and that she would pass on to Hallie. She watched as the music lifted Ellen and the daughter beside her; drew them into the pain of their memories, separate and shared; and swept them into a story of tragedy and hope. She could see her sister's muscles tighten and draw as she embodied the memories of a child sitting on her mother's lap as her fingers caressed the keys.

Ellen's fingers moved easily, and memories of Mona's mother spun through the air and linked mother, daughter, sister, and niece as the music rose and fell and entwined them all. Grief poured out in the strains, an agony of pain and searching. And in the end, in one final progression of chords and resolution of dissonance, the notes converged in one final strain. Joy.

"The Heart Knows."

Mona listened and heard the beat of past, present, and future that embraced them all. She closed her eyes as she felt the steady pulse of life in Adam's fingers. She felt the pulse of life in the music as it filled the room, the throb of her mother's heart, of Harold's, of Ellen's. The song embraced them—a song of joy beyond the pain. Harold had heard its strains in each of their lives and had stirred it in them, even in his death. A song of joy. The gift of his heart to theirs.

Chapter Twenty-four

Mona sat across the table from Adam at Red's on the River in Rockford as he gripped her hand lightly across the white linen tablecloth and leaned toward her. His white oxford cloth shirt lay crisp beneath a navy linen jacket he'd pulled from the back seat of the Suburban and slid over his broad shoulders. A surge of wonder pulsed through her. To think that God had brought her to this stunning man with gentle eyes in spite of her short-sightedness and skepticism and stubbornness.

"I suddenly feel underdressed. I thought we'd be stopping for a burger on the way home. This is too much, Adam."

"You deserve something special tonight, Mona. I thought this might be a hard day for you." He gestured to the linen-topped tables, open fireplace, and view of the Rogue River through the wall of glass on the west side of the restaurant. "What do you think?"

Mona looked past the stone promenade where outdoor tables and chairs were clustered along the walkway to the curtain of trees that lined the river. Gratitude flooded over her for the serenity of their surroundings.

"It's lovely. And you're right. I was dreading today's appointment. But it means everything to me that you were with me. I'd avoided facing Dr. Bailey for a long time. I thought that if I never had to hear him speak anything negative to me out loud, I could control what was happening.

"Then one day Harold was smiling at all of us with that funny grin he's been wearing for the past few months, and the next day he was in the hospital, and suddenly God reminded me that I don't control anything in my world. It was too much when that same afternoon Dr. Bailey called to tell me he suspected I might be having TIAs and he was worried my brain was warming up for a stroke. For those next few days, I looked into Harold's face and I thought about how close I'd come to dying the day I was swept onto the rocks on the pier and about the second chance I'd been given. My friend was dying, and I'd fought so hard to recover from my accident, only to have someone tell me I could lose it all again . . . it just seemed like too much.

"And I felt guilty thinking about myself while I sat at Harold's side, realizing he was slipping away. Then I'd hear his voice in my head telling me soon he was going to be better than he'd ever been in this life and that I needed to take care of myself and get on with what God still had ahead for me."

Adam tightened his grip and leaned forward. "Harold knew what he was facing and made his decision. He knew his glioblastoma was aggressive, and he refused treatment that could be as deadly as the cancer itself. He chose to shorten his stay with us by a few months because he knew the price of the struggle.

"But you're facing a different picture, Mona. We're fighting for your long-term health, and you're going to have to work harder than most people. You saw Dr. Bailey's face. This is serious. You're going to have to stay on blood thinners and track your migraines and neurological symptoms. We're going to schedule the follow-up tests he suggested. And we're going to make sure you're watching your diet and exercising. No more extra butter at the movies, Miss VanderMolen. For purely selfish motives, I plan to keep you around for a good, long time."

Mona smiled. "Selfish motives? I think I like the sound of that."

"Yes. We'll discuss those later. Right now, I'm instituting the beginning of our collaborative plan. For starters, we're going to work together on the list you've made for cleaning out Harold's house. We'll sort through one room at a time. I'll do the grunt work while you sit and order me around. I've got the church youth group lined up to pick things up on Fridays from Harold's garage to cart them off to be sold on eBay. They're working on a fundraiser to build a church in Mexico this summer. Seems that Harold already knew that and wanted funds to go to that project. He had that covered in his file."

"It appears you're getting a bit bossy, Adam. And what if I don't agree with your plan?" Mona tossed her head playfully and waited for his response.

"Then we'd have to negotiate. I would be willing to consider making certain concessions, based upon concessions on your part."

"I see. And what would those concessions include?"

"Well, the first would be a kiss, of course."

Mona felt her face flush red, as a plump and slightly balding young waiter moved to their table and presented their menus with a nod. Adam waved him away.

"I'm sorry, young man, your timing is off just a bit. This lovely young woman was just getting ready to kiss me."

Mona's head jerked up, and she swatted Adam's hand across the table. "Adam!"

The waiter muttered an excuse and prepared to step away, but Adam caught his arm.

"Just one minute. I'd appreciate a little moral support here. The lady can hardly refuse me, don't you think? After all, we are engaged. Show him your ring, Mona."

"Adam! What do you think you're doing?" She felt the blood surging to her head, but he pressed on.

"You know, she seems to be a little reluctant about the kissing thing, don't you think? And I guess I can hardly blame her. Here we are engaged to be married, and I've never given her a ring. You'd think I'd be more of a gentleman than that. I don't imagine you have one up your sleeve do you, young man?"

The waiter broke into a sudden smile, unbuttoned the cuff of his shirt sleeve, withdrew a small black satin box, and handed it to Adam. "Here you go, sir. Congratulations, ma'am." He nodded and backed away from the table as Mona stared at the box in Adam's hand. Suddenly she felt the blood draining from her face.

"What have you done, Adam Dean?" Mona's hands suddenly gripped her long-stemmed water glass, and they began to shake.

He smiled. "Once again, I have been in cahoots with your sister. Open the box, Mona." He reached slowly across the table and placed it in her hands.

From her peripheral vision, Mona realized that the eyes of dozens of people in the restaurant were on her as she slowly drew back the lid of the small black box. Her heart was pounding, and for a moment she was certain she could hear the sound of her blood rushing through her ears.

She gasped, and her eyes filled with disbelief, then with tears.

"My mother's engagement ring!" She pulled the ring from the box and stroked the stone lightly. "Where did you get it? How did you get it?" She raised her head, and Adam's eyes caught hers and held them.

"Will you accept it as if it were mine to give to you, Mona? Ellen came to me a week after Harold's funeral and gave the ring to me. She thought it should be yours. She believed it would mean more to you than any other ring, and I agreed."

The tears flowed down Mona's face, and she knew her mascara would leave streaks of black where the droplets dripped onto the linen. She didn't care.

"Of course I'll accept it. It's perfect. You're perfect. My sister is perfect. Hallie is perfect, except that we're all really a mess, but God loves all of us anyway, and isn't that perfect? Welcome to the mess of my life, Adam. I love you. Now about that kiss . . ."

He slid the ring on her finger, and then his hands cupped her face and drew it to his own. And somewhere in the distance Mona heard the sound of applause as Adam's lips met hers.

A week later, Ellen told Mona about the drinking.

She couldn't handle it on her own right now. Too much had happened too quickly. She was alone too much in a big old house that reminded her of Harold and the wife he'd lost and the daughter he'd lost. Maybe life was about losing people after all. Hallie was gone most of the time, and Phil was never coming back. She'd grieved for too many people, and she needed to go back to Fairhaven, just for a while. She'd already called, and a program was starting in three days. Debbi Cunningham had agreed to drive her down. She was the one woman besides Mona who'd been willing to listen to a drunk these past few weeks. Debbi was even talking about starting a faith-based program at their church for people struggling with addictions. It helped that her sister worked at Fairhaven and could give a start-up group some direction, and maybe if Ellen came back from Fairhaven strong enough, a program like the one at church would be the extra hand she'd need. And maybe people in Stewartville, Greenville, Alma, Middleton, and Stanton could use an accountability group, too.

Mona looked into her sister's eyes as they'd sat together on Harold's Herculon couch and known her sister was right.

Ellen had to leave again.

She couldn't control her drinking, and she'd been asking for help in her own way for weeks. Meeting with Debbi and asking Mona to come sit with her sister late at night wasn't enough. They would never be enough.

Mona knew Ellen was scared, but this time there were no excuses. She was talking about her problem and what she had to do about it.

They'd packed up the few things she'd need, and she'd made her explanation to Hallie early one Saturday morning at breakfast before Debbi came to pick her up, just before Mona moved her own things into Ellen's bedroom. Hallie had kissed her mother quickly and told her she loved her, then headed out the door. Mona wasn't sure where she'd gone, but she hadn't come home until well after supper time.

What started as a rough couple of weeks stretched into a tedious succession of months. Ellen hadn't wanted visitors, and Hallie seemed content to comply. She struggled with her focus in school, and her grades slipped. And Adam and Mona couldn't help but notice Hallie's more frequent slamming of doors as they dove into the task of cleaning out Harold's house—sorting through his personal items, cleaning out closets, the attic, and the storage areas in the basement. For a few months, while the renovations at the shop were at their peak, Mona and Hallie moved into Harold's house. It was spring when Mona moved back to the loft and Ellen returned.

Throughout the long winter, Adam was Mona's only constant, a quiet presence who spoke to her fears, drew them out, and helped her to face them time and time again. His presence became her lifeline. The weekend after Harold's death, he began staying in the Cunningham's basement on weekends, staunchly sitting each Sunday in a row of women—Mona, Ellen, Hallie, Cara, and Elsie.

Mona felt the first stirrings of hope again as the hard-packed, barren earth of winter gave way to spring. In the first glimmering light of the predawn hours, she sat with Hallie at Harold's kitchen table, his Bible and the curled pages of his journal before her, and her prayers changed—no longer pleas for what God should be doing, but praise for what God had already done, was doing, and promised to do.

In those moments, Mona's eyes began to open to new gifts that had surrounded her all along—even the gifts of sorrow and pain— and she found thanks even for the tears.

Chapter Twenty-five

Halfway through her morning walk on the streets of Stewartville, Mona VanderMolen made her final decision to run away with Miss Emily. To run away from Adam, from Ellen, from Hallie, from the constant pull of decisions. What she needed most was peace, and at this moment of her life, she was not going to find it in Stewartville. But she knew exactly where she could find it.

She'd pondered her decision as she made her ninth lap around the block north of the antique shop. By the time she'd hit lap ten, her cell phone was in her hand and she'd hit speed dial. Two phone calls and ninety minutes later, she'd slipped into the alley with a writhing Miss Emily slung under her arm and slid into the seat of Ellen's red Corvette. If it was going to be all-or-nothing, she might as well make it good.

Sixty miles passed before her actions finally sank in. She could hardly believe she'd had the nerve to leave them all behind. Hallie had thrown a fit and begged Mona to let her go with her, but Ellen had refused, and Hallie had finally stormed out the front door of the shop, the door slamming in her wake. Even as she watched Hallie disappear up Main Street, Mona knew it was best for all of them. It was time to push the child into the arms of her mother and step out of the way. God would help them figure out how to take it from here.

The open road and solitude beckoned. Mona headed west along M-59, the low-slung ride of Ellen's Corvette gripping the road as she slid around the corner and headed south on U.S. 131. She accelerated hard and felt the race of the engine as she merged into traffic.

It was time to put Stewartville behind her. To put the months of struggle with Ellen and Adam behind her. To put her struggle with her soul and body, and the small strokes that had almost swept her away, behind her.

It would be good to be alone. More than good—it would be heavenly. The sound of the surf sweeping its fingers in the soft beach sand. The iridescent glow of pulsating sunsets. She would sleep in the loft, nestled beneath the low rise of the ceiling where she could trace the movement of the water from a mattress in a nest of blankets on the floor. She would eat strawberries and chocolate and walk at midnight to the Prayer Tower at Gilead and remember why she was there.

To be alone. Completely. Unequivocally. Finally.

She would sit in the stillness of the night and pour out thanks for everything that had been and everything that was and everything that would be and know that, in the solitude, God surrounded her. He had been in every moment that had gone before and would follow. In spite of everything each one of them had been through, his gifts in the days ahead would be enough.

In all the months since her accident, she'd had so little time alone with God. She craved it. She needed it now more than ever—time alone with God before she and Adam became husband and wife.

She was proud that she didn't cry until she pulled to the end of the lane and caught her first glimpse of the beach house through the trees. *Tomorrow, I will become Mrs. Adam Dean.* The weight of her decision settled over her soul as she pictured Adam in Harold's house, alone and praying for her here, and she buried her head in her hands and wept.

The sound of high heels punching against hardwood floors drifted through the grate near Hallie's bedroom door.

There wasn't much time.

She opened the small drawer in the left-hand box and pulled out a thin gold chain hung with a heart-shaped pendant. It nestled in her hand, the multi-colored stones glinting against the morning light that fell through her tall, bedroom windows.

Stacy's necklace.

She'd taken it off two days after she'd fled with her mother to Stewartville. It had been easier to abandon it to the dark corner of a dresser than to face the questions someone might ask. Questions she hadn't wanted to answer.

But things had changed since then, people had changed. There were times to move on and times for grief to be marked and claimed.

She reached into the matching right-hand drawer and pulled out a worn and creased note lying on top of a stack of papers. She'd nearly memorized it, but today it was important to feel the paper between her fingers:

> *Dear Hallie,*
>
> *By the time you find this note, I'll have gone ahead and met Stacy and introduced her to my precious Lynn and Minnie. I plan to tell your sister*

*how much you miss her and all you're learning about
the many faces of love. Mark the moments with your
mother. Each one is a gift both to her and to you. You
are her eyes of hope and her song of joy, even in the
dark days. God's love promises us each the gift of that
power.*

*The dresser is the gift of my heart and hands.
The boxes on the top are called Bible boxes. My
deepest hope is that they become a special place for
your treasures and gifts of love.*

Your friendship was one of my most treasured gifts.
Love,
Harold

Hallie folded the note carefully and traced the shape of the heart
where it rested in her palm. Then she slipped Harold's note back
into the drawer on top of her mother's letters.

The sound of the high heels drifted through the grate.

She turned toward her bedroom door. It was time to mark a
moment.

Ellen stood before a wide, gilt mirror nestled between a collection
of mosaic inlaid trays displayed on the east wall of the shop as she
swept mascara onto her short, blonde lashes. Count on Hallie to
hog the bathroom on the one day of the year when they couldn't
afford to be late.

She had less than five minutes to finish her face and get her daughter out the door to pick up Cara. If Mona hadn't run off with her Corvette, she could have made up time in air-conditioned comfort. But now she'd have to pray that the forty bucks she'd shucked out at the Curl Up and Dye wouldn't fly out the windows of the cab of the truck. She'd learned the hard way that stomping the gas pedal never coaxed another drop of life from the engine when that bucket of bolts was fully loaded.

Ellen caught Hallie's reflection behind her as she flew down the stairs in a pale yellow Diane von Furstenberg dress borrowed from Ellen's closet. A pair of white sandals dangled from her hand as she worked to stab a pair of Swarovski crystal chandelier earrings into her lobes.

"You're gorgeous," Hallie called as she headed through the tapestry curtains to the back room, and Ellen heard the thump of the door of the commercial refrigerator. "No one would ever suspect you could be the mother of a sixteen-year-old."

Ellen turned, laying her tube of mascara on a table draped in ivory antique linens and set with mismatched pink and yellow china and crystal and paste bracelets serving as napkin rings. She waited as Hallie flew back through the curtains carrying a cluster of daffodils, roses, and hyacinths in her hands. Her eyes swept her daughter. She was stunning. Somewhere between fifteen and sixteen, Hallie had become a beauty. Her red curls tumbled nearly to her elbows, and her face glowed with the quiet composure of a woman.

Hallie laid the flowers on the counter near the rear of the shop and walked toward her mother. Ellen's eyes swept her daughter's face, but she couldn't read the emotion she saw there.

Hallie reached up and pulled her hair forward over one shoulder. "I need your help, Mom. I don't want to do this alone."

It was a simple statement, yet Ellen saw the flush of hesitation. Hallie opened her hand, and a chain and jeweled heart spun down from her fingers.

"I thought we needed Stacy with us today. I haven't worn it since we've lived in Stewartville because I wasn't sure I could talk about her—about me and what happened. But the necklace is part of her, and I need to wear it today. It would mean a lot if you'd be the one to put it on for me."

Ellen waited for the familiar rush of fury that always came with the mention of Stacy's name.

She could see that Hallie was waiting for it, too.

But seconds ticked by, and with each second that passed, a swell of hope rose in Ellen's heart, until at last it folded in on her in one crashing wave of joy.

She reached for the chain and fastened it around Hallie's neck as she faced her daughter. "I've been praying for the day you'd ask me to be a mother again, even if you only welcomed me back with the tiniest request. And I've never believed you'd ever ask for anything really important, like strength or courage or hope, because I've never believed I had any of those things to give. Thank you, Hallie."

Ellen turned her head and blinked against the tears. So this was why Mona had left—to force this moment. She'd known that once she was gone, it would come.

She gripped the linen-draped table beside her as Hallie leaned forward quickly, kissed her cheek, and suddenly spun, her dress swishing around her legs.

"I love you, Mom. And I came to you because I need your strength. Now what do you think? Will Dan Evans notice I'm sixteen?"

Ellen took a deep breath and took a quick dab at her eyes. "You're giving me emotional whiplash, girl. Can you stay on a topic for more than fifteen seconds? I'm not ready to have you interested in a college guy, so I hope he shows up wearing blinders."

"Well I, for one, do not. We e-mail tons, and he's called a few times, but I haven't seen him in ages, and besides, Cara gets to meet him today. How cool is that? So you finish up here. I'll be back in five to pick you up after I go get her."

Before Ellen had a chance to reply, Hallie grabbed the bouquet from the counter and disappeared through the tapestry curtains and out the back door of the shop. Ellen sighed. Two more years, and she'd be gone. And then what?

She turned and looked around her. The shop was exactly the way she'd envisioned it—filled with decorative gifts and artwork she'd crafted from cast-off antiques. From the high, pressed-metal ceiling, she'd hung an assortment of elegant chandeliers created from silver teapots, serving pieces, silverware, and crystals. Colorful mosaic work was splashed about the store, overlaid into dressers, tables, boxes, and trays. The mismatched dishes she'd collected at yard sales and antique sales—items people thought to be worthless—had been arranged in artful table settings interspersed with Adam's reproduction antiques. Striking groupings of pinks, greens, yellows, reds, and ivories were set off by bits of antique linen, lace, pearls, and vintage jewelry.

Ellen's eyes moved to the west wall of the shop and the glowing rosewood of the Story and Clark upright piano that stood against the ragged brick. Lynn's piano. It was the one thing in the shop that wasn't for sale. A collection of vintage music fanned out artfully across the front. On the right side of the lid, a birdhouse rested next to a large wooden sign—a replica of the one that hung above the front door of her shop. A sign Hallie had crafted with Harold's tools and Adam's help: Gifts from Morningsong.

It didn't seem possible that six months had passed since Harold had died. But he'd envisioned the gifts that would enter her life before Ellen believed anything good could ever exist again. In the months after his death, his presence had lingered in the house, a thread that had somehow bound her to hope when drinking and despair had overwhelmed her a second time. In the dark of winter, she'd asked Mona to take her back to Fairhaven. And when the divorce had been finalized and the time had come to move out of Harold's house and into the home he'd prepared for them above the shop, she'd driven one night to an AA in Alma and joined. Two weeks later, she'd called Debbi Cunningham and asked if they could begin studying the Bible together over coffee. Her evening had slowly faded, but the morning Harold had faith to believe in had dawned.

Ellen walked through the wide archway that connected her store to her sister's. It had taken three days to tear out the wall and put up the load-bearing beam that bore the weight of the dividing structure. Two months to finish the new apartment above her store that was now the home she shared with Hallie. Six months to learn to begin living as a recovering alcoholic and a mother to her daughter. And she knew it would take a lifetime to explore the hope that was growing within her.

"I'm beginning to know joy, Harold," she spoke into the stillness of the room. "Of course, you knew I would." She closed her eyes and felt a rush of gratitude.

Adam checked his watch. Only five minutes.

The Suburban was loaded, and the keys and directions had been delivered to Pastor Cunningham. Everything on his list had been checked and double-checked. The house was spotless, thanks to Elsie and Jessica, who had dusted, doused, and disinfected every nook and cranny. Thank heaven, Jessica had signed on permanently. It appeared that there was nothing the woman loved more than the smell of Lysol and Lime-A-Way, and Adam had managed to strike a bargain for once-a-week cleaning that would keep everyone happy.

He sat at the chipped Formica kitchen table, an open Bible in front of him. No matter where Adam flipped in the yellowed pages, Harold's underlinings could be found neatly scribed beneath a favorite verse, many with dates and names penned beside them. He folded the Bible shut and pulled it toward him. He'd found the verse he'd been searching for.

He glanced through the archway that connected the dining and living rooms. Little had changed since he'd moved in. He'd given Harold's worn couch and recliner to the church youth center and moved in his cranberry couch, leather chair, and a few of his reproduction pieces. Lynn's bedroom furniture had been kept in place in the front bedroom, and the piano had been given to Ellen, as Harold had asked. The furniture in the other bedrooms had been replaced by other reproductions from his collection.

It had been hard for everyone to see changes in Harold's house and to admit that he was truly gone. But once Ellen and Hallie had moved into their new apartment and he'd moved into the house, he'd tried to make changes slowly, even though Harold had made certain in his will that the house would be his.

He picked up his cell phone off the table and hit redial for the third time, and for the third time that morning, Mona didn't answer. He was certain she'd turned off her phone or had chosen to bury it in the beach sand. She'd learned to protect her solitude and her time away with God since the MRI. When she needed space, she made it. And she'd made it more than clear that, right now, she needed it. Packing up and leaving on a moment's notice for her overnight prayer vigil was about as clear as she could get. Her strong will was certain to make life exciting. Over the past few months, he'd prayed hard and fast as he'd battled his memories of Julie's headstrong nature. And more than once he'd struggled not to panic and throw Mona in his Suburban and force her to have her MRI on his terms.

Harold had been wise enough to help him understand that Mona would need to face the source of her struggles on her own. Forcing her to do anything would almost never be right for either one of them. He could trust her to work things out with God on her own. And so Adam had swallowed hard as she'd driven out of town yesterday with barely a moment's notice. But in spite of his shock, he'd heard the passion in her voice, and he'd understood. She'd needed time alone.

Adam snapped the phone shut and slid it into the pocket of his slacks. He glanced at his watch as he stood and pulled his jacket from the back of the kitchen chair. Then he reached for Harold's Bible. It was the one thing he'd promised her not to forget.

And then it was time to go.

Dan Evans stood at Mona's side on the deck of the beach house. The waves broke on the sand in gentle swells, and the rhythm of their cadence settled over Mona's thoughts like a gentle prayer as they looked out over the water. She turned and gave a firm adjustment to his yellow necktie against a crisp white shirt.

"You drove in yesterday? I see you have Ellen's Corvette."

"Yes. I kind of stole it at the last minute. I wasn't really planning to make a break for it like this, but when I finally decided to run away, I thought I should do it with flair. There was something that just felt . . . right . . . about taking off in a hot Corvette. And Ellen finally relented and gave me the keys."

"Nervous?"

"No. That was yesterday. But I knew it was time for me to be here, alone with Miss Emily and God and to get away from all the hovering. It's been a tough six months since Harold died, and the three months before that was . . . was a long journey of its own. I needed time—just me and God. Doctor's orders, you know." Mona gave the tie a final pat and glanced north up the beach and toward the Prayer Tower. The wind teased her hair, and she shoved a tendril of red behind her ear.

"We have ten minutes, Miss V. Do you think we should start? It's a slow walk through the sand."

Mona laughed and smoothed the front of her white silk dress as she turned. "Adam will be waiting no matter how long it takes me. There's a part of him that's been waiting for me at that Prayer Tower since the first day we met. So if you'll do the honor of escorting me barefoot through the sand, I believe the time has come for me to make my appearance at my wedding."

It was the simple ceremony Mona had planned, with family and friends crowded together into the small space of the Prayer

Tower. Adam's uncle Elmer and aunt Florence stood alongside his cousin Steph, her new husband, and Sadie, Steph's daughter. Elsie was decked out in a lovely pink chiffon dress and dyed-to-match shoes, and tiny pink rosettes had been artfully sprinkled through her lavender updo. Jessica's family stood beside Debbi Cunningham, and Dan Evans and his mother were crowded toward the front near Hallie, Cara, and Ellen. By the time the bridal party filled in, it appeared that Mona and Adam might have to be slathered with cooking spray in order to slide through the crowd.

But Mona wasn't aware of the crowd. She didn't see their smiles or nods or hear the click of their cameras. Somewhere walking up the wooden stairs toward the tower above, even the young man at her side faded away, and Mona walked into the memory that had first drawn her to Adam. She was standing outside the tower door, barefoot and tear-stained, strengthened in her spirit, held in the gaze of a man she barely knew.

Ellen had hung the small space with wind chimes borrowed from the shop she would share with Adam and Mona, and their music mingled with the rustling of the pines and the cadence of the waves breaking on the shore as Pastor Cunningham's voice spoke the simple ceremony.

With a final word and a kiss, Mona and Adam sealed their vows before their witnesses with their hands clasped on the verses Adam had marked in Harold's open Bible:

> *You answer us with awesome deeds of righteousness,*
>   *O God our Savior,*
> *the hope of all the ends of the earth*
>   *and of the farthest seas,*

Shelly Beach

who formed the mountains by your power,
having armed yourself with strength. . . .
Those living far away fear your wonders;
where morning dawns and evening fades
you call forth songs of joy.

About the Author

Shelly Beach is a Christian communicator who speaks at women's conferences, retreats, seminars, and writers' conferences. She is a college instructor and writing consultant in Michigan and the author of *Hallie's Heart*; *Precious Lord, Take My Hand*; *Ambushed by Grace*; and *The Silent Seduction of Self-Talk*. *Hallie's Heart* won a Christy Award in 2008, the same year *Precious Lord, Take My Hand* was named an ECPA Christian Book Award finalist.

Shelly can be found online at shellybeachonline.wordpress.com and shellybeachonline.com.

DON'T MISS THE BEGINNING OF MONA'S STORY!

Hallie's Heart, winner of a 2008 Christy Award, is available wherever books are sold.